A Reluctant Melody

Books by Sandra Ardoin

CONTEMPORARY ROMANCE
Hidden Veil Hometown Series
A Musician's Heart
A Horseman's Mission

Love at Christmas Inn Series
Love in Second Bloom
Leaving the Past Behind
Lost in Winter's Wonderland
Box Set:
Longing for Second Chances: Three Second Chance Romance Novellas

HISTORICAL ROMANCE
Widow's Might Series
Unwrapping Hope
Enduring Dreams
Rekindling Trust

Barnes Brothers
The Yuletide Angel
A Reluctant Melody

ADDITIONAL NOVELS, NOVELLAS, AND SHORT STORIES
A Love Most Worthy
Daphne's Day Out

A Reluctant Melody

Barnes Brothers

SANDRA ARDOIN

Corner Room Books

ISBN: 978-1-7334630-9-6

All Scripture quotations, unless otherwise indicated, are taken from the Kings James Bible.

Let us therefore come boldly unto the throne of grace, that we may obtain mercy, and find grace to help in time of need.

Hebrews 4:16 (KJV)

Chapter One

North Carolina, 1892

Joanna Stewart's fingers waltzed across the silk covering her lap. Had the stripes of the dress fabric been piano keys, the cab of her brougham would be filled with the melody of Sullivan's "Let Me Dream Again."

She halted the romping digits and gripped the material of her skirt in a tight fist. *Dreams.* She awoke to the pain they caused years ago ... after the lie of romantic love dealt its deadly blow.

A horse car rattled past on the tracks running down the middle of Broad Street. The bell dangling from the animals' collars jingled with each plodding step.

Joanna's driver, Liam McCall, turned onto Cleary. When the carriage stopped, she peeked out the window and scanned the dry and dusty street in front of the Stewart Broom Factory. When was the last time she'd ventured out of her house and into the midst of strangers? A month? Two? She wouldn't be in town now if Perry's note hadn't stressed the importance of their meeting.

A man on a bicycle passed too close to the carriage and thumbed the bell on his contraption. Her horse shied and the brougham rocked. Joanna grabbed the window frame to brace herself.

Using coarse language and the power of brawny arms, Liam brought the animal under control. A moment later, he yanked the door open and held out his hand. "Foul things, horses. If it were up to me, I'd shoot 'em all."

Inwardly, Joanna cringed. "Even work animals deserve our respect and compassion, Mr. McCall." As he helped her down, his callused fingers swallowed her lace-gloved hand.

What she wouldn't give to rid herself of the drunkard with the bloodshot eyes and whiskey breath. She had never met a more unsavory individual than this man, her best friend's husband.

She picked coins from her purse. "It's near noon. Get something to eat. I should be no more than an hour." He grunted and reached for the money. She pulled her hand back. "Something to eat, not drink."

Liam's lower jaw worked back and forth, and his stare hardened. He would be a handsome man if the surliness ever left his face, and drink hadn't bloated it. Looks were a fool's delight, especially when wasted on a man with a fondness for alcohol. Joanna learned that lesson the hard way.

"Yes, Miz Stewart."

She placed the coins on his palm, then lowered the brim of her hat and turned toward the two-story brick building containing the broom factory's offices.

"Excuse me, ma'am."

The husky male voice jolted her. She glanced up and into the somber, brown eyes of a man whose scarred face, off-center nose, and tattered clothing said he'd witnessed some of the worst of life.

He whipped off his hat and lowered his gaze. "You wouldn't happen to have more of those coins, would you? It's been a couple days since I've eaten."

Most likely, this rough-looking man had spent his money at one of the local bars like Liam was wont to do, yet something about him struck a chord of empathy in Joanna. She dug into her purse a second time, handed him the same amount of money she'd given Liam, and added a brief smile. "Go with my driver to the café down the street."

The man dipped his chin. "Thank you, ma'am."

"You're welcome, sir."

Joanna ignored Liam's scowl and escaped to the building. Inside, she nodded to a gentleman seated behind a desk and climbed the L-shaped staircase to her right. At the end of the hallway, she stopped outside a door marked *Perry Stewart, President.*

As she clutched the knob, a tall shadow formed on the other side of the frosted glass. Before its presence fully registered, the door swung open and the knob jerked from her hand. A soft squeak emerged from her throat.

Perry stood in the doorway, a column of strength and masculinity. As usual, he was impeccably dressed in an expensive black suit, and his hair, short and dark, was combed back to form waves on top of his head. With a narrow face and aqua eyes, he resembled his mother more than his father.

"Good morning, Joanna. I'm sorry if I startled you."

At his warm smile, she lowered her gaze to the hands

clutching her purse. Perry had been her friend for more than five years. Sadly, her visits meant more to him than to her. Somewhere there must be a rule she could recite to him that discouraged grown stepsons from becoming romantically involved with their younger stepmothers.

"You simply took me by surprise. How did you know I'd arrived?"

"The transom." He laughed. "A woman's light step is apparent. I must say, in your case it was eagerly anticipated."

He eased back into the room where English landscapes hung from mahogany paneling, and an antique oriental carpet covered the wood floor. The latter's intricate patterns in red, gold, and deep blue matched the richness of the walls. Unlike his frugal father, Perry had excellent taste and an appreciation for quality.

A breeze wafted through two open windows and carried the essence of the adjacent factory into the room: broom corn, machine oil, dust, men's shouts. The factory had prospered under Perry's management, but its income hadn't provided the Stewarts' fortune—a fortune that dwindled under her late husband's control.

Although her husband had chosen to bequeath her—his disgraced spouse—little more than a rundown, old mansion, Joanna didn't begrudge Perry his inheritance. Nor had she blamed Clayton for leaving her a symbolic reminder of the state of their marriage. She had earned his contempt when she confessed her shame a week after they married.

She entered the room and stopped between a pair of hand-carved chairs facing a mahogany desk. Papers covered the surface of the desk and were stacked inches high on each end.

"You look busy." She kept her back to Perry. At thirty-two, he was six years older, but she often felt as ancient as the carpet under her feet.

"You know I'm never too busy for you. I hate seeing you waste away in that crumbling relic alone."

"I'm not alone. I have Rose and Annie." And Liam. She attempted a smile, but it faded before it began. "Why did you send for me?"

The door clicked shut. "Someone is interested in buying the house."

This time the smile blossomed, inside and out. *Finally.* "That's wonderful news."

Instead of walking around the desk, Perry stopped behind her. He gave her shoulders a light squeeze, and then slid his hands down the full, green and white-striped sleeves covering her arms. "I'm happy to see you finally treated yourself to a new dress. You've worn those old frocks for too long."

Pressed between her stepson and the desk, she turned in his arms. "Perry—"

Behind him, glass rattled with the opening of the office door. Joanna hid from view.

A throat cleared. "I'm sorry for interrupting. I was instructed to walk right in."

Kit Barnes. Even after all these years, the familiar voice left her weak. She peeked around Perry and drew back before Kit could recognize her.

What was he doing in Banesville? How had he found her?

Joanna's vision blurred, and her head grew light. If Perry hadn't caught her, she would have fallen to her knees.

***

Mr. Stewart caught the woman as she collapsed. "My dear."

Kit strode forward. "Is there anything I can do?"

"I'll handle it." Southerners were touted to be hospitable, but Perry Stewart's abrupt response made it clear he didn't welcome assistance. Kit backed away to give the couple room, while Stewart helped the woman into a chair and crouched beside her, his profile sharp with worry. "Darling, are you all right?"

"Yes." The voice barely reached a soft hum.

Kit had spied only a sliver of white-gold locks piled under a black straw hat. "Shall I summon a doctor?"

"No." The feminine whisper turned harsh.

Perry Stewart ran a hand through his hair. He glanced at Kit, his expression shifting from displeasure to anxiety. He turned back to the woman. "Did you eat this morning?"

She shook her head.

"We've had this discussion before. You must let Rose fix you regular meals. It's near noon. I'll order lunch for the three of us."

"Don't bother." She started to rise, but Stewart pushed her back into the chair.

"You must revive your strength."

Her back stiffened. "I ca . . ." A shout from the factory yard covered the rest of her reply.

"If the lady isn't feeling well, perhaps we should postpone this meeting." Kit clutched the brim of his hat in a tight fist and waited.

"Perhaps it would be best." Stewart led him to the door and ushered him into the hallway. "I regret your wasted time, sir."

The moment he'd received the attorney's letter indicating the availability of the house on Hickory Grove Road, Kit dropped everything to travel to North Carolina. He discarded the idea of going back to Pittsburgh without at least discussing a possible purchase.

"I'll be at the Hotel Ambrose and won't consider my time wasted as long as we can meet again soon."

"I'll send a message with a new appointment time once Joanna is able to join us again. Good day, Mr. Barnes."

The door snapped shut behind Kit, and he stood in the stuffy hall with the brim of his hat curled in his hands. Joanna? He dismissed the sinking feeling in his gut as ridiculous. Numerous women with that name were born into the world, even some with hair the color of a midday sun. He loosened his grip on the tortured head covering, rolled his shoulders, and trudged down the stairs.

Why had he been so quick to suggest postponing their meeting? Though he questioned the need for Mrs. Stewart's attendance, how long would he have to wait for another appointment?

Time was running out. He must purchase that house or it would be the alcohol-obsessed men of Banesville who would suffer.

Chapter Two

Kit walked out of the office building and into the sunshine of the early June day with his hands stuffed in his trouser pockets and his shoulders hunched.

His partner, Benton Greer, stood with one foot on the ground and the other propped against the bricks of the front wall outside the broom factory. "Well?"

Kit stopped at Ben's side. "I don't know."

Using the sole of his boot, the lanky giant pushed away from the building. "What does that mean?"

"The meeting was postponed. There's a woman involved somehow. She became ill, so I suggested we wait until she felt better." Kit marched through the opening in the picket fence surrounding the broom factory with Ben walking in his shadow. "We might as well head back to the hotel and eat lunch. Mr. Stewart said he'd arrange another meeting and send a message."

The two men strode in silence down Cleary Street. They

waited for a two-wheeled cart to pass before crossing to the other side of Broad and turning left.

"When that last deal went sour, we lost a lot of time, Kit. We need to be ready to open the mission in just over two months. If we don't find a place soon—"

"I know what's at stake."

He and Ben had ridden by the house soon after arriving in Banesville and noted its perfect size and location. They were told the structure needed wide-ranging repairs, inside and out. Kit wasn't convinced they could finish in time, yet the real estate agent assured him it was a perfect fit to house those requesting physical and spiritual assistance to break their dependence on alcohol.

Regretting his sharp response, Kit rested a hand between his friend's shoulder blades. "I didn't mean to bark at you. The Lord provided this opportunity, so I believe we can count on Him to work everything out, don't you?"

Ben snorted with humor. "You're preaching to me now, son?"

Kit laughed at the former pastor, his elder by a mere five years. "I prefer it to the other way around, old man."

Their pace slackened as they walked down Seventh Street and up the steps of the Hotel Ambrose.

I can do all things through the Christ who strengthens me.

Kit wanted to believe the Apostle Paul's words with his whole heart, mind, and spirit, but he couldn't brush away the nagging sense of trouble to come.

***

The brougham stopped under the porte-cochere in front of

Joanna's house. She didn't wait for Liam to help her from the carriage, but threw open the door and jumped to the ground, then rushed up the porch steps.

The screen door stuck when she tried to open it. She yanked on the pull until the door scratched an arc in the porch planks. She'd add planing the bottom of the door to Liam's growing list of repairs to the 1850s structure. The sooner she sold the place, the better.

But never to Kit Barnes.

She hurried through the house and beyond the spiral staircase. Behind her, Rose called her name, but she ignored her friend and burst into the music room, seeking solace in the only place she'd known to find it since childhood.

Joanna dropped onto the seat at the grand piano, ripped off her gloves, and tossed them toward the nearby davenport. She closed her eyes and savored the cool and sleek ivory beneath her fingertips. Calling forth memorized notes, she strived to retreat into another world where time ceased to exist. There was nothing but the present moment, and in that moment she could be whomever she wanted. She longed to be Joanna Cranston at eighteen with the ability to see into her nineteenth year and how her silly and shallow character would affect her future happiness. She would prevent all the mistakes she had made and the hurt she'd caused. She would never relive the greatest sorrow of her life over and over.

Her hands crashed on the keys, but the calm she sought refused to take hold. Her every thought centered on Kit, his impact on her past, and the damage he could unleash on her future.

"You rushed through the house like your backside was on fire."

Joanna twisted on the piano stool. Trying to fool Rose McCall with a phony smile was useless. They knew each other too well. "I assure you it's not."

"Funny, I was certain I smelled smoke as you rushed by me." Rose crossed her arms. "Is Perry pressuring you again?"

"No." Joanna grimaced at the memory of his hands running down her arms. "No more than usual."

"Then what's upset you?"

Less than a handful of people knew the darkness of her sin. Only her friend Rose knew everything it had cost her. She hadn't planned to say anything, but the words "He's here" spilled out before she could catch them.

"Who's here? Perry?" Rose glanced around the paneled room.

"No." Although, if Joanna hadn't put her foot down, Perry would have escorted her home. As it was, he'd insisted she stay and eat something before leaving. Half the ham sandwich remained on the plate when she crept out of the office. The other half sat like an iron ball in her stomach.

"Then who?" Confusion saturated Rose's voice as she studied Joanna's face. After a moment of silence, Rose hiked her strawberry-blonde eyebrows. "You don't mean . . .?"

Joanna nodded.

"In town?"

"Worse. He came to Perry's office today." She explained the reason for Kit's unexpected and untimely entrance.

"Do you think he knew you owned this house and has some plan to discredit you? Please don't tell me he mentioned your previous . . . relationship . . . in front of Perry."

"No, he didn't. And one time does not amount to a relationship, Rose, especially when the other party despises you afterward."

The brows lowered and compassion replaced the surprise on Rose's face. "I'm sure Kit Barnes never despised you, Jo. After all, it takes two."

Joanna wandered to a window and leaned into a panel of the heavy brocade curtain. On the other side of the glass, a stand of pine trees blocked her view past the north side of the house and the neighbor a block away. A white butterfly flitted past, its path meandering as its wings beat against the air. She touched the window as if her hand could pass through the glass to caress the blithe insect.

"I hid my face and pretended to be ill until Kit went away."

Rose released a heavy sigh. "If you hid from him, I'm not surprised he didn't realize it was you. I'm sure his being there was a coincidence. That would be a blessing, wouldn't it?"

A blessing? Perhaps. If Joanna believed in such things anymore. "What if he did catch a glimpse of my face and didn't recognize me? Have I aged so much in seven years? Or maybe he's forgotten all about me. Maybe I'm just one in a hundred who . . ." A sob clogged her throat.

The shame still turned her stomach. At nineteen, she'd lost everything—her future with a good man, her virtue and self-respect. Even her family deserted her when her father pronounced her beyond redemption and condemned to eternal judgment from God.

Why had she allowed herself to fall in love with a drunken cad?

"Isn't being forgotten by Kit Barnes no more than I deserve?"

"Shh . . ." Rose stepped behind Joanna and squeezed her shoulders. "Don't work yourself up into a tizzy."

"I can't see him again, Rose."

"Then tell Perry he'll have to handle the sale without you."

Joanna sniffed and pulled a handkerchief from her sleeve. She wiped her eyes and blew her nose. "I don't care if the walls crumble around me. I won't sell this place to a man who treated me like a harlot and promptly forgot me, not after all I've been through."

Chapter Three

Kit and Ben sat at a table in the hotel dining room. Quiet voices droned around them in soft, drawn-out syllables. Outside, dusk covered the land in shadow, and low light from gas lamps on the walls flickered across the faces of Kit's two companions.

Stewart leaned back in the chair across from him and sipped the golden liquid of the brandy in his glass. Kit ran his tongue across his bottom lip and shut his eyes. His gut grew warm with the remembered taste of an expensive cognac. The man couldn't realize the temptation Kit faced simply by being near alcohol.

Over time, he had learned to deal with the momentary urges like this—the demons that tried to convince him one glass couldn't hurt. Those moments were a personal thorn in the flesh, but intruded less and less into his life. Rather than give in, he used it to strengthen his faith and remind himself he was a new man.

That was the basis of their work—showing men they could become new creations, both in Christ and in the world. They provided the spiritual tools to help inebriates cope with the difficulties of withdrawal and remain sober. It was their calling.

Stewart pointed to the letter he'd handed Kit. "Mrs. Stewarta asked me to deliver that in person. Under the circumstances, she felt obliged to put her decision in writing."

Kit leaned forward with his arms crossed on the table. "*Her* decision? Your wife decides about the house?"

"My wife? I'm afraid you misunderstood, Kit. I hope you don't mind if I call you Kit." Stewart smiled as if they were old friends.

"Not at all. And I'll call you Perry."

The man nodded. "To be clear, Joanna is not my wife." He added something under his breath that sounded like "not yet."

"Then I don't understand her role in the sale of the house."

"Joanna inherited the property from my father. She's my stepmother." Perry's lip curled on the last word, the smile long gone. "And before you ask, yes, she was much younger."

The disgust in the man's voice prodded Kit to recall the embrace he'd witnessed that morning. Obviously, Perry preferred a different relationship to exist with Joanna Stewart—one that had nothing to do with stepmother and stepson. Did the widow return his feelings?

Every time he heard the name Joanna, Kit's mind raced back seven years to the night he betrayed his brother's trust. God had forgiven Kit's past but had his Joanna found . . .? His jaw clenched. Not *his* Joanna. She should never have been his.

He worked his tense jaw muscles back and forth. At this moment, his only concern was obtaining the house and grounds for his work, not the immorality in which he'd participated with

Joanna Cranston, the woman his brother had hoped to marry.

Kit held the envelope away from his body, preferring to hand it right back. "This is what I think it is then?"

He and Ben exchanged pained glances. They had prepared for bad news as soon as Perry asked to meet them here rather than in his office, but the idea of starting their building search over at this late date churned his stomach.

"I'm afraid so."

Kit opened the envelope and pulled out a single sheet of paper. He scanned the contents and read the words out loud to Ben. "'Dear Mr. Barnes. I have decided not to sell my home at this time. Joanna Stewart.'" He turned the paper over. Blank. "That's it? No explanation?"

Ben stirred a spoon through his coffee. "Short and to the point."

"There isn't even a 'Sincerely.'" Kit regarded Perry. "Did she disclose to you why she won't sell?"

"I'm sorry. She told me nothing." Perry's pleasant facade slipped and his lips compressed. "I only know that, once she makes a decision, she can be stubborn."

"Yes, well, it was my understanding she'd *decided* to sell."

Ben cleared his throat and raised one brow with a silent warning to be more circumspect. But really, how stubborn could she be if she changed her mind within eight hours?

Kit folded the paper and slipped it back in the envelope, holding in the desire to rail against the woman's fickleness. The only thing that stopped him was his belief that God had a plan, even if He kept it to Himself for the time being.

"Why couldn't she tell us in person? You said she no longer felt ill."

Perry examined his well-manicured fingernails, running his

thumb over the rounded edges. "Joanna is somewhat reclusive. She rarely goes out."

"The home Ben and I established in Pittsburgh three years ago has helped a number of men battle alcoholism, Perry. With the right place and the financial donations we've been promised, we can accomplish the same good here. We've worked hard with town officials and your local temperance group, especially Mrs. Lucinda Brockhurst. She insists we open our doors by August twenty-second, the anniversary of her son's death, or the group she leads will rescind an offer of monetary support. That leaves us only two-and-a-half months. Will you speak with Mrs. Stewart again on our behalf?"

"As I said, I'm as much in the dark about her motive as you, gentlemen, but she was adamant."

Ben slumped in his chair. "What if we talked to her and explained our purpose?"

"As I mentioned, she's reclusive. I doubt she'd see you." Perry dropped his hand and frowned. The chair screeched across the floor as he pushed away from the table and rose. "Now, if you'll both excuse me, I have plans for this evening."

Kit waited until Perry walked out of the dining room before he turned to Ben. "Something isn't right with the situation—or the woman."

"It bothers Stewart, too. I could feel it." Ben gulped the rest of the coffee in his cup.

Kit left the table and the dining room. That same disturbance swathed him from the moment he'd walked inside the man's office at the Stewart Broom Factory. A sense of mystery surrounded Joanna Stewart. It had piqued his interest earlier and even more so now. She acted secretive, not even allowing him to glimpse her face. Why? Because she withdrew from people? If that were the case, perhaps she deserved more pity than censure.

Ben followed Kit into the lobby. "Guess we should head upstairs and get some sleep. It's a long trip back to Pittsburgh."

"You go ahead and take the train. I won't be leaving tomorrow."

"Kit—"

"We have to find another building." He slapped the hat on his head and started for the door.

"Surely not right now. It's after eight."

Kit checked the clock in the hotel's lobby, ambled back to his friend's side, and covered his embarrassment with a grin. "No. I guess not."

"You plan to see Mrs. Stewart yourself?"

Ben knew him well. "Maybe."

"You read the letter and heard Stewart. She's made up her mind. What good will confronting her do?"

"Probably none." But what choice did he have?

***

Morning heat warmed Joanna's face, and a bright light pierced her shuttered eyes. She threw off the sheet and blinked several times, fighting to keep her eyes open. Eventually, she won the battle with sight, but her body protested the command to rise.

Propped on her elbows, Joanna squinted at the clock on her bedside table and groaned. She thrust her arms to the side, and her head fell back onto her pillow. After nine? She should have been up hours ago.

She rubbed her eyes and crawled out of bed. Not even splashing with the tepid water from the basin on the washstand roused her. She dressed as if under the effects of a sleeping powder.

Once downstairs, Joanna padded toward the kitchen, expecting to hear Rose's singing or Annie's sweet giggle. She paused at the dining room.

Quiet. Too quiet.

Rose was a cheery bird most mornings, singing and capering around the kitchen. They often teased one another about how she trilled while Joanna snarled.

In the kitchen, her friend sat at the table near the wall with her back to Joanna, head bowed. Oddly, Rose's russet hair still hung in the nighttime braid running along her spine rather than pinned atop her head.

"I'm sorry I slept late."

Rose's shoulders stiffened. She lifted her head, but didn't turn around. "After yesterday, I'm sure you needed it."

The muffled words sent apprehension skittering through Joanna and shook off any remaining fatigue. She inched closer. "Where's Annie?"

Rose stood and shuffled to the stove, still keeping her back in view. "Sleeping."

"Please, look at me."

Rose hesitated. When she twisted to face Joanna, her dainty chin quivered beneath a lower lip twice as large as normal. A gash snaked out from the right corner of her mouth, and an ugly bruise surrounded it.

Joanna stood rooted to the floor, wide-eyed and heart thundering. "How . . .?"

Rose ducked her head. Her shoulders shook with noisy sobs.

"Oh, Rose." Joanna wrapped her arms around her friend. "What are we to do about this?"

A tempest swirled inside Joanna. Men. Did God not make one who was better than a selfish brute?

Chapter Four

After Ben's train left the depot, Kit wandered the streets of Banesville. Overnight, his temper had cooled, and he'd agreed to Ben's request to approach Mrs. Stewart again only if a meeting with the real estate agent provided no other possible properties.

Kit started across an alleyway on Lee Street not far from the Crossroads Bar. The sound of a snore slowed his pace. He peered into the alley to find a man slumped against a brick wall. Memories of Kit's own past drunkenness assaulted him.

There but for the grace of God . . .

He wandered into the alleyway and hunkered down next to the sleeping man. The stench of sour liquor overwhelmed the space between them. Stubbles of graying whiskers dotted the middle-aged man's face. Stains and dust clung to the worn and wrinkled suit.

Kit jogged the man's arm. "Wake up." Once more. Harder. "Wake up, sir."

When his efforts produced nothing more than an indiscernible mumbling followed by a growl, Kit gently slapped each side of his face. "Come on. Wake up."

Quick as cannon fire, the man's fist crashed into Kit's jaw, sending him sprawling backward onto the dirt. Pain radiated throughout his head. He massaged the battered and throbbing side of his face, thankful his jawbone remained solid.

Kit eyed his semi-awake attacker. The crooked and flat nose, old scar running along his right cheek, and quick reflexes boasted of a background as a fighter—either by profession or temperament.

"Nice move."

More mumbling before the man fully opened his eyes and slid upright. "Who're you?"

"Kit Barnes. Who are you?"

"Donovan. O'Connor." He rubbed his eyes and ran a hand down his face. The lines of confusion creasing his forehead softened. "Yeah. Donovan O'Connor."

Kit's aching jaw slipped. "As in bare-knuckled-fighter 'Dynamite' O'Connor?"

The man's eyes narrowed before he sighed. "No more. Those days are long over."

Kit had attended one professional fight in his life, ten years ago between "Dynamite" O'Connor and "Lefty" Lloyd. It ended in two minutes with a knockout blow from the man in front of him, and bestowed on Kit an aversion to fisticuffs. Unfortunately, his work with men in their cups led him to break up amateur bouts from time to time, but until today, he'd never been the victim of a punch.

When Donovan struggled to rise, Kit jumped up and grabbed an arm to assist him.

Donovan shook off his hold. "I can do it myself."

Kit raised his arms and backed away. He believed in the concept of "turn the other cheek," only not to a man trained to knock him unconscious.

"How about some breakfast?"

Donovan wobbled on his feet. "What?"

"There's a restaurant down the street." Kit clutched the fighter's elbow to steady him as he listed sideways. "I suppose you're penniless after last night."

Donovan patted his coat and reached inside the pockets of his trousers. "Guess I am."

"Then come on. I'll buy you breakfast. I haven't eaten, either." The ache in Kit's jaw warned against chewing, but compassion and an empty stomach overruled his good judgment.

Kit turned the man toward the entrance of the alley. Donovan stiffened as if about to protest, but stumbled into the early-morning sunshine. He squinted at the light and grimaced. "Sure. Why not?"

A hot meal of eggs and ham, along with strong coffee and some well-placed questions, loosened the fighter's tongue. His story soon spilled out—a story of increasing losses, both personal and professional, and fewer fights, then none at all. All too often, Kit had heard similar tales with different settings, different circumstances.

Donovan shoveled eggs into his mouth like he was scared someone would snatch his plate. "A man's got nothin' without his work."

True. And due to Mrs. Stewart's unpredictability, Kit's work in Banesville was in danger.

He lifted a forkful of egg and eased it into his mouth, chewing with caution. These days, to atone for the mountain of havoc he'd raised in his youth, he built up men such as Donovan O'Connor, set them on a more productive path in this life, and pointed them to eternal life in the hereafter.

How would he do that in this town without a proper place to meet their physical needs and keep them out of the local saloons?

Later, outside the restaurant, Kit asked, "Do you have a place to stay?"

Donovan wheezed a chuckle. "Sure. You saw my mansion."

"I have an extra room at the Hotel Ambrose. You can use it to get some good sleep and a, uh, bath."

The fighter's brown eyes narrowed again. "Why're you doing this?"

"Like you said 'a man's got nothin' without his work'."

"And what is your work, Barnes?"

"I'll tell you after you wake up."

Kit escorted Donovan to Ben's second floor room in the hotel. Once the man was settled, he raced down the stairs again and out the front door.

There must be another suitable property in Banesville besides Joanna Stewart's, and he intended to find it.

***

Joanna yanked what was left of the cube of ice from the tin-lined compartment of the icebox and slammed it on the counter. She grabbed a pick and stabbed the cube over and over until chunks flew off. She gathered them up and wrapped them in a towel.

"The drinking is bad enough," her voice caught, "but I won't let this happen to you again." She led Rose to the table, urged her into a chair, and handed her the compress.

"I'm not afraid for myself." Tears streaked over Rose's pale skin. "But what if he hurts Annie?"

What if? Liam's threats and short temper frightened the six-year-old enough without him laying a hand on her. If he ever harmed the child, Joanna would . . .

"Where is Annie?"

"After she awoke"—Rose touched the corner of her mouth—"I carried her to a bed upstairs and stayed with her."

"And Liam?"

"In our quarters, sleeping it off."

Joanna stepped toward the door leading to the rear veranda and peered out at the wooden structure twenty feet away. It had been built in the days when the kitchens of such large homes were constructed separate from the main residence as a precaution against fire. Now it served as a cottage for the McCall family. The longer she stared at the area of the building in which Liam slept, the greater her fury.

"I don't know what to do."

Joanna turned to Rose. "You don't have to do a thing. I should have fired him the first time."

Rose jumped from her seat. "Fire him? If he leaves here, he'll take Annie and me with him."

Joanna pointed to the misshapen lip. "We'll go to the sheriff and show him what he did."

"Why should he do anything when it's my word against Liam's?"

"Times are changing, Rose. The authorities take these things more seriously."

"I won't drag you or Annie into another scandal." Rose winced in pain.

Joanna rubbed her forehead. "Fine. I'll tell Liam he's to leave without you. If he doesn't, I'll threaten him with arrest."

"But what if he—"

"Rose." Joanna closed her eyes and willed her temper to settle. "Do you want to live this way the rest of your life? Do you want to be a woman terrified of her husband and raise a child who's terrified of her father?"

"What if he's willing to change?"

"Has he yet? I'm tired of the man. I'm tired of seeing him belittle you, and I'm tired of seeing Annie cower around every male she meets because of him."

Rose wiped her eyes with an apron. "We weren't much good at choosing our men, were we?"

"No." Joanna opened the door and paused before stepping outside. "You and Annie are all the family I have. You've been my friend and protected me since that horrible time in Philadelphia. Let me help you now."

As she approached the cottage, the fire of Joanna's wrath flickered, and uncertainty almost snuffed it. Did she have the nerve to throw Liam out? What if he refused to go? Worse yet, refused to go without his wife and the child? Joanna had only threats to stop him. And if he did leave, would Rose grow to resent her interference?

When doubts jeopardized Joanna's resolve, the mental vision of her friend's swollen face strengthened it. She pounded on the door of the cottage until the side of her hand ached. She wasn't foolish enough or courageous enough to barge inside and risk being trapped with Liam.

Finally, the door opened and exposed Rose's husband, half-dressed and looking like a grizzly waking from hibernation. "Rose isn't here."

"I know exactly where Rose is. She's in my kitchen, holding a cold compress to her mouth."

He shrugged. "Clumsy woman. Fell and hit a chair."

"Get your things together and get out."

His body stiffened. "Out? You firing me? You don't want to do that, Miz Stewart."

"Why? Will you hit me, too?" Was it fear that flashed across his face? Surprise? It came and went too quickly for her to tell. "Leave my property and never come back."

He regained his typical swagger and leaned a shoulder against the door post. "And how do you, a slip of a thing, think you can make me go anywhere?"

His gaze ran from her face to her toes, lingering on various spots in between and sending a chill along her spine as if a gust of mid-winter wind slid down her dress. The man disgusted her.

Joanna swallowed the revulsion climbing her throat. How was she to make him leave? Certainly not through besting him physically.

"Can't think of a way, can you?" Liam bent forward until his nose was less than six inches from hers. "Bet I can think of one."

The stench that blew from his mouth nearly knocked her over, but she stood her ground and waited, determined not to give him the satisfaction of asking what he meant.

He straightened. "You're awful high and mighty."

"You have ten minutes." She turned to leave.

"Five thousand. Dollars."

Joanna pivoted. "What?"

"I'll leave for five thousand dollars."

Had she not been so shocked, she might have burst into laughter. "You'll leave because I've told you to."

"Don't press me, Miz Stewart. I know three things you want

to protect more than anything." A smug grin shot one side of his face upward. "My wife, the girl ... and your secret."

Joanna stepped backward and tripped over her skirt hem. She flailed her arms. Liam reached out and caught her, drawing her close. If only he'd let her fall rather than touch her.

She stared into bloodshot hazel eyes. What did he know about her? Surely Rose never told him. Why hadn't she thought things through, taken time to plan before approaching him, or gone straight to the sheriff? If she believed God answered the prayers of sinners, she'd ask for wisdom. But she was long past being worthy of His generosity.

"Let go of her, Liam."

Joanna wriggled out of his hold and spun around. Rose stalked down the path toward the cottage, the ice pick clutched in her fist. "Rose, go back inside."

"No. This is my concern."

Liam laughed at his wife. "Woo-ee! You oughta be more careful, sweetheart. Looks like the chair you tripped over fought back."

Rose pointed the ice pick at him. It quivered in her trembling hand. "I want you out of here and away from me and Annie."

"Miz Stewart and me were just negotiating about that when you arrived. I told her I'd gladly leave. I'll give her you and Annie." He winked. "And keep my mouth shut about her indiscretion."

Rose's hand opened, and the ice pick fell to the ground. "I never said anything, Joanna. Believe me."

Joanna studied her friend's crinkled brow. If Rose never told him, how did he find out? "You know nothing."

"Suit yourself. It'd be a shame if I was forced to leave here. Of course, I couldn't think of going without my precious family." He pointed to Rose's face. "You can see how awkward my wife is.

Probably won't be long before the girl takes on that trait."

Rose shot past Joanna. "You leave Annie alone."

He shoved her away and glared at Joanna. "Well?"

"You know I don't have that kind of money."

"Not in cash. Not yet." He lifted his gaze to the house.

Joanna's stomach clenched with the realization of what he'd say next.

"But you know where to get it. Real fast."

Chapter Five

While Donovan O'Connor slept off the effects of the previous night's binge, Kit roamed the streets of Banesville. Rows of two- and three-story brick and wood-framed buildings lined Broad Street and the first couple of blocks of side streets.

Houses ringed the business district. The larger and more elaborate dwellings were located in a neighborhood on the east side. A development of industry and median-priced housing was planned for the area around the new Fairview Park, not far from the Stewart residence. It made the location of that particular property all the more enticing to Kit.

Rolling hills of cotton and corn, a granite quarry, and a handful of old gold mines dotted the county. Manufacturing businesses extended the town limits to include the formation of neighborhoods with rows of small, identical houses built for the workers in the two cotton mills.

Kit bought a peach from the stand outside the grocer's and savored the sweetness of both the taste and fragrance as the juice dripped onto his hand. He breathed in the fresh air that lacked the constant haze from steel mill smokestacks.

With nearly five thousand residents, it would take close to fifty Banesvilles to equal the population of Pittsburgh, but the town promised continued growth into the next century.

During his visit with the real estate agent that morning, Kit had learned of another possible location. The Simmons Avenue house was not equal in size to the Stewart residence, and it hadn't the yard for privacy and proper exercise, but with some additions, it would do as a start. He also worried it was too near the Moondog Saloon for the men to fight the temptation to sneak away. As he knew well, theirs was a lifetime battle with the enemy always surrounding them and too often victorious.

Perhaps it wasn't God's desire for him to establish a place here. Maybe he and Ben had stumbled ahead of the Lord in accepting the offer from Lucinda Brockhurst and her temperance friends to fund a second home. Yet he couldn't free his mind of the fact that, within a mile's circumference of his hotel, he'd counted six brick and wooden churches to support the spiritual needs of the people. As many bars supported the physical cravings, and alcohol distilleries operated county-wide. Who knew how many stills were located within woods and rundown shacks?

Kit stopped in front of the barber's and glanced in the direction of Joanna Stewart's house. From what he had been told, in spite of the necessary repairs, her house fit their requirements to near perfection. If his being here wasn't in God's plan, why did his fascination with her place continue to border on obsession?

He leaned with his back against the rough boards of the building and closed his eyes. *Lord, it's out of my hands and dependent on You. Provide your guidance and wisdom.*

Kit checked his watch. Donovan might be up by now. Even if God brought him here simply to help the former fighter, he would be satisfied that the trip was worthwhile.

He returned to the hotel, knocked on Donovan's door, and waited until asked to enter the room. The man stood at the washstand, splashing water over his age-lined face. Even from a distance, he smelled better.

"Rested?"

Donovan rubbed a towel over his skin. "I'll admit, a soft pillow's more comfortable than a brick wall."

Kit grinned. "It's possible for you to sleep on a pillow every night, you know."

The towel dropped onto the marble top of the washstand. "I'm not that desperate for a good night's sleep."

"You don't desire a normal life?"

"I don't desire what you have in mind."

"I haven't even told you yet."

Donovan glared at him. "Mister, I've heard tell of other poor sots falling for get-rich-quick schemes from men like you. I may be a drunk, but I'm an honest one."

The course of the conversation stymied Kit. "What is it you think I want from you?"

The man sat on the edge of the bed. He pulled on a scuffed boot and stomped his worn heel on the floor. "You think I'm so low down I got no scruples, that I'll jump at the chance to make money, even if it's tainted."

"I'm not offering you money, and I'm not asking you to do anything dishonest." Kit stood next to the bed. "My job is to help men defeat the enticement of alcohol."

Donovan paused in the midst of pulling on his other boot. He stared at Kit, then shook his head. "So you want me to snitch on my friends and tell you where the local rot gut is made? Nope."

One day Mrs. Brockhurst and women like her might be successful in shutting down the local saloons and stills, but that wasn't his concern, and he doubted it would help much anyway.

"I want to show you how to turn your life around."

Donovan broke eye contact and stomped the second boot heel on the wood planks. He grabbed his shirt and headed for the door. "You're one of those do-good preachers, trying to set the world right for God? Sorry. Not interested in that either."

Kit had dealt with men like Donovan before. Pressing his point never achieved good results. The men they supported had to be willing to receive assistance. "I leave the preaching to my friend, Ben, but if you ever need help, Dynamite, you know where to come."

"Thanks for the breakfast." Donovan dipped his head in a curt nod and walked out of the room.

Kit watched from the window as the old boxer left the hotel. If it were God's will that he remain in Banesville, he and Donovan would meet again.

***

Joanna's fingers skimmed the piano keyboard and created a soothing sound that opposed her muddled thoughts about Liam and the choice she must make. She closed her eyes, immersed in the music. Her body swayed with the rhythm of spontaneous notes.

"That's beautiful."

Her eyes popped open, and she lifted her hands from the keys. The notes evaporated in the room's stale air.

Rose stood in the curve of the instrument's frame. The swelling was gone, but the bruise around her mouth was more pronounced. "What is it called?"

"I'm not sure. I suppose I heard it somewhere once."

"Or you composed it. God gave you a rare talent. I've always thought you would do well on a concert stage."

Joanna turned her attention to the window and the sunshine gleaming through the glass. She forced a smile. "My music teacher told me the same thing when I was sixteen. He suggested I pursue it."

Rose frowned. "What did your father say?"

Reverend Edward Cranston's poisonous outlook on life was no secret to Joanna's friend.

"According to Papa, anything other than holy music was sinful." *According to Papa, living was sinful.* "He canceled my lessons and ordered me to play only hymns for his Sunday services."

"Singing God's praises brings joy to people."

"Not the songs Papa chose. They were dark and heavy with God's judgment."

"What an unhappy existence your father must lead."

"Once I overheard Mama complain that, in Papa's eyes, earthly pleasure had no place in the life of a person bound for heaven."

Whenever Joanna thought of the trials she'd been through since her mother left years ago, she resented God. Did He enjoy watching her stumble from one poor state of affairs into another?

"If that were true, Joanna, why would God have given us the ability to laugh?"

Deep in a cave-like corner of her soul, a voice cried out that Joanna's turmoil broke God's heart. Oh, that it was true, and she could turn to Him for comfort. But if He cared, why did she always feel so alone? Not even Rose and Annie filled that need for something more to satisfy each day.

Her breath caught. Had she followed in her father's footsteps—basking in misery?

"I know you're worried. We wouldn't be in this predicament if I hadn't given in to my fear and married Liam." Though she had come to the Stewart house a widow in Joanna's employ, Rose had believed raising a child was easier with a man to lean on—evidently, any man. Yesterday, they had driven him away.

"We've both made mistakes."

Rose gripped the top edge of the piano. "You're not responsible for my problem, Joanna."

"If it hadn't been for me, you never would have met Liam. We'll go where he can't find us."

If Joanna sold the house to Kit, the money would go to Liam, along with much of her savings, and she would have a pittance to start over somewhere else. Yet, she couldn't bear knowing Kit was near, that she might meet him around any corner at any time.

"Are you sure you want to sell to Mr. Barnes to save us from Liam?"

Joanna laughed, the strident sound devoid of humor. "A matter of choosing between two evils, isn't it?"

***

The next afternoon, Joanna leaned back in the parlor armchair. Her head rested against the scallop-edged antimacassar draped over the back.

Perry towered over her. "Why, Joanna? Why change your mind again?"

Joanna sighed and lifted her head. With no word from Liam since Wednesday, she had begun to hope she could ignore his threat and almost talked herself into believing they were safe, that he had gone away, fearful she would report his abuse and blackmail. The note Rose found tacked to the cottage door that morning proved her ignorance.

My best to you while you heal.

Liam had been careful to disguise his threat, but Joanna read between the lines, something Rose refused to do.

"I don't understand." Perry shoved aside the pillowcase stretched inside Joanna's embroidery hoop and dropped onto the sofa. He crossed his legs and stared at her as if she were a stranger. "First you want to sell, then you don't, and now you do. You don't normally display a capricious nature."

How did she explain her odd behavior without revealing the truth? Liam made it clear their agreement was to be secret or not at all. Not that she wanted it shouted from one end of town to another anyway. "You know I didn't feel well the day Mr. Barnes arrived for our meeting. I made a rash decision."

"And now you want me to offer him the house?"

"I'm sorry if I've inconvenienced you."

"I don't mind a bit of inconvenience when you're involved, but why not tell him yourself?"

She smiled to ease the tension between them. "You are more capable when it comes to conducting negotiations, and you were willing to act as my agent before. Are you unwilling now?"

"Perhaps so, if I'm going to look like a fool in Kit Barnes' eyes." He huffed. "I'll send him a message that we'd like to meet—"

"That's not necessary."

He cocked his head. "I beg your pardon?"

"I would prefer that you see to everything. When the papers are ready, they can be sent here for my signature."

Joanna sat rigid as he studied her, his dark brows drawn in a "V." Finally, his features relaxed. He uncrossed his legs and rose from the sofa. "If that's what you want, I'll notify him."

"Thank you."

She followed Perry through the foyer to the porch. He stopped and turned toward her. "Barnes seemed anxious to purchase a property. It's possible he's already found another location to suit his needs. What will you do then?"

She laid a hand against the burn in her stomach. What if? "I'll contemplate that problem should the need arise."

"I wish you would contemplate us." His aqua gaze held hers before he reached out and, with the tip of one finger, raised her chin. Perry bent forward and Joanna stiffened. Her heart thundered in her ears. But instead of pressing his lips to hers as she'd expected, he kissed her forehead. "Goodbye, Joanna."

Perry walked to his carriage parked under the porte cochere. After a last look in her direction, he urged his horse into a turn and back down the drive.

Joanna touched the spot where he'd kissed her. Contemplate them as a couple? She didn't dare.

Rose stopped alongside her. "Maybe you should marry him."

"He doesn't deserve someone like me."

"Nonsense."

The carriage turned onto the road and vanished in a cloud of dust. "Perry deserves a wife with an honorable past, not one who wasted her youth and God's patience on vain pursuits."

"I've never met that woman, Joanna, and I doubt she ever

existed, not to the degree you remember. Despite everything, God loves you. So does Perry. Both will forgive you if you ask."

She faced her friend. "Now you're the one speaking nonsense. Why should I expect Perry to do what his father refused to do?"

They stepped inside the house. Annie peered from behind the staircase. Her chestnut hair poked out in various places from a pair of braids she'd plaited herself. "Is he gone?"

Joanna glanced at Rose, who held her arms out for the child. "He's gone, my girl."

Annie rushed to Rose and received a reassuring hug. She gazed up at Joanna. "I don't like him, Aunt Jo."

"It's all right, sweetheart."

Both women knew Annie's dislike had more to do with Liam than Perry. The latter had never so much as raised his voice to her. In fact, he ignored her. Did Perry not like children? The question never occurred to Joanna before.

She climbed the stairs to change into a dress better suited to helping Rose clean the house. The child's reaction reinforced Joanna's conviction that she had no choice but to sell to Kit. Even without Liam's threat hanging over her, it was the right thing to do—for Rose and Annie.

The girl was young. Once she was free of the loathsome Liam McCall, she would regain her trust in men.

Unlike Joanna.

Chapter Six

Kit boarded the horse-drawn streetcar and found an empty seat at the back. Once settled on the wooden bench, he reached into his coat pocket, removed the envelope he'd received from Perry Stewart, and withdrew a sheet of expensive paper. He ran a finger across the tiny embossed symbol at the bottom, a stationer's mark, then reread the succinct message.

Sir,

> *If you are still interested in the purchase of Mrs. Stewart's home, please contact me at my office, and we will begin the process of sale.*

Kit's heart thrummed. The woman had changed her mind—again. He'd never met a more fickle female. A chuckle erupted. In actual fact, he still hadn't met one, since they'd never been introduced. Before he replied to Perry's message, he intended to meet this mysterious stepmother and decide for himself the level of her seriousness. What did one say to the person who held the well-being of others in her unpredictable hands?

As the car rolled south down Broad Street toward the outskirts of town, Kit eased back and grabbed the paper a former passenger left lying on the seat. He read the news of last Sunday's flooding and fires that engulfed the Pennsylvania communities lying on the banks of Oil Creek. The calamitous event ran all the way from Titusville to Oil City. He whispered a prayer for those affected by the extensive loss of life and property. With all they were going through in his home state, how could he complain about an indecisive woman?

The conductor frowned at Kit. "You know your destination?"

"How far is Hickory Grove Road?"

"Get off at Peeler and Limestone. It's another half-mile northwest."

"We're headed in that direction?"

"We are." The man leaned against the back wall of the car and tucked his thumbs inside the armholes of his vest. "You reckon to make Banesville home?"

"Not permanently." Kit held out his hand and introduced himself.

The conductor pumped his hand once, then let go. "William Rainer. You got something against our glorious South, Yankee?"

Kit ignored the man's good-natured prejudice and explained his purpose for being in town. To end, he added, "Problems with alcohol exist in all corners of our country, Mr. Rainer—north, south, east, and west."

The conductor straightened, his face pinched with disgust. "Most drunkards don't have a problem with alcohol. The problem is the quantity they consume."

"That's one way of stating it. However, with God's help, people can change." Kit hesitated. It had taken him several years before he'd grown accustomed to admitting to strangers his weakness. Still, it wasn't a comfortable admission. Each time, he held his breath while awaiting the other person's reaction. "I'm one who has changed."

The statement drew raised, silver eyebrows. "You don't say? So you reckon you can help others?"

"With God, all things are possible, sir. But to answer your question, we help those who seek help. Until a man has the will, success is doubtful."

They discussed the house he and Ben planned to open. "In general, we approach it three ways. Doctors handle the physical issues and care for the body. We rely on pastors such as my partner, Ben, for spiritual guidance. As for the practical matters of finding them work and repairing family relations, I take responsibility for many of those tasks. Mostly, I manage the daily operation of the ministry. We want our men to know it's possible to conquer the lust for liquor, and to see the glory of a sober life."

The conductor eased onto the empty seat across the aisle. He leaned forward and lowered his voice. "Do you think you can help my wife's brother?"

Once more, Kit discerned the hand of God on his work and his purpose for being in this particular town at this time. "I'd be happy to talk with him, but as I said, there are men who refuse our help, and we aren't successful with everyone who comes to us. I'm staying at the Hotel Ambrose. Have him contact me."

Kit exited the car blocks from Joanna Stewart's home and waved to the conductor. Once he reached the house, he strolled up the long drive and paused about ten yards in front of a two-story, white structure at the top of a low hill. Over the years, its broad porch and portico had been augmented with a porte cochere. The mansard roof imparted pride, distinction, and elegance to a country dwelling standing in the midst of simpler farm houses.

On his last visit, he and Ben sat inside a rented buggy parked at the edge of the road and missed details of the home's condition. Today, he could see the outside needed a new coat of paint. Several rotting boards along the foundation were splattered with rust-colored dust from the clay soil. He tilted his head back. A number of slate shingles were missing from this side of the roof.

What was the inside like? He rubbed his hands together. There was only one way to find out. After seeing the extent of the required repairs, he might follow Mrs. Stewart's example and change his mind.

Kit climbed the porch steps and pulled on one of the double screen doors. He frowned as the bottom scraped along the porch flooring. Once he squeezed through, he lifted the iron knocker and announced his arrival.

Moments later, the inner door creaked open and a child peered at him from inside the house. She clutched a stuffed cat, crude and homemade, but well-loved. Round eyes, pale blue like his own, studied him. Those eyes grew fearful, and she swung at the door in an attempt to slam it shut.

"Wait." Kit slapped his hand against the wood panel. "Is Mrs. Stewart home?"

She turned and screamed, "Ma-ma!"

A woman rushed into the foyer, her focus solely on the child. Tendrils of blonde hair poked from the back of a bright red, calico headscarf wrapped around her head. She wore a dingy work dress covered by an apron and carried a feather duster in her left hand.

With her back to Kit, she knelt in front of the girl. "Good heavens, Annie, what's wrong?"

The child's stare drew the attention of the woman—Mrs. Stewart's housekeeper?—to what was behind her. When her wide, blue-gray gaze bore into Kit's, the air *whooshed* from his lungs with the force of another of Donovan's punches.

He should have turned his back on this town and left on the train with Ben.

***

As Kit Barnes stood on the other side of the threshold, memory after memory rushed through Joanna's mind in a humiliating flow more powerful than she had experienced in Perry's office and the days since. Vivid images, tingling senses, and grief—mind-numbing grief.

The feather duster clattered to the floor.

She struggled to drag in a breath, and an absurd thought jumped to the forefront. To him, she must look like a fish dying on desert sands. On the other hand, from his parted lips, pale face, and heaving chest, she surmised Kit fought his own battle to catch his breath.

When he found his voice, he managed to sputter a feeble, "J-Joanna Cranston?" He had not recognized her in Perry's office after all.

She swallowed, but it failed to ease her dry throat, and she almost choked when uttering the word "Stewart."

"I beg your pardon?"

Once the initial shock wore off, Joanna realized that she still knelt by Annie's side. Looking up at Kit put her at a disadvantage, so she pushed to her feet and steeled herself to deal with him as a mature adult—a widow—not the naive young woman of seven years ago.

"It's Joanna Stewart." She pronounced each word slowly and with feigned confidence. "Or if you prefer, Mrs. Clayton Stewart."

Kit's slackened jaw clenched and his icy-blue gaze hardened—a gaze that lacked the red, glassy effect she had noticed often during their short time together. Regardless of his recklessness in those days, he had been charming and striking in looks, only two years older than her.

Standing before her today, he had come of age and devastated Joanna with a clean-shaven and sober appearance, a square jaw and stubborn chin. The only blemishes to his attractiveness were the yellowing bruise at the side of his face and the ferocity in the stare that held her awestruck.

"You knew me when I walked into Perry's office on Tuesday, didn't you? Why hide and pretend to be ill?"

"Because I had no desire to see or speak with you. If I had known you were interested in my home, I would never have agreed to a meeting in the first place. Why do you think I asked Perry to contact you today? You were to deal with him, not me."

From the top of the paper collar and up, his skin reddened with outrage until the color matched the deep blush of her favorite rose. Wherever she went from here, she'd never plant another such bush and let it forever remind her of him.

He crossed the threshold and stopped within a foot of her. She squelched the instinct to retreat. Hot breath fanned her face as he said, "If I had known who owned this place, *Mrs. Stewart*, I would have canceled the meeting myself."

At his raised voice and fierce expression, Annie grabbed Joanna's hand and slid partially behind her. Kit's eyebrows spiked. Evidently, he had forgotten the child's presence. So had she.

Joanna bent and ran a comforting hand over the soft hair covering Annie's head. It twisted her heart to see fear in those young eyes. "Take Kitty and run along to the kitchen, sweetheart. I smelled cookies baking earlier."

"For my birthday?"

"No. Mama has something special planned for your birthday."

Annie eyed Kit one more time, as if she were unsure about leaving Joanna alone with him. Finally, she backed away, then whirled around and escaped down the hall toward the kitchen. The soles of her worn boots tapped the floor in an excited rhythm.

Joanna turned to Kit. "Please keep your voice down. You scared her."

"It wasn't my intention." He exhaled with a heavy sigh. "She's partial to that stuffed cat, isn't she?"

"The child is partial to animals, real or stuffed." Once they were settled elsewhere, Joanna would get the child a puppy or a kitten. She should have done so long ago.

They stood in uncomfortable silence, both gaping at different walls of the foyer. She slid a peek at him. By the faraway look on his face, Joanna suspected Kit never noticed the garish and peeling wallpaper. Sooner or later, he would.

Now what? They couldn't stay this way for the rest of the afternoon. He said he would have canceled their meeting had he known her identity. Did he despise her so much he'd turn down her current offer to sell?

No. No. No. Joanna refused to lose the two people she cared for most to a mean and drunken lout. She'd use the Devil himself to be rid of Liam for Rose and Annie's sakes. It just so happened he stood two feet away.

"We may as well make ourselves comfortable in the drawing room."

Chapter Seven

Past history prodded Kit to run back down the drive and all the way to Pittsburgh if he must. Instead, he removed his hat and followed Joanna into a large drawing room where she sat on the sofa with her back straight and chin held high.

Kit glanced around the room. Their illicit tryst cost him five years of estrangement from his older brother, Hugh, while she surrounded herself with opulence. He ground his back teeth. Hugh had no idea of the favor Kit had done him.

To this day, he cringed at the memory of seducing the woman his brother loved. Knowing God had forgiven him for the sins he'd committed—still committed every day—should bring him peace of mind. Not now. Not while standing here and looking one of his biggest mistakes in the face. As dishonorable as his own actions had been, he never would have succeeded in betraying

Hugh without Joanna's all-too-willing participation.

Although he'd been unaware of it at the time, he'd caught her in her stepson's arms on Tuesday. She hadn't changed.

Kit regretted upsetting the girl, though. Annie. Had Joanna been so vain as to give her daughter a portion of her own name?

A burning sensation rose in his chest. Why had he never thought of her as a mother ... as another man's wife?

Had Clayton Stewart been a man fierce enough to make his own child cower at the sight of a male? Kit's fingers curled into a tight fist. Had he had the same effect on his wife?

Joanna gestured for him to occupy the chair across from her and began to straighten her dress. Her fingers stilled, and she glanced down. When she lifted her chin, her eyes were closed, and he imagined her counting to ten. She raised a hand toward her head and dropped it before touching the cloth tied around her hair. Kit gripped his lower lip between his teeth to keep from laughing aloud.

She opened her eyes and her lips spread in a failed attempt at a smile. "Excuse me. I'll ask Rose to prepare us refreshment."

What would she do if he told her he didn't want any? Would she concoct another excuse to remedy her disheveled appearance? He might as well go along with her ruse. He hadn't eaten since breakfast. "Coffee and those cookies you mentioned sound good."

A dignified Joanna Stewart stood and, with her back rigid, crossed the room at a well-bred snail's pace. She turned into the hall and disappeared. At the skitter of running feet, he laughed.

The laughter ceased as he sniffed the scent of furniture oil. A nearby table held a rag as gray as Joanna's apron. He'd caught her cleaning house? Why? With a place this large, she must employ servants to accomplish the job.

For the first time, he focused on the sparse and shabby furnishings scattered throughout the large room. He could say Joanna had done well for herself if it weren't for the obvious surroundings that shouted neglect. The once glittering luxury of the Stewart home had dulled.

The carved mantel of the fireplace, gilded sconces, and wide trim reminded him of his grandfather's house in Philadelphia. Though he and his mother's father battled endlessly during Kit's wayward youth, he thanked God the two of them reconciled before Grandfather Mullins passed on.

Joanna returned without the apron and head covering and eased onto the settee again. "Rose will be in shortly." She fluffed the material of the blue, cotton dress—one better suited for cleaning than entertaining—and squirmed on the seat. Her gaze darted everywhere, except in his direction, and her fingers moved across her lap as if she played a lively and imaginary song.

Did her awkward fidgeting have less to do with anger or vanity than it did nerves? Kit slumped in the chair at the thought of making the audacious Joanna Cranston Stewart nervous.

A slim, red-headed woman, close to Joanna in age, carried a silver tray into the room. It supported a matching coffee service, china cups and saucers, and plates covered in silver dollar-sized sugar cookies. After setting the tray on the table next to Joanna, she snatched the dusty rag and tucked it into her apron.

"Thank you, Rose."

"You're welcome. Call out if you need anything else." Kit battled frostbite to his face under the servant's glare. "I mean anything."

Rose left the room, and he said, "Pleasant woman."

Joanna's expression darkened. "Rose McCall is my best friend. She's been my rock through every trial I've faced and the one person I could count on. Don't ever speak ill of her."

Every trial? What had the years since he'd last seen Joanna wrought?

Slivers of sympathy worked their way under Kit's skin. Irritated, he brushed them aside. Why should he feel pity for Joanna when he'd been the one to suffer through the sorrow of a broken family relationship?

She jabbed the dessert plate in his direction, and the cookies slid along the smooth china. Kit caught them before they landed in his lap. Then she reached out to pass him a saucer holding a cup brimming with coffee so hot it produced a high cloud of steam. He held his breath, wishing he'd asked for lemonade.

After her short, but intense, tongue lashing, dare he broach the topic of their past? It hung like a black shroud over their heads and would continue to do so if he passed on this opportunity. "From your friend's attitude toward me, I suppose she knows about us."

"Obviously, your memory is poor. There was never an 'us,' Kit."

She'd thrown in his face the angry words he'd shouted long ago. *"Joanna, there is no 'us.' There's you and me and one night that meant nothing."* The steam that swirled above his coffee fell short of taking the chill from the air.

"How is your brother?"

Employing a smile, he countered her attempt to provoke him. "He's well, thank you. Hugh opened a grocery in Northern Virginia and married last year. Violet is a lovely woman, so sweet and . . . innocent." He gained momentary satisfaction in hearing her soft gasp.

The starch left her posture, and she murmured, "I'm sure she's a perfect angel."

Odd that she chose that term to describe Violet, a woman known as the Yuletide Angel. "She may not be perfect, but Hugh found a godly and noble woman."

"I am happy for him."

The sincerity in her voice added to Kit's shame. Why was he acting like a cretin and rubbing Joanna's nose in Hugh's happiness? Because she tried to put him in his place after he insulted her and her friend with unkind remarks? He leaned forward. "Joanna—"

"Do you still want to purchase my property?"

He drew back at the meekness in her voice. Regardless of her less than principled character, she had always been a confident woman. He'd seen this side of her only once. While it didn't sway him years ago, it pained him to witness it now.

Kit looked around. Did he still want this place if it meant dealing with Joanna Cran ... Joanna Stewart? The Lord had given him a choice between best and second best, between this place and the Simmons house. Shouldn't his cause rise above his personal animosity?

"I'd like to discuss a purchase."

Joanna set her saucer on the tray. The cup produced a gentle rattle. She clenched her hands on her lap, her gaze fastened on them. "Since you ignored my wish that you deal with Perry, we may as well settle the terms while you're here."

Kit opened his mouth to say he'd like to see the whole house first, but Perry Stewart burst into the room without waiting to be greeted. With his attention fixed on Joanna, he marched forward. "Joanna, I sent a message to the hotel for Mr. Barnes." Perry removed his hat and tossed it on the settee. "I've heard nothing from ..." the words drifted away once he noticed Kit.

"Good afternoon, Perry. I received your message."

He frowned. "What are you doing here? Mrs. Stewart requested I handle the negotiations of her sale."

"So I've been told."

Perry crossed his arms and glared, increasing Kit's vigilance. If the housekeeper knew about them, had Joanna also confided their indiscretion to her stepson in the past days?

"I'm sorry if I overstepped my bounds." Kit set his coffee cup on a nearby table and stood. "I was about to ask Mrs. Stewart for a tour of the property before I decide whether or not to make an offer."

Perry patted Joanna's shoulder. "You wait here, dear. I'll show him around."

She glanced between the two of them. Nothing in her stoic manner suggested a romantic involvement with her stepson. "Thank you, Perry."

Kit grimaced when Stewart squeezed Joanna's hand. He waited for her to bat her eyelashes or bewitch him with a smile, a flirtatious response to Perry's show of affection. When she pulled away from his hold without the expected coquetry, Kit's lungs caved with the release of his breath.

More than an hour later, they had toured the downstairs rooms, five upstairs bedrooms, the cottage and outbuildings and walked the garden and grounds adjacent to the house. When they returned to the drawing room, Joanna occupied the same place on the settee. He would think she'd remained there the whole time if it weren't for her change into the fashionable green and white striped dress she wore on Tuesday—the dress he'd spotted hanging in an upstairs bedroom earlier. The Joanna he'd known would never have been seen in the same clothing twice in one week.

He'd rushed through her room, reluctant to invade her

private domain. Like the other rooms in the house, its furnishings were old and sparse. Taking into account other tidbits he'd gleaned this afternoon, he suspected she had been selling the furniture bit by bit. The only valuable piece to remain was the grand piano in the music room.

"Well?" Her glance shifted from one to the other of them, then lingered on Kit.

How did she manage to place such curiosity and demand into one word? She was that desperate for his money? "I'm interested."

Had he not been studying her, Kit would have missed the delicate relaxation of her shoulders. "Then you may have the property for five thousand dollars."

"Five thousand?" Outrageous.

"Joanna," Perry crossed the room to stand behind the settee, "may I speak with you? In private?"

She held up her hand. "It isn't necessary. Mr. Barnes wants to buy. I want to sell."

Kit stuffed both hands in his pockets to prevent himself from throttling her. "The real estate agent mentioned four thousand, which I find more than fair considering the age of the structure and the amount I'll spend in renovations."

The one pristine area Kit found was the garden with its meandering paths and variety of flowering and foliage plants. Years ago, he had appreciated Joanna's horticultural talent in every sprout and bloom surrounding her father's house. Back then, she'd had a knack for growing medicinal herbs. She had accomplished the same here. No doubt the men would find the half-acre of greenery a place of comfort and serenity during their trying times.

"My benefactors have—"

"Your benefactors?"

"Yes." Kit dropped onto the chair he'd occupied earlier and leaned forward. "This purchase is not for my personal use, Joanna." He explained about the home in Pittsburgh and the offer from Mrs. Brockhurst and her friends.

A moment of open-mouthed silence followed. "You come to the aid of men who consider alcohol a balm for the troubles in their lives? Kit, you couldn't pass a bottle of whiskey without it following you home. I always figured Mrs. Brockhurst for a snob, but I never thought she lacked common sense. Has she seen that bruise on your jaw?"

Kit smiled. "It's clear only one of us has changed."

Her stare spit nails, but his comment halted her mockery.

Perry's puzzled gaze ran from Kit's dusty shoes to the top of his head. "You two knew each other before today?"

Joanna shifted on the seat as if she sat on a cactus-stuffed cushion. "We met in Philadelphia."

So Perry hadn't been aware of their past and, apparently, she wasn't eager to tell him even a portion of the story.

Perry's nostrils flared and his chest heaved. "I see."

Kit figured he saw more than she intended. Over the years, she had become quite the lady of the Southern manor, but the slight tremble running through her fingers betrayed her detached expression. He had gotten one thing right. Perry wanted more from Joanna than a stepmother-stepson relationship.

You've landed in a hornet's nest, Barnes. He would be fortunate to leave this room without being stung.

A shrill child's giggle echoed in the foyer—Annie with the brown hair and blue eyes. After scaring her with his angry voice, Kit welcomed the glee coming from the . . . what? "How old is Annie?"

"She'll be six on her birthday."

Six? A cold wind raked his core. "When is that?"

"The fifteenth." Joanna narrowed her eyes. "Why?"

Kit subtracted the years and months. A June birth. Every degree of warmth drained from his body as his gaze shot to Joanna.

God, tell me it isn't possible.

All right, what did he know for certain? Incapable of speech or movement, he reasoned through the facts. The child had called for her mama, and Joanna responded within seconds. Annie turned six in less than a week. From what he'd learned, that made her older than Joanna's marriage to Clayton Stewart. She had Kit's coloring.

"Kit?" Joanna's voice broke through his preoccupation.

He jumped to his feet, hat in hand, and prepared to leave. "I'd like to think . . ."

"What is your decision, Barnes?" Perry blocked his path to the foyer.

Kit considered the condition of the structures and grounds, the lack of servants, the fact that he'd caught Joanna in the midst of cleaning her own house, the meekness in her voice when she asked if he was still interested in a purchase. Breaking through the confusion, all he saw were Annie's eyes and hair color.

Much of the inheritance from his grandfather remained in a trust for the next three years. Kit wouldn't see the bulk of it until he'd been sober and trouble-free for ten years. Until then, he lived on an allowance, much of which maintained the Pittsburgh house. However, he had set aside modest savings. Could he afford to agree to Joanna's ridiculous price?

Somehow, he would make up the thousand-dollar difference himself. What he wouldn't do was let Joanna's daughter know want. Not when he could provide for her . . . his own child.

Chapter Eight

Joanna sat on the flat lid of the trunk in the attic. Dust swirled in the narrow beam of sunlight cutting across the dry, wooden floor in front of her. Not even opening the windows rid the space of the summer heat.

She coughed and, with the back of her hand, swiped perspiration from her forehead. "I wish I had my fan." She waved musty air at Annie, who sat at her feet and giggled.

"You were smart to suggest we start this job in the morning. I can't imagine what it will be like working in the mid-afternoon heat." Rose swiveled to glance around the rest of the space. "What will you do with all this . . . clutter?"

"Much of it was here when Clayton bought the house. Frankly, it's rubbish that I plan to leave for Kit to sort through."

Rose planted her hands on her hips. She tried and failed to hide her smile. "Joanna Stewart, just because you don't like him, is it a proper Christian attitude to saddle him with the job of cleaning out what you don't want?"

"I abandoned proper Christian attitudes long ago, remember?"

What would the angel named Violet do? Contrary to everyone else's opinion, Joanna had never felt more than friendship for Hugh Barnes and wished him well in his marriage. But the affection in Kit's voice when he spoke of his sister-in-law two days ago, not to mention the veiled taunt, still stung.

"Don't tease like that."

"You think I'm teasing?" At Rose's scowl, she said, "All right, so you won't consider me a total heathen, I'll ask Perry if there's anything he wants. I'm certain some of his mother's things are still here."

Annie tugged on Rose's apron. "What's a hee-then?"

"Never mind." Rose leaned down and gently tapped a finger on the tip of Annie's nose, and then addressed Joanna. "Perry has never struck me as being the sentimental sort."

"I don't think he is, but I should give him the chance to look." Joanna doubted he'd risk dirtying his clothes to rummage through the collection of odds and ends. "I only want what will bring a decent price when I sell it, and I don't see any of that kind of thing up here. There's not much of value left on the other floors, either."

"What about the piano? I know it means a great deal to you."

Joanna's stomach muscles constricted. Since she was seven, she'd only lived a short time without expressing her joys and frustrations through music. Those were the months between being cast from her father's house and marrying Clayton— months she had needed the comfort most. That period of separation from playing the instrument she loved had hurt with a magnitude that intensified the loss she had suffered.

"A piano that big would never fit into the size place we'll be able to afford, and would cost too much to transport."

Asking Perry if he wanted to buy it was out of the question. He owned a similar grand piano already, one she suspected he purchased to please and impress her, to encourage her to feel at home when she visited, and bribe her into a more permanent stay.

"It's possible Mr. Barnes wants it for his ministry."

Joanna shook her head with an emphatic fervor. "He's taken too much from me already. I'll find a buyer for the piano because I will not leave it for him."

She had survived one turbulent period brought on by Kit. She would survive this one and plead that God make it the last. Maybe He would find her pathetic enough to take pity on her.

Joanna tapped her toe on the floor in an irregular rhythm. Kit had appeared stricken just before he bolted out the door. Had he taken ill? For a moment, it troubled her. After all, the last thing she wanted was for him to die in her house. How would she explain that to Mrs. Brockhurst and the other biddies in town who already considered her a murderer?

"I'll ask Perry if he knows someone who might want the piano."

Rose grabbed an old bonnet from a box and tried it on. She strutted across the floor, dodging furniture and trunks.

Annie jumped to her feet and reached upward to Rose. "I want a hat."

Joanna laughed, her mood bolstered by their antics. "I think you'll enjoy playing with the old dresses and toys we've found today."

"Can I, Mama?"

"Whatever is all right with Aunt Jo." Rose removed the

bonnet and set it on Annie's head.

"Take whatever you want, sweetheart."

"Can I have this, Aunt Jo?" Annie held up a cheap, wooden box with a badly carved cover. Its unsophisticated design would attract only a child.

"If you want it." Joanna hopped off the trunk and raised the lid to dig through her husband's clothes. She wrinkled her nose at the smell of the moth-repelling naphthalene flakes and removed the protective paper covering the vulnerable cloth inside. She reached for the top article, then drew her hand away, amazed by the sudden sorrow that gripped her over the loss of a man who barely spoke to her when they were alone.

After a successful fight against pneumonia, the doctor had diagnosed Clayton's recovery to be all but certain. Within forty-eight hours, her husband died.

Almost three years had passed and too many people still looked askance at her. She couldn't walk through town or enter a business without feeling followed by curious stares. They tickled like ants crawling along her scalp. She'd heard the talk. An older man. A young wife. The interest of an adult stepson. Her husband's unexpected death. As a whole, the circumstances made for tantalizing rumors, but scarce facts.

"Surely, there are men who can use Clayton's things."

Rose reached over Joanna's shoulder and removed a wool suit coat. She shook it out and examined it. "I see no moth holes in this one."

"Then put it in the pile to sell. We need money if we intend to live somewhere other than on the street."

"Where will we go? The sale will be legal soon, and you haven't decided."

"After we pay Li—"

Rose gripped Joanna's arm, and both women glanced at Annie in silent acknowledgment that little pitchers had big ears.

"After everything is settled, there will only be a few hundred left, but I want to get as far away from Banesville as possible."

"I understand."

Rose's soft reply pinched Joanna's conscience. So far, she had made all the decisions regarding the move, giving her friend insufficient say in the matter. Maybe Rose didn't really want to leave town.

Or maybe she didn't want to leave her marriage.

Joanna led Rose out of Annie's hearing and lowered her voice. "I'm sorry. We haven't talked much about how you've fared since Liam left."

She paused to rethink what she was about to suggest. Could she stay, even for Rose and Annie? "I can't bear the thought of him hurting you again, but I won't press you to leave if you'd rather stay."

"But what of Mr. Barnes and the others around town who offend you at every turn?"

"We'll find an inexpensive place. Maybe near one of the mills where I doubt we'll run into anyone of their class. And I'll need work."

Rose's eyes popped. "Surely you're not saying you'd work in a cotton mill?

Joanna's father may have become a minister, but he'd never forsaken his wealthy roots for the sake of the Gospel. Even though Clayton held a tight rein on the purse strings while they were married, she had been content with the things her husband had provided, considering life with a miserly husband to be a penalty for her past behavior. Now the state of her finances forced her to consider employment, but could she go so far as to seek mill work?

"Those places are meant for a person like me, not you, Joanna. You know nothing of operating machinery or weaving cotton into cloth."

"And you do?"

"No, but if anyone works in a mill, it should be me."

The idea of either of them working more than sixty-five or seventy hours a week in a hot, humid, and dusty factory for inadequate pay disheartened Joanna. Most people would say their best option was remarriage. That disheartened her even more.

"Annie will require someone to care for her during the day."

Rose eyed the child skipping across the open space she found in the attic. "Pretty soon, Annie will be of an age to work in such a place. I won't let that happen. I won't stand by while either of you ruin your health and die of the brown lung or lose a hand in the machinery."

Joanna didn't care for herself, but how could she ever subject Annie to such a dismal future?

Rose brushed a tear from her cheek. "Jo, I want better for the child. I want better for her than a man who drowns his disappointments with liquor." It wasn't necessary for her to add that she wished Liam were the man she thought she'd married. It was written in every sad line on Rose's face.

"Then perhaps we'll go to Raleigh, or maybe to a town along the coast. Surely we'll find work in a shop while Annie attends school."

Rose laid a hand on her arm. "I don't know how to thank you."

"I'm the one who owes you, Rose." Joanna glanced at the child. "And we both owe Annie a happier childhood."

Chapter Nine

Joanna crept toward the front door and wished for a window panel so she could see who had knocked. What if Kit tried to surprise her with another visit? She was too filthy, tired, and cranky to deal with him today.

She waited, willing the person to go away. The door knocker beat against the wood once more, and she jerked the door open. "Perry?" He normally entered without knocking.

His smile faded at the sight of her.

"Yes, I look a fright. I wasn't expecting visitors. Rose and I have been in the attic all morning."

Perry dropped his hat onto the half-moon side table along the wall. "I came to apologize for my shortness with you the other day." He lifted a cobweb from her tousled hair, then frowned and pulled a handkerchief from his pocket to wipe his hands. "I was caught by surprise. I had no idea you and Kit Barnes were—"

"We were nothing." Joanna attempted to relax the tight muscles in her neck and shoulders. "Please, come in."

She led him to the family parlor and stood near the front window so she wouldn't be tempted to sink into a chair and dirty the fabric. Despite her mood, a smile lurked on her lips. The poor, fastidious man. What a sight she must be to him. All the better if it helped him get over his infatuation with her.

"I came to tell you I've received the contract. Kit and I will meet this afternoon to discuss it, and then if all is satisfactory, I'll bring it to you for signature." His gaze pinned her. "Unless you would like to meet with him yourself."

"No. I'm content to let you handle it."

Perry leaned against the fireplace mantel. With his finger, he traced a rose leaf on a hand-painted vase. "I noticed the friction between the two of you." His finger stilled, and he waited. What did he expect her to say, that she and Kit were lovers who'd had a spat? He'd have a long wait.

"His brother wanted to marry me. It didn't work out." The truth and yet a lie.

Perry stepped away from the fireplace. He stopped before coming into contact with the dust wafting around her. "You aren't obligated to sell to him, you know."

You're wrong, Perry. "He's shown the only interest."

Kit's purpose for the house was absurd, and completely unlike the young man who had tossed her aside. What had she ever seen in him other than his looks?

The question breached the dam holding back memories, both good and bad. Kit had fascinated her from the moment she first saw him in Philadelphia. His easy laughter and devil-may-care attitude were the antithesis of her father's sober and pessimistic outlook. Yet, underneath that shallow exterior, she'd perceived a smoldering fire—an emotion she longed to explore—never realizing how badly she would be burned.

While she'd danced and flirted with the other young men at the Everspring Ball, her gaze continued to stray in his direction. Finally, he noticed her and made up his mind to approach. Then his brother stepped between them and blocked their view of one another. It was the last time she saw Kit that night. He left the dance without ever speaking to her. They didn't meet again until Hugh introduced them before a dinner at his grandparents' residence.

"You need money for the upkeep of this house. Let me pay for the repairs and you won't have—"

"Perry, I can't."

He forgot himself and grasped her dusty sleeves. "It makes sense, Joanna. I have the money."

What would he say if she told him she needed five thousand dollars? Would he have that for her? "We've discussed this before. I won't allow you to support me or pay my debts."

"You're family. I want to help."

Joanna eased out of his hold. "I'm leaving Banesville for good."

Perry's eyes widened, and he retreated a pace. Had he never taken her spoken wishes seriously before now? "Where will you go?"

"I don't know yet. Rose and I are discussing it." As soon as she said those words, Joanna clamped her mouth shut. Judging by the set of Perry's jaw, she'd made a mistake in mentioning Rose.

"She's going with you?"

"And Annie."

"Your housekeeper is a married woman. What about her husband? What does he have to say about it?"

"Liam no longer lives here. I fired him Wednesday morning."

"You fired . . .? Why? Why didn't you tell me before now?"

Joanna raised her chin. "I fired him because I won't stand by and let anyone physically abuse a friend—not even if he is her husband."

Perry turned his head away. "Of course, you were right to let him go. Last Wednesday, you said?"

"Yes."

"Where is Liam now?"

"I wouldn't know."

They had heard nothing more from Liam after Rose received the note on Friday. It gave no indication of where to reach him. Even if it had, she'd never tell Perry and risk his confronting the drunkard, possibly getting hurt in the process. Though she believed he had been bluffing, she couldn't risk that Liam truly knew a damaging fact about her past with Kit. She would pay thousands of dollars to the lout if it assured her that no one ever learned the truth, especially not Perry . . . or Kit, for that matter.

"You've lived here without a man's protection for several days and didn't tell me?" Perry faced her and took her hand. "I've told you before that it isn't wise for you to live alone such a distance from me. A burglar entered the Jackson residence two nights ago. What will you do if he comes here? Let me take care of you, Joanna."

"Perry—"

"Stay at my house until the sale is final and you've chosen another place to live. There's no need to leave town. I'll ask around. Perhaps there's a house available in my neighborhood."

Live in his neighborhood? After she finished paying Liam she couldn't afford a month in a nice hotel room, much less the purchase of a residence in the better part of town.

"Perry, others will find it improper, and I've had my fill of rumors concerning our relationship."

He dropped her hand with a force that sent a dull pang through her shoulder. "Pay no attention to what a bunch of old hens think."

Joanna had dealt with the opinions of old hens since she was eight, the day they learned her mother had walked out of the Cranston house in the company of a man other than her father and never returned.

She rubbed her shoulder. Gossiping old women weren't the ones who came to mind this time. As much as it pained her to admit it, Kit's opinion concerned her most. Would she ever be free of the man's hold on her?

"If I accepted your offer of a temporary place to stay, what about Rose and Annie?"

"You know I already employ a full staff. I'm sure a number of ladies would be happy to hire Rose, if it weren't for the child."

Joanna thought as much. Perry had never made secret his disapproval of her having befriended a household servant. Annie's existence doubled his objection.

He patted her arm. "Don't worry. I'm sure Rose will find an employer who won't mind the presence of the child. In time, the girl will be an additional help to her mother. I might be persuaded to hire her myself after the child grows to a point of being useful."

"I have greater dreams for Annie than being someone's household help or working in a factory." But if the two women barely kept a roof over their heads, how would she manage to provide the child an education that would bring her a brighter future?

"She's not your responsibility, Joanna." Perry waved away the subject. "Let me return home and instruct my housekeeper to prepare a room for you. It will give you time to gather your things. I'll come back for you this evening before supper."

"I'm afraid I can't accept your hospitality. I'll be fine."

"Don't be foolish. What if a stranger entered this house? Who would protect you? Rose? Obviously, she couldn't protect herself from her own husband."

Joanna bit her tongue. Any response would provoke further argument, something she hoped to avoid. Perry had been too good to her over the past three years.

"Suit yourself." He strode from the room, snatched his hat from the table, and marched out the door.

Joanna lumbered up the stairs and down the hall to her room. The last thing she wanted was to hurt another Stewart man. Apparently, she was destined to do it over and over. The sooner she left Banesville, the better off Perry would be without her.

***

Not long after Perry drove away, the door knocker sounded again. Joanna skipped down the stairs, presuming he had returned to smooth over their troubled parting. She smiled and opened the door to a woman, a stranger. She couldn't be more than twenty, young and pretty, with high cheekbones, green-tinted hazel eyes, and rosy lips. Reddish-brown hair reminded Joanna of the fawn that had followed its mother through her yard that morning. Wave after wave fought the restraints of combs and pins under a straw hat decorated with red, silk roses.

"Yes?"

The woman inhaled a deep breath, planted a cheerful smile on her face and asked, "Are you Mrs. Stewart?"

"I am."

"My name is Darcy Baird, ma'am. I'm looking for work. I'll do anything you need—wash, iron, cook, clean."

The exuberance in the young woman's gentle drawl and anticipation in her hope-filled eyes provoked Joanna to say, "I'm sure you're a competent worker, Miss Baird, but—"

"I can sew, and I make fine lotions. Would you like a sample?" She thrust her arm out to reveal the scent of lavender. "What do you think?"

"It's lovely. However—"

"Please, ma'am, it's been difficult to find employment." She rubbed a hand over her ample middle.

The unconscious reaction drew Joanna's attention to a bulge under clothing that hung more slack than fashion dictated, even in these days of physicians warnings against tight corsets. At her stare, Darcy Baird jerked her hand behind her back, straightened her backbone, and tightened the muscles in her middle—a ploy to make the baby inside her look as if it didn't exist.

"I-I'm a widow, Mrs. Stewart."

A lie if Joanna had ever told one. While Darcy's dress, manner, and speech indicated an educated woman, the white-knuckled clutch of the purse and the lip caught between her teeth revealed desperation. Another woman who allowed a rogue to take advantage of her and paid the price?

Compassion warred with an urge to shut the door in Darcy's face and on Joanna's guilt. "Miss Baird, my house has been sold. I'm preparing to move from town shortly."

"Oh." Darcy's chin dropped. She took a step backward. "Well, I thank you for your time, ma'am."

Joanna pushed the door, intending to close it. Halfway, she stopped as the inner battle continued. "Would you like something to eat before you go?"

Darcy displayed a sad smile. "No, thank you."

Joanna remained in the doorway as Darcy trudged back down the drive. Once she reached the street, Joanna shut the door and leaned against it, tempted to lift a prayer on the woman's behalf—tempted, but not persuaded. Coming from her, it might do more harm than good.

Chapter Ten

Kit stopped in front of a massive, moss-colored Queen Anne structure with a turret on the right and a wide porch that wrapped the front and both sides. He hiked the brick walkway leading to the Brockhurst house, rang the buzzer, and waited until a maid opened the door.

When she gazed up at him, he slipped into his Philadelphia-bred manners. "My name is Christopher Barnes. I sent word earlier of my intention to call upon Mrs. Brockhurst this morning."

"Yes, sir. She's expecting you."

The maid led him into a drawing room where a thin, middle-aged woman draped in black was seated on the settee near the fireplace. The room equaled Joanna's drawing room in size but contained the extravagant furnishings the Stewart house lacked.

Mrs. Brockhurst's eagle-eyed stare focused on him. Joanna's assessment of the woman's personality was exaggerated, but not wholly incorrect.

"It's a pleasure to see you again, Christopher. Please be seated." With a royal sweep of a hand, she gestured to the straight-backed, ornately-carved chair across from her, then said to the maid, "You may bring the tea now, Mavis."

"Yes, ma'am."

Kit shifted on the hard chair in search of a comfortable position. He gave up. "I wanted to inform you of our progress in the establishment of the ministry here."

"The Spencer Brockhurst House."

It was a mouthful he preferred to shorten in private to the House. "Yes, of course."

Research revealed her sixteen-year-old son died from a fall down the stairs. If Kit's majority benefactor insisted upon honoring her late son by naming the home after him, they would do so. He didn't care what name the place went by, only that it succeed in its purpose.

After Mavis brought the tea, Mrs. Brockhurst poured and handed Kit a delicate cup and saucer. "You have secured the location you sought?"

"Yes, ma'am. We'll be on Hickory Grove Road, well away from the drinking establishments."

"Good." The shadow of a question crossed her face. "Hickory Grove, you said? Which house?"

"The Stewart house."

She reached for her tea and added a dollop of cream, then stirred until there was no doubt the two had melded. "Are you sure you've chosen well?"

Kit straightened his shoulders, alert to the quiet admonition. "It's an ideal location and the size will allow room for growth. I signed the contract yesterday. I'm afraid Mrs. Stewart asked more than I'd expected, but I'll make up the difference from my personal funds." At the distaste written in the pinch of her lips, he asked, "Is there an issue I should know about?"

Mrs. Brockhurst sipped her tea and seconds ticked by before she set the cup on the table. "I'm not one to believe in every rumor that comes my way, Mr. Barnes, but there are those in Banesville who hold Mrs. Stewart to be less than, shall we say . . . honorable."

A swift and unforeseen irritation rose in Kit. He'd grown up in the shadow of a shiftless and irresponsible father, so he attributed the reaction to a desire to protect Annie from her mother's reputation.

He swallowed the weak tea and waited for his hostess to continue. People like Mrs. Brockhurst—people who claimed not to believe in rumors—always continued, until others knew every sordid detail.

She shrugged as if to dismiss whatever gossip she intended to pass on. "Some people believe Mrs. Stewart's sorrow over her husband's sudden and unexpected passing was inadequate for a grieving widow. She displayed no tears during the funeral or in the days that followed."

"People show grief in different ways, Mrs. Brockhurst. Perhaps Mrs. Stewart is not one to cry openly in public."

That had not been the case when Kit left her years ago. She had wailed and begged him to stay. How different might their lives have turned out had he given in to her then as she had given in to him an hour before?

"My concern comes from perception, Christopher—the perception which an unemotional young widow leaves, especially when a handsome stepson is involved."

Perry's affection for Joanna was obvious, but Joanna's for him hadn't been as evident, not to Kit's notice on Friday.

"It led people to wonder if . . . well . . ." She left the rest of her statement hanging in mid-air.

"Wondering what, Mrs. Brockhurst?"

Her brown-eyed gaze bore through him. "People wonder if Clayton Stewart died a natural death."

Kit sank against the back of the chair. He had expected her to talk of adultery on Joanna's part, but murder? Ridiculous.

Lucinda Brockhurst waved a fan in front of her face. "Frankly, I'm afraid the purchase of that particular property may alienate other donors who feel Mrs. Stewart should not profit from—at the least—apathy toward Clayton's death."

A financial threat? Kit brandished the grin meant to charm the beholder. "Then, Mrs. Brockhurst, I'm glad to know you take no stock in whatever rumors are circulating about Mrs. Stewart. A woman such as you wields the influence among your peers. No doubt you'll persuade them that the Stewart property is the best possible location for the Spencer Brockhurst House, regardless of who owned it in the past. In the long run, what is more important, the men involved or a rumor?"

Her stare and the twist of her lips told him she saw through his attempt at flattery. She answered his question with a stilted smile.

***

After leaving the telegraph counter at the railroad depot, Kit dreaded a return to the emptiness of his hotel room, so he strolled down side streets and then Broad.

He had sent Ben a telegram but included nothing more than that he'd signed an agreement to buy Mrs. Stewart's house. He also requested that his partner return to Banesville within the week. There would be plenty of time to tell the rest of the story after Ben arrived and before the final papers were signed. They'd both need to work hard to prepare the house for opening on schedule.

Although he'd never confessed to Ben the details of his relationship with Joanna, he had admitted to being the cause of ruining his brother's hope for a future with her. The preacher would be surprised to learn she was the seller. Yet, his friend's surprise could not possibly outdo Kit's.

His steps slowed as he approached a man and woman blocking the walk ahead of him. She was on the young side of sixty and faced Kit. The deep orange day dress she wore flaunted white polka dots, and her voice carried for a good half a block. "What do you mean you have no idea who is responsible?"

Kit stopped behind them. Should he step into the street and go around? Neither looked destined to move soon.

"What do we pay you for if you can't find a simple burglar? I heard he nearly put poor Mr. Jackson in his grave on Friday night. Lands sakes, it's gotten to be a body can't feel safe in her own home."

Though eavesdropping was frowned upon by polite society, the subject of their conversation caught Kit's interest. He pretended to study the advertisement for a new wonder cure displayed in the drug store window to his right.

"I assure you, Mrs. Chandler, the rumors of Mr. Jackson's brush with death are false. He slept through the event. Still, the sneak thief left no clues behind."

"What do you need with clues? Everyone knows he's one of

those drunkards from the saloons." She shook her finger at the deputy. "If you were on your toes, you would search those places first."

Her comment froze Kit's feet to the boards. Over a year ago, the Pittsburgh house had been subject to scrutiny when a rash of burglaries involved one of the men staying there. The investigation forced Kit and Ben to consider closing the ministry. Fortunately, they proved themselves innocent of participation in the crimes without permanent harm done to their cause. What if Mrs. Chandler was right? A similar situation here could cost them dearly.

"Assign men to guard our neighborhood until you find the scoundrel."

"I have men already set to watch the west side, ma'am."

The west side? The wealthy side of Banesville and Mrs. Brockhurst's neighborhood. Was Mrs. Chandler one of the temperance women who had agreed to help fund the house?

"See to it you remain vigilant."

The deputy eventually calmed her but failed to convince her of the proficiency of his office. The two of them parted, and Kit tipped his hat to the woman as she passed him.

He said a silent prayer that Mrs. Brockhurst had as much influence as he'd given her credit for earlier. If the rest of his donors were as starched and difficult as the two he'd met, the project could be doomed before it started.

Kit also asked God's forgiveness for slipping back into his old character long enough to try to beguile his benefactress. These days, he sought to atone for his sins, not to practice them.

Mrs. Brockhurst had gotten in the last say, though. With one breath, she spoke of hosting a lavish reception in honor of the opening of the Spencer Brockhurst House. With the next, she made it clear no residents would be invited to attend.

He entered the narrow building that housed Medford's Ice Cream Parlor, a side shop of Medford's Mercantile, and pulled out a chair from the table nearest the front window. This was the only kind of saloon he frequented nowadays. When concerns overwhelmed him, sweets helped to alleviate the desire for something stronger. Today was a two-scoop day, and he ordered one each of vanilla and chocolate.

The frozen cream cooled his tongue and coated his throat. As he sat there, the noise and street traffic outside the window vanished, replaced by scenes from his visit to the Stewart home. He'd told Joanna she hadn't changed, but that wasn't true. The romantic overtures of a young lady had been replaced by the sober and mature air of a sophisticated widow.

Perry said she preferred to remain at home rather than venture out. Again, it was a trait so unlike the woman he knew in Philadelphia. Back then, she flitted from house to house like an iridescent hummingbird sticking her beak into one flower after another and savoring the societal nectar.

What had Joanna seen in him in those days of hedonism? The ice cream curdled in his stomach. He had never been blind to her interest in him or her flirtations—only deaf to the crying afterward. In those days, he was his father's son, and he'd spend the rest of his life making up for it.

Had the rumors Mrs. Brockhurst mentioned been the catalyst that forced Joanna into the reclusive state Perry claimed? From what Kit gathered, Clayton Stewart died almost three years ago. Joanna no longer wore the dreary colors of mourning. If the rumor of an adulterous relationship was correct, what stopped the two Stewarts from marrying after the older man's death?

Laughter drew Kit's attention to a pair of children seated

across the room. The girl with her caramel-colored hair reminded him of Annie. Did Joanna ever bring her daughter here? His daughter?

Kit dropped his spoon in the bowl and pushed it away with half his ice cream uneaten and melted into a lumpy, brown pool. He left the building and ambled down the street toward his hotel. *If* Annie was his child, how could Joanna have dared keep her from him?

What if it were true and his donors found out? His senses reeled. How could he acknowledge Annie as his without risking the loss of donations from those who would condemn him for his former moral failure? Regardless of his present lifestyle, if that part of his past became public knowledge, he doubted Mrs. Brockhurst wielded enough clout with her peers to help him, nor would she attempt to use it for his sake. No donations, no ministry.

He approached a narrow building that housed a saloon. Raucous laughter burst through the open windows, and the smells of beer and tobacco smoke reeled him in. His steps slowed and his hands trembled as he fought the hook that dug deeper into his craving.

The past days had taken a toll. It had been a shock to discover the house belonged to Joanna and to learn of Annie's existence. Now, the threat of losing his benefactors hung over him.

Shouts and laughter echoed in Kit's ears. His mouth watered, remembering the smooth taste of bourbon. His breathing deepened. His heartbeat accelerated. His hands curled into fists, and his soul cried out, *Father, I can't battle this temptation alone.*

Someone bumped his shoulder. The blow knocked him sideways, and he stumbled, but that one moment's distraction freed him from the lure of the saloon.

He glanced at the man's back as he staggered down the street. Donovan. He should follow and help him, but his own fight with liquor's enticement was too raw. What good was a blind man in helping to guide another blind man? They would both land in the proverbial ditch. He must wait until his vision cleared.

Minutes later, he entered his hotel room and glanced at the bed. A tremor ran from head to toe at the thought of how close he'd come to falling into the hole he'd crawled from years ago.

He pulled the leather bag from under the bed. Ben could handle the preparations for this mission.

Kit never made a secret of his alcohol-related past, but his relationship with Joanna was best left a private matter . . . best for him, best for her and the child, and best for the men he tried to help. By staying in town, he risked the revelation of that secret and the failure of the House.

The image of Joanna gazing upon Annie with love and concern stopped him in the middle of opening the bag. He and Ben taught the men they worked with to face their problem with alcohol and not run from it.

Maybe God provided this opportunity for Kit to meet a child he'd known nothing about, and allow him to face the past. He slid the bag back under the bed, unable to go anywhere until he learned the truth. He would trust God to help him deal with the consequences.

Chapter Eleven

"Here I come. I'm going to get you." Joanna trotted through the yard behind the house in pursuit of Annie. She reached out as if to grab the girl, but held back.

Annie shrieked and ran faster. "You can't catch me, Aunt Jo."

"Is that right?" She swept the child into her arms and planted a kiss on her hot cheek.

Rose walked onto the ground-floor veranda running along the back of the house. She placed a chocolate cake on a table they had moved there for the summer. Glasses for lemonade and two paper-wrapped packages covered the rest of the table's surface.

Joanna set Annie on her feet, took her hand, and led her to Rose. "I've brought you the birthday girl." She poured each of them lemonade and closed her eyes in bliss as the tart liquid flowed down her dry throat.

Annie drank half her lemonade and turned to Rose. "Let's

jump rope."

Rose issued a playful groan. "I think this girl intends to make the most of growing a year older."

"And tire us in the process." Joanna set the glass down. "All right, let's see how much you and I remember from our childhoods."

Each woman held an end of the rope as it swayed with gentle back and forth motions. Annie called out rhymes in a sing-song voice and tripped more often than not. After a while, she fell on purpose. All three laughed, and the child rose to do it again.

"Your turn." Annie grabbed the rope from Joanna.

Joanna lifted her skirts and hopped from one foot to the other as the rope swung in uneven motions. One way or another, she managed to keep her feet from tripping her up while all three of them laughed at her efforts.

Without warning, Annie dropped her end of the rope and stood motionless, her eyes as round as the daisies blooming behind her. Joanna halted. Her heartbeat—already racing from the exercise—could outpace a bicycle. Had Liam returned? Would the man ruin their party when he cared nothing for the girl?

She inched around with a sense of dread. Not Liam. Nevertheless, the pulse in her neck continued to throb. "What are you doing here, Kit?"

He stood at the back corner of the house and offered a smile meant to cajole a glacier to sing. It certainly tempted her to burst into song. "I understand someone celebrates a birthday today, and I found a present she might enjoy."

A gift? What possessed Kit to bring Annie a birthday present?

Joanna gripped her hands in front of her. Did he think that by charming a child she adored he could worm his way into her life again? Why would he want to? She had signed the contract and had given him no indication she planned to back out of their agreement. In another week, she would be gone, and the place would be his to do as he wanted.

He approached them with nothing in his free hand. The other was tucked inside his coat. A bulge under the material moved, and Joanna drew back.

A muffled and pitiful *meow* brought Annie from her hiding place behind Rose's skirt. "What is that?"

Kit struggled to keep his gift from escaping. "What is what?"

She pointed to the bulge. "That. It's moving."

He looked down with exaggerated surprise. "Oh, this. Let's see, shall we?" He knelt in front of her. With both hands and a good deal of effort, he freed the stubborn animal's claws from the linen material of his coat and paid for it as the kitten dug dagger-like teeth into his skin. "Well, what do you know, a cat."

Annie gasped. "A kitty. An orange kitty."

The ends of a yellow ribbon tied around the squirming animal's neck were frayed from the same sharp teeth that now pierced Kit's flesh.

"So it is." Kit held the cat toward Annie, and she shrank back. The kitten clawed what was left of the unmarked skin on his hands. "It won't hurt you."

Joanna snorted. "Yes, we can see by the scratches."

Rose crouched in front of Annie. "What is it, Mr. Barnes? A him or a her?"

"Definitely a female. I have the claw marks to prove it." He held out his hands and smirked. "She didn't appreciate my method of surprise."

A female not appreciating your surprises. Fancy that. Joanna pinched her lips together to keep the comment from spilling out.

It was a waste of breath to compete with his sarcasm.

Kit placed the cat in Annie's arms and looked up. "On the way to the hotel earlier, I passed a group of boys pleading for homes for a litter. This one caught my eye. Do you mind?"

Annie planted kisses on the kitten's head and stroked the fur, enraptured by the gift. How could they say no, now?

"It's a bit late to ask." Joanna smiled at Annie and scratched the kitten between her ears. "What will you name her?"

The child thought only a moment before saying, "I'll name her Jelly, 'cause she's orange."

Rose cocked her head. "Jelly?"

"Like what you make."

Joanna chuckled. "I think she's referring to your orange marmalade."

"Ah." Rose swiped her hand over the cat's fur. "Well, just keep Jelly out of my kitchen, hear?"

"Yes, ma'am." Annie hugged the kitten. "Thank you, mister."

Kit reached out as if he wanted to pat her head, but withdrew his hand. "You're welcome, Annie."

Rose climbed the back porch steps. "We were about to cut the cake. Would you like a piece, Mr. Barnes?" She glanced over her shoulder but avoided the glare Joanna sent her.

Kit eyed the dessert on the table. "How can I resist, Miss McCall?"

"It's Mrs. McCall. Rose is . . ." From the corner of her eye, Joanna caught her friend's grimace. "It's Mrs. McCall."

"I'll get another plate and glass." Rose walked inside the kitchen, leaving Joanna to entertain Kit. Annie sat in the grass, playing with her birthday gift, one that overshadowed Joanna's present of shiny, new boots.

Kit whipped off his hat. A tiny rivulet of blood from a long scratch oozed and mixed with the light brown hair on the back of his hands. The teeth and claws must have been painful, but he never flinched whenever the kitten attacked.

"Those scratches should be cleaned."

Kit gave the rising welts a momentary glance before his gaze fixed on her. "You're probably right."

Neither of them moved. In the silence, Joanna's conscience prodded her to volunteer to clean them for him. Instinct told her to ignore the urge.

"If I could use the pump inside . . .?"

Allow him inside her house again?

Oh, for heaven's sake, he'd own the place soon. She pointed to the door leading into the kitchen. "In there. While you clean up, I'll find the yarrow salve."

When she returned, Kit sat at the table on the porch. He held the backs of his clean hands toward her and waited. Oh, how she despised that enticing grin.

Joanna paused near the door, suddenly afraid to get too close. One bite from the snake's charms had proved one too many. If she'd learned nothing else in her life, it was to be cautious when around Christopher Barnes.

She danced from one foot to the other.

He meant nothing to her.

She stepped forward.

Kit no longer possessed any power over her emotions.

Another step closer.

Anyway, with Rose and Annie around, why worry?

A third step.

For the dare in that smirk alone, Kit deserved whatever pain the cat caused him.

Joanna marched forward, closing the space between them. She dug into the jar and then snatched his right hand. Warmth from his skin spread up her right arm like a flame. Several times, her fingers wanted to curl around his, and she forced them to straighten. She rubbed the oily salve into his wounds, pretending a calm that the tightening of her chest negated. The act of mercy took an eternity.

Kit turned his attention to Annie, who trotted through the unkempt grass as she played with the kitten. With Liam gone, the yard was growing ever more neglected. The women hadn't the time to care for both the inside and outside. The garden was the only area Joanna maintained.

"Where will you and Annie go when you leave this house?"

Unprepared for Kit's question, she said the first thing that entered her mind. "As far from here as possible." He tried to jerk his hand away, but she caught the tip of his finger in a vise-like grip.

"You're leaving Banesville?"

"Yes." She tugged the hand closer and continued her ministration.

"What about Perry?"

She stopped dabbing salve on the long scratch running the length of his index finger. "What about him?"

His questions, his endeavor to be cordial and interested in her life, clanged like warning bells. At one time, he'd shown a similar interest, drawing her in and raising her hopes—only to destroy her through his desire to hurt his brother.

She would pay into eternity for her lapse in judgment, for loving a man who used her and tossed her aside. Hadn't her father said as much before he cast her out of his house? If Papa were here this minute, he would remind her again of the sin she'd committed, and the mercy she would never find from the almighty and judgment-prone Creator.

"Given your relationship with him—"

"Relationship? Are you implying there's more than friendship between us?"

"Have you forgotten I caught the two of you in an embrace?"

"When?"

Kit leaned forward, his gaze steady and none too gracious. "In his office. The day I arrived and you pretended to be ill."

If he were a man who held her in the least esteem, she would suspect jealousy in his tone. "You call that an embrace? You must be out of practice, Kit."

Finished with the right hand, she let go, and the warmth connecting them fled. In its place, she erected an emotional wall of ice. "Now that I've shown you how it's done, I'm sure you can manage the other hand yourself."

After shoving the jar of ointment closer to Kit, she walked away with annoying tears welling in her eyes. She should have refused to tend his scratches. She should never have allowed him in the house last week, much less agreed to sell to him. She should have left Banesville long ago.

If so, these emotions she'd locked in a tiny compartment of her heart would never have broken free. No matter her precautions, the frozen remnants of her love for Kit Barnes melted and flowed like black venom through Joanna's veins.

Forever and always.

Chapter Twelve

Remember. You owe me.

Joanna found Liam's not-so-subtle reminder slipped under her kitchen door. She wadded the paper, threw it in the stove, and watched it shrivel and curl into black ashes. While the first message rattled her, this one infuriated her. He really thought she could forget that the entirety of Kit's payment for her property would go to him?

"Good morning." Rose rushed into the house later than usual, hurried to the ice box, and pulled out the pitcher of milk. "I'm sorry I'm late. I see you've made coffee already."

Joanna poured them each a cup of the strong brew and set Rose's on the stove, glad she'd destroyed Liam's note. Mentioning it would only upset her friend. No matter what Rose claimed, Joanna recognized, in the lines and facial gauntness, the image of regret over a failed marriage and uncertainty over the future. Hadn't her own mirror reflected the same worry numerous times during her union with Clayton?

"Where's Annie?"

"In bed." With her finger, Rose tested the heat on the iron surface of the stove and reached for more kindling from the wooden box on the floor. "She has a fever this morning."

Joanna froze with the coffee cup halfway to her mouth. "How high?"

"Not bad." Rose tossed kindling into the firebox and shut the door.

"Why don't I bring her here and put her in bed upstairs where we can keep a better eye on her?"

"There's nothing to be concerned about right now. I gave her tea with willow bark earlier, and she's sleeping soundly. I'll check on her in a bit."

Over the years, Joanna had lived through Annie's teething, the coughs and sniffles from colds, a scare with measles. Children became sick, and there wasn't anything one could do to prevent it. At these times when a mother's care was needed, a part of her experienced the envy of a woman who must remain content with being called "Aunt Jo" rather than "Mama."

"Why do you think Kit Barnes brought Annie a present?"

Rose's question startled Joanna from her self-pity. "I wish I knew. I don't trust him."

"Aren't you being too skeptical?" Rose shut the icebox door after retrieving a bowl filled with eggs. "Maybe he's trying to be a friend."

"After ruining my life? I'm sure there are plenty of other people in the world he's damaged. Let him be their friend."

"I'm only saying that he seemed a nice enough man. If you

give him a chance, you might find he's changed."

Joanna stood with her hands on her hips, in awe of her friend's naiveté. "Or I might be taken in by him again. I want to forget our history, not repeat it."

"Have you ever thought that it might take facing that history together for your wounds to heal?"

"There's nothing to heal."

"You know that's not true."

Was Rose suggesting that Joanna tell Kit what happened after he left her? "Kit gave up any right to learn the truth long ago. Even if he has changed, I won't let him dredge up those days now so he can achieve a sort of self-serving penance."

Rose shook her head and cracked the eggs on the edge of a bowl. "I may not agree with your viewpoint, but I do understand it."

"Good." Joanna paced across the kitchen floor. "He had a motive for giving Annie that kitten, and I don't appreciate that he's using her in whatever plan he's concocted."

Rose cracked eggs in a bowl. "When it comes to using Annie, I'm afraid he's not the only one."

Joanna stopped in the middle of the room. "Are you talking about Liam? Have you heard from him? Has he threatened Annie?"

Rose beat the life from the eggs and said nothing more. Why would she want to protect her husband after all he'd done, the threats he'd made to each of them?

Joanna marched to the back door. "Annie shouldn't be alone in the cottage. I'll carry her over here while you make breakfast."

She rushed outside, the slam of the cast iron skillet on the stove merely background noise.

***

Joanna swept through the foyer, carrying another dose of the doctored tea to Annie, who rested in a bed upstairs. The door knocker sounded, and she frowned at the intrusion. With the cup and saucer balanced in her right hand, she opened the door with the left and forced herself to inhale a steadying breath.

"Kit." Again. Why couldn't he leave her alone?

"Good morning, Joanna." His voice was smooth, but cool. He offered no smile today, genuine or taunting, but removed his hat and gestured to the towering beanstalk of a man beside him. "This is my friend and partner, Benton Greer."

The man whipped off his hat. "Just call me Ben, ma'am."

Joanna spied a third man standing behind them, inspecting the crack in a column supporting the portico. He held a pencil and book, and his mouth puckered as if he sucked on a lemon.

"This is Mr. Culbertson," Kit said. "He's the contractor we've hired to make necessary repairs."

Mr. Culbertson dipped his head. "Ma'am."

"Sir."

Perry had mentioned the possibility of Kit bringing a professional to evaluate the repairs to her house before the final papers were signed, but she didn't welcome the arrival of these men without an appointment. Had she known in advance, she would have arranged to be elsewhere.

Joanna turned her attention to Kit. "I'm afraid this isn't a good time. Annie isn't well today." She held up the saucer. "In fact, I was just taking her something to ease her fever."

Concern marked Kit's face as he eyed the staircase behind her. "What's wrong with her?"

"Nothing serious."

"I'd like to look in on her, if I may."

At his request, Joanna narrowed her eyes. "And when did you receive your medical degree, Dr. Barnes?"

Kit's jaws twitched as if he ground his back teeth. "I won't disturb her."

"She's resting."

"I said I wouldn't disturb her."

Mr. Culbertson's curiosity shifted between the two of them. No doubt he memorized each word of their discussion, planning to return to town with quite a story. Her desire to argue flagged in the face of potential gossip and Kit's determined and stony glare. "You may say hello from the doorway of her room."

Ben Greer rested a hand on the contractor's shoulder. "Why don't we take a stroll about the outside and let you get a better look at what needs to be done?"

The two men walked away, leaving Joanna alone with a sour-faced Kit. The cup rattled on the saucer, so she steadied it with her free hand. Halfway up the stairs, his grunt halted her. She turned to find him shaking the banister. "Is there a problem?"

He shook the top rail one more time as if she didn't already know there were loose spindles. "I'll bring this to Mr. Culbertson's attention. It should be fixed right away, before anyone is hurt."

Joanna continued up the stairs. "I hope your contractor brought an adequate amount of writing paper to make notes."

She led the way toward a bedroom at the front of the house. That morning, she had opened the outer doors at each end of the hall to allow the scarce air that stirred to travel from the front to the rear of the house. It helped, but after climbing the stairs, she wanted to wipe the back of her hand across her forehead and upper lip to rid her skin of the beading moisture.

Who was she trying to fool? She tramped up and down these steps numerous times a day without this result. But those trips weren't made with Kit walking at her heels.

Joanna stopped outside the door of Annie's room. Kit bumped her back and grabbed her shoulders to keep her from tripping forward. The now lukewarm tea in the cup sloshed and spilled over into the saucer and splashed her hand.

She squiggled from his hold and faced him. "Why are you so intent on seeing Annie?"

Kit backed a step and lifted a shoulder. "I'm concerned. I'd like to pray for her health."

Pray? Kit? Joanna would have laughed if his expression didn't gush with sincerity.

"Aunt Jo?"

Barely discerning Annie's whimper, she hurried into the darkened bedroom, careful not to leave a trail of tea on the floorboards. She lowered the cup and saucer to a nearby table, next to the carved box from the attic, and eased onto the mattress. Curled at the foot of the bed, Jelly awakened and stood, then arched her back in a stretch that ended with her claws coiling into the chenille spread.

"What is it, sweetheart?"

"Are you talking to the mister who gave me Jelly?"

"Yes. His name is Mr. Barnes, and he'd like to say hello." Joanna brushed strands of hair from Annie's face and paused with her fingers on the child's brow. Still warm. "You need more rest. I'll ask him to leave."

Annie propped herself on one elbow and scooped Jelly up next to her. "Can't I see him?"

This child who feared most men asked to see Kit? Apparently, the going rate for her trust these days was the gift of a kitten.

"All right." Without glancing in his direction, she motioned Kit into the room.

He crossed the floor and stopped next to her. To Joanna, the dimly lit and quiet room heightened the spicy scent of his hair oil, the heat from his body, and the sound of his breathing. As he crouched beside the bed, his arm brushed Joanna's knee. She sprang to her feet and crept to the window.

"What's this I hear about you not feeling well, Annie?"

Joanna peered through the glass. Attempting to ignore the wisps of their words and soft exchanges of humor, she concentrated on the antics of several robins as they pecked the dirt. Kit had a knack for befriending children. They flocked to him like those robins flocked to the sounds of insects underground.

A flash of memory weakened Joanna, and she slumped against the windowsill.

So long ago, she'd lain on a bed in a miserably hot and dreary room with her ears covered to block the continual roar of her father's chastisement and her own screams. Pain had quaked through her and perspiration soaked her clothing. Rose wiped her face and whispered assurances of God's care to counteract Papa's claims of eternal destruction. All the while, Joanna held to a feeble hope of forgiveness. Before that day ended, her hope died.

And why not? It never stood a chance against God's judgment.

Chapter Thirteen

Kit followed Joanna down the stairs. This time, he avoided running his hand along the wobbling rail. What other problems with the house posed a threat to Annie's well-being?

Once they reached the foyer, Joanna nodded to Ben and Mr. Culbertson, who waited near the door. She excused herself and rounded the back side of the staircase before Kit could thank her for letting him talk to the girl. Was she angry because he'd insisted upon seeing for himself that Annie wasn't terribly ill?

As they approached the bedroom earlier, he'd thought the child called for an aunt, but in light of Annie's feeble voice, he must have heard wrong.

Ben stepped away from Mr. Culbertson and leaned in close to whisper, "Is she all right?"

"Annie? I'm sure it's nothing. We had a pleasant conversation." Kit could accuse Joanna of a number of unflattering things, but he'd never accuse her of raising a disagreeable child.

"What about Mrs. Stewart? She was upset."

Kit stared down the hall toward the music room. "I believe that's her natural state these days."

He eyed the inquisitive contractor who ran a plump hand over the papered walls of the family parlor. Mr. Culbertson made a notation in the book he carried. "How do things look, sir?"

The man raised his gaze to the ceiling. "Got to check the upper floors."

Kit climbed the stairs once more and stopped to point out the loose spindles. "For the child's safety, will you send a man to fix these immediately? I'm afraid she'll be hurt."

Culbertson nodded and made another notation. Joanna had a point with her comment about the contractor needing plenty of paper.

Each of them halted on the stairs when the piano chords encompassed them. On one side, they filtered up from the hallway next to the staircase. On the other, they drifted through the wall, tickling Kit's ears with the rise and fall of the melody. Thanks to the piano lessons his grandmother foisted on him as a youth, he recognized, yet couldn't recall the correct Mozart concerto.

Ben grinned. "Heavenly music. You never mentioned Mrs. Stewart's artistry on the piano."

Kit nodded, hesitant to destroy the beauty of the performance through the sound of his voice. He glanced at Mr. Culbertson. The man stood with his eyes closed, breathing in the music as if it came from Mozart himself. A smile tilted his lips, and his toe tapped the tread of the stair.

The lively allegro tempo gave way to a slower andante before the movement changed again. Kit imagined Joanna's fingers floating over the keys with the precision of one who performed concertos for her livelihood, which sparked a memory, both ephemeral and electrifying. It was a memory of those same long, lithe fingers as they caressed his face from his temple to his jaw.

Shame worked on him like Jelly's claws. He closed his mind to the inappropriate thoughts and replaced them with Wednesday's vision and the sound of feminine laughter. The glee had enticed him to the back of the house. There, he watched Joanna jump rope, unable to turn away from the pure, carefree enjoyment in her behavior. Once she spotted him, the merriment vanished.

If given the chance, he'd intended to bring up the subject of Annie's father that day. Not knowing was driving him to distraction. Then he learned Joanna intended to leave Banesville, and his purpose splintered like the wood on the outside of this house. If she confirmed his suspicion about Annie, what would he do? Until he could answer that question, he'd bide his time.

"Let's carry on with the upper floors, shall we?" Kit's words spilled out in a razor-sharp command.

After inspecting the second and third floors, the three of them entered the foyer again. The music swirled around them with the same intensity as before. Surely, she'd worn her fingers to a nub by now.

Kit raised his voice to be heard over a crescendo. "Well, Mr. Culbertson?"

The man jerked his head, imploring them to follow, and walked out the front door. He stopped under the porte-cochere. "As beautiful as Mrs. Stewart plays, I couldn't hear myself think."

Mr. Culbertson opened the book he carried and ran his finger down the page. "I've made an extensive list of repairs. The worst involves the chimney on the southeast side of the house. I counted a number of bricks to be replaced. The roof needs patching. A number of the slate shingles are missing."

Mr. Culbertson pointed to a column supporting the portico. "See that crack? Runs vertical about ten feet. It'll only get worse with time. Inside, I found walls with holes in the plaster, and water has leaked through the roof to stain a ceiling in a second-floor bedroom. Everything needs new paint."

Ben turned to Kit. "You sure you want to go through with this?"

Mr. Culbertson added, "Considering its age, I'd say that, overall, the place is solid."

If Kit read Ben's glance at the front door correctly, his friend hadn't referred to a concern over the condition of the house. He weighed the cost of the repairs with the cost of losing the opportunity to learn the truth about Annie's parentage.

"I'm sure."

***

Kit stood across the street from the Moondog Saloon as the sun descended behind the building. On this Saturday night, a clear, twilight sky replaced the earth's halo of pale yellows, oranges, and pinks—tranquil colors that ran contrary to his mood since conducting the inspection of Joanna's house yesterday.

Annie's quiet humor had dispelled his concern over her health. It wasn't the child's situation or Mr. Culbertson's list of repairs that sent his mood south. It was Joanna. With each moment in her company, he felt like a reprobate.

Ben brushed against a young poplar tree he surpassed in height. The tree's trunk, hardly thicker than a broom handle, leaned toward Kit and knocked his hat cockeyed with its switch-sized branches. "There was another burglary Thursday night."

Kit moved to stand on the other side of his friend. He straightened his crooked hat. "I heard."

"It wasn't too far from the Stewart house. I'm concerned about the ladies living there by themselves."

"They won't be there much longer." Kit's casual answer ran contrary to the taut muscles running along his abdomen. "No one has been hurt, and from what I've seen, Joanna hasn't much to steal."

"I keep thinking about the Pittsburgh incident."

"We proved we had nothing to do with that situation, Ben. If we let fear keep us from helping those who ask, what good is our purpose?"

"True." Ben ground a heel in the dirt. "I wonder if Mrs. Brockhurst and her friends are aware of what we went through."

"She's never mentioned it, and I'm sure it's not something she would have let pass. There's no sense in borrowing trouble by bringing it up."

They both stared at the narrow brick building of the saloon. The inside glow from the gas lighting spilled onto the walkway through open windows. Every now and then, men stepped into the drinking establishment or stumbled out of it. The front room overflowed with a Saturday night crowd. So far, Kit hadn't spotted the one man he'd hoped to see.

"Sure is a noisy place. Between the banging on the piano, the shouts, and the off-key singing"—Ben rubbed his ear—"it's a wonder the neighbors' dogs aren't taking up the chorus."

"It's early. They may yet join in." At least, with the setting of the sun, the air had cooled to a more comfortable temperature.

"You want me to go inside and see if he's there?"

"No." God had healed Ben's addiction so completely that nothing about alcohol affected him any longer. The Lord worked that way at times, but not for Kit. He checked his watch. Eighteen. "Let's give it another twenty minutes. If he doesn't show, we'll head back to the hotel."

"Why are you so eager to meet up with Donovan O'Connor? You told me he showed no interest in changing his ways."

"I recognized something in him. I don't know. Call it a melancholy desire for help, even if he won't admit it. I want to give him a purpose again. I want him to see he's still a person of worth and that God sees him that way, too."

Ben smoothed the hairs of his dark beard. "Hmm. I've heard those words before."

"You've said them at least once . . . to me."

"Now that you mention it, you're right. Guess I'm a smart man."

The heavy mood weighing on Kit lifted long enough for him to grin at his friend. "You're also a good friend."

Ben's brow furrowed. "You've come a long way since I found you freezing in that field in '86."

Kit nodded. Six months after betraying his brother, he'd been at the lowest point he'd ever been in his life. Numbed by liquor and guilt. Feverish and weak. Only through God's mercy did he survive that night in late March long enough for Ben to find him and proclaim the news of a blessed and heavenly redemption—news he'd grabbed hold of as if it were the last bottle of spirits on earth.

"People can change."

Kit studied his friend. Ben often cloaked deeper thoughts in pithy sayings. "Why don't you just tell me what you're thinking."

"All right." His friend's glib expression turned serious. "I'd suggest you go easy on Mrs. Stewart until you get to know her better. You're no more than strangers now."

Kit turned his focus back to the rowdy saloon, the muscles of his shoulders tense. "I know all I need to know."

"Do you? Until arriving in Banesville, you hadn't seen her in years." When Kit remained silent, Ben huffed. "I'm not aware of the details of what happened between the two of you, but I'm no rube, Christopher. There's enough friction between you to set every tree afire from here to the Virginia line."

What would his partner and best friend say if Kit told him it was possible he'd fathered a child—a daughter he'd recently met—with the woman Ben urged him to get to know better?

"Kit, how do you expect to help men in need of extending and receiving forgiveness when you're not willing to do the same?"

While he wanted to say he had been forgiven already, the words stuck in Kit's throat. It wasn't at all what his friend meant. "I understand your point, but Joanna will leave town once the property purchase is complete, so it doesn't matter."

Ben frowned but refrained from saying the obvious, that it mattered to God, and it mattered to Kit. Instead, he asked, "Did she say where she's going?"

"I don't think *she* knows where she's going. Even if she does, I don't expect her to share the information with me."

"You'll never know for sure unless you sit down with the woman and talk to her. Don't miss this opportunity to clear up the past. What if it's the only one God gives you?"

Ben was right about his need to talk to Joanna. The Lord had instilled that fact in Kit for days. But how did he initiate the conversation when she was as cold toward him as a Christmas morning in Alaska?

The saloon door opened and the light from inside the building drew Kit's attention to Donovan O'Connor. He stood in front of the building in the presence of another man.

"There he is." Kit's thoughts about Joanna fell away as he tipped his head in the direction of the saloon. The hour was early, but Donovan's gait was unsteady as the two men staggered east along the paved walk. "He must have started this afternoon."

Kit crossed the street with Ben at his side, the noise from the drinking establishment growing ever louder. The two of them closed the distance between the former fighter and his companion, remaining several feet back. The bruise on Kit's jaw had healed, but he didn't fancy receiving another one.

"Donovan." He called out the name with only as much volume as required to be heard over the laughter and music.

Through the darkness broken by a streetlight in the distance, Kit noticed the rise of beefy fists. Donovan turned and relaxed his hands. "Preacher."

"Here's the preacher." Kit introduced Ben, then the two of them angled toward the stranger at Donovan's left. Kit held out a hand in greeting. Though no taller than Kit's five feet and ten inches, the burly man's stiff posture warned against expecting too much geniality.

After a momentary hesitation, he shook Kit's hand. "Name's Liam."

The dim light kept Kit from discerning details of the man's appearance, but the potent smell of alcohol filled the air between them. "Good to meet you, Liam." He turned back to the man he'd come to see. "How are you, Donovan?"

The fighter elbowed his companion. "The preacher here has a mind to reform me."

Rather than take offense, Kit smiled. "I prefer to think of it as forming a new friendship with the hope that I can help you."

"Yeah, well, it was good to see you again." Donovan spun on a wobbling heel and began to walk away.

"I'd like to offer you a job." Even without a flicker of movement from his friend, Kit sensed Ben's surprise.

Donovan halted but kept his back to them. "We've been over this."

"I told you why Ben and I are here. We're purchasing an old house that stands in need of repair and renovation." Kit paused when Liam sniggered. "Would you be interested in helping us?"

Rotating on the balls of his feet, Donovan faced Kit. "And the conditions of taking the job?"

"Three meals a day and a place to sleep." Knowing his response wasn't what Donovan wanted to hear, he added, "There will be no drinking at any time whether working or not."

"Bah." Rather than walk away, Donovan stared down at his boots. "What makes you think I know anything about construction, anyway?"

"I only know you're a hard and capable worker when given a worthwhile task to work toward. I trust you to do the best job possible. After all, you once said a man is nothing without his work. It's up to you."

Donovan raised his head, and Kit's chest tightened at the reflection in his watery, reddened eyes. "I'll ponder it."

Darkness enveloped the men, and a bawdy tune from the saloon swallowed their laughter.

Ben ran a hand down his beard. "Now I know what you meant by the melancholy in the man. I'll pray for him. Why didn't you offer the same opportunity to Liam?"

Had Kit ignored a man God placed in his path to help? Maybe he should have offered Liam a job . . . if he needed one.

"I think Liam bears watching. His smugness rubbed me wrong." Kit started in the direction of the hotel with Ben at his side.

"I'm not one to give up on an insensitive character." Ben gave Kit a good-natured shove sideways. "If I were, you wouldn't be here."

"Praise the Lord for that."

Chapter Fourteen

"What about Chicago?" From her seat across the dining table, Joanna spread a number of Clayton's old papers and several photographs over the cherry wood surface. She shuffled through them and waited.

Waiting had become routine each time she suggested a place where they might move after the house sold. "No" to New York. "No" to Richmond. "No" to Timbuktu.

"I've never been to Chicago." Rose picked up the cardboard-backed photograph of Perry as a child. He stood in front of his mother, a lovely woman with ebony hair. A much younger Clayton sat in a fringed, velvet-covered chair to their right. "It's a big city."

"True, but that allows us many more options when it comes to employment."

"It burned to the ground."

Joanna stared at Rose in disbelief. "That was over twenty years ago. They rebuilt with brick structures to guard against that happening again."

She picked up a dry goods bill from 1884. With the yards of lawn and taffeta listed, she surmised it was material ordered by Clayton's first wife. "The Columbian Exposition will be there next year, and we'd be right in the middle of the excitement. People will travel from all over the world for the exhibits. Don't you want to see the latest inventions and architecture? Think of the glimpse we'll get into the way we'll live in the next century."

Her friend shrugged. "I can only take one day at a time. What would you do in Chicago?"

"I could teach music." Another possibility rose in Joanna's mind. "There will be theaters. Do you think it's naive to believe people might want to hear me play?"

"Not at all." Rose bit her bottom lip. "You could do that here, you know. I'm sure people would hire you to play for parties."

"Oh, Rose, what are you thinking?" Joanna crumpled the receipt and tossed it into the trash stack to her left. "You know that would never happen, not while they blame me for Clayton's death. Anyway, this is not a good place for either of us to remain while Liam lives here. I can tell you from experience that it's certainly not good for Annie to grow up amid the gossip of a broken marriage."

Her friend blenched and then raised her chin in a rare act of defiance. "I'm the one to decide what is or is not good for Annie."

The words as well as the chilling tone caught Joanna by surprise. "Of . . . of course you are. She's your daughter."

"Please, don't forget it."

What on earth had gotten into the woman? "I didn't mean to

imply—"

"You never mean to, Joanna, but it happens all too frequently." Rose left her seat. As she walked toward the butler's pantry with her back rigid, she said, "I'll give Chicago thought."

Joanna leaned forward with her elbows propped on the table and her face cupped in the palms of her hands. What had she said or done to anger Rose? Had she exceeded her position when it came to raising Annie or did Rose use that as an excuse to end the conversation about moving away? Clearly, she balked at the idea. But why?

As soon as she paid Liam off, Joanna would board a train departing this town with its rumors and the snide remarks of people who thought they knew everything about her. She'd leave Perry and his constant offers of marriage. Most of all, she'd leave Kit and the memories that swirled around her at all times of the day . . . and night.

One more week and she'd be gone. Joanna straightened in her chair and cast a glance over her shoulder toward the kitchen. Would she leave alone?

***

Joanna dragged her feet down the stairs and approached the kitchen with caution. She peeked through the doorway. Plates rattled as Rose stood at the sink and washed the breakfast dishes.

Rarely hungry in the morning, Joanna tended to neglect the early meal. Instead, she preferred two cups of strong, black coffee. Today was no exception, but she dreaded walking into the tense atmosphere in the kitchen to face a repetition of last night's strained supper.

She should apologize, but for what? What had she done other

than helping see to Annie's needs and assisting Rose with her care?

Joanna slipped inside the kitchen and poured a cup of coffee without saying a word. She hastened to the dining room with it. When Rose carried in the pot and refilled her cup, Joanna risked thanking her.

"You're welcome." Rose tromped back through the butler's pantry to the kitchen.

When finished, Joanna wished to leave the china cup and saucer on the table and go straight to the music room, but she carried them into the kitchen. Rose stood at the sink drying a skillet, her back to Joanna.

"Just put them down. I'll wash them in a minute."

Like a scolded child, Joanna set the cup and saucer on the edge of the counter. She wanted to walk away, but her feet refused to move, so she stood next to Rose and stared out the window. "It looks like rain today."

"Mmm ..."

Joanna's heart sank with the non-committal response. This was ridiculous. "At least tell me what I did wrong. Why are you so angry with me?"

Rose set the skillet on the stove with a clang. Her shoulders heaved, and she breathed a long sigh. "I'm angry with myself. I should never have lost my temper and spoken to you that way. It's just ..." She laid the damp flour-sack towel on the counter, flattened it, folded it lengthwise, creased it. Fold, crease, fold— over and over, until it was six inches square and Joanna longed to yank it from her hand. "I couldn't ask for a better friend, but there are times when you make me feel as if I'm not the one raising Annie."

"That's absurd."

"Is it? When Annie was sick on Friday, I said she should stay in her own bed. You went to the cottage and brought her here against my wishes. When Mr. Barnes brought her Jelly, you accepted the gift without consulting me."

"But Annie's always wanted a kitten. You said when she was old enough, she'd have one."

"Yes, when *I* deemed she was old enough. Besides, that's not the point." Rose's voice grew shrill. "Time after time, you've taken charge of her and left me out. It has to stop, do you hear me? You are not a mother."

The breath whooshed from Joanna's lungs as if Rose had pummeled her chest instead of the counter.

Rose's eyes grew wide, and she slapped her hand over her mouth.

Joanna reached out to steady herself and her arm bumped the cup. It tumbled off the edge of the counter, hit the floor, and shattered into tiny pieces scattered from one corner of the kitchen to another.

Why had she even sought to discuss this? Why hadn't she left well enough alone? Rose would have gotten over her pique, and things would have returned to normal between them.

Rose laid a hand on her shoulder. Joanna flinched at the touch. "Oh, I'm sorry. I've been so worried about Liam and the loss of my marriage. I never meant to take it out on you."

Joanna eased out of Rose's hold and searched for an excuse to leave, to flee the rooms that once served as a haven for her. "I think I'll take Perry the photographs I found."

Bits of china crunched under the soles of her shoes as she trundled from the kitchen. Were all her relationships meant to eventually end like the cup—broken and irreparable?

Chapter Fifteen

At the end of the drive, Joanna glanced in one direction, then the other. Why had she blurted this solution to putting space between herself and Rose? She'd rather suffer slivers under her nails than face the people of Banesville who snubbed her. With the sales of the horse and brougham, there would be no hiding in the cab of a carriage for this trip.

Besides, the late morning was hot as red coals and molasses-sticky. Perry probably didn't want the photographs anyway. She should return to the house.

A perverse mind-set seized Joanna. Turning right, she hiked down the road. Beads of moisture dotted the skin above her eyebrows and along her chin, and her underclothes clung to her skin. Not far in the distance, thunderclouds rolled up from the southwest to remind her she hadn't brought an umbrella.

After almost a half-mile, she squinted at movement ahead.

The horse car drew near. Should she travel the rest of the way alone and on foot or ride in relative comfort inside a car likely filled with backbiters and busybodies? She craned her neck to see how many people occupied the conveyance. From where she stood, she couldn't tell.

A rivulet of perspiration wended its way down the side of her face, and she brushed it away with her sleeve. Perry would chastise her for walking the whole distance. Gathering her courage—or maybe she didn't care enough anymore—Joanna waved to the driver.

After he stopped the dappled draft horses alongside her, she peered up at the open windows to glimpse into the car—not that she could see much beyond the side on which she stood.

"You fixin' to board, ma'am?"

Joanna hesitated, then climbed the steps and handed the conductor on the platform her nickel. Before she'd chosen a place to sit, the car jerked and rolled forward on the tracks. She fell onto the nearest seat and grabbed her tilted hat. Its pins pulled at the roots of her hair.

A snicker rolled up the aisle from the back. She twisted to glance over her shoulder at the person who laughed at her. A young man erupted with humor again, but his attention was fastened on the lovely girl beside him. No one else paid Joanna any mind. She faced forward and slumped in the seat, irritated with herself for being so sensitive.

The clouds arrived, as did the rain. By the time they reached Broad Street, surprisingly, she had relaxed to the point of sitting straight. The rain had stopped, and the rest of her walk was muddy but uneventful.

Joanna entered the Stewart Broom Factory building to the soft and distant rumble of thunder. She'd reached the bottom tread of the stairs on her way to the second floor and Perry's office when the young man behind the front desk called out, "I'm afraid Mr. Stewart is not in his office, Mrs. Stewart."

She returned to the desk. "Do you know where he is?"

The clerk rose from his chair. "In the factory. I'll tell him you're here."

"That's not necessary. I'll find him." She marched down the hall and out the back door of the office building.

Head down and dodging puddles, Joanna hurried across the red, muddy yard toward the brick building where Perry manufactured his brooms. At the approaching creak and rattle of a horse-drawn wagon, she stopped and waited for it to roll past, its tarp-covered load of crated brooms tied down in the bed. She knew enough about the operation to expect its destination to be the railroad depot.

Clayton never took an interest in the company Perry managed. He'd bought it to give his son experience in the business world, but considered it beneath a Stewart's serious attention. However, Perry built it into a profitable venture. Stewart brooms were sold in stores on both sides of the Mississippi. One day, Perry hoped to ship his products as far as California—farther if he could arrange it.

She stepped through the doorway of the two-story factory and stopped to let her eyes adjust to an interior darkened by more threatening weather.

Bales of broom corn, each weighing over two hundred pounds, and multiple crates of handles were stored in the loft covering the opposite side of the room. Dust from the materials formed a constant gray layer of grit on the windows. Tiny particles danced in the light from gas lamps around the open space while shadows occupied the corners.

The intermittent buzz of a saw came from an adjacent room where wood was cut into the proper lengths for the various types of brooms, and lathes molded the handles.

The making of a broom was more a craft than mechanized labor, and Joanna never tired of watching Perry's employees use the foot pedals on machines to turn the wire that tied the damp broom corn to the handle. Sections of the brush were added a few at a time, and with skillful twists, turns, and cuts, shoulders formed and the broom took shape, all held in place with tacks and thin strands of wire. Once the material dried, the brooms were placed in a clamp device and sewn to hold their structure. Those who were proficient constructed a broom in a matter of minutes. Perry hired only those who were proficient.

Almost two dozen men, women, and children, a couple of the latter no older than ten, were busy with various tasks from toting the broom corn and handles to putting together the goods. In the far corner, two women bound a stack of finished brooms to be shipped. Each employee was too busy with his or her own job to notice Joanna.

Last Christmas, she had purchased a child-sized broom for Annie to play housewife. When were these children allowed to play? Would a ten-hour workday soon be Annie's fate? Not if Rose would let Joanna be of help. That looked less likely after this morning. From now on, she would try not to alienate Rose further. Joanna had no child, never would, and she had better remember it.

After failing to see Perry, she tapped the nearest woman on the shoulder. "Excuse me, do you know where I'll find Mr. Stewart?"

The woman, wearing an apron over a faded calico dress, jerked her head. "He left through that door a short time ago, ma'am."

"Thank you."

Joanna walked across the room to the side door, looked around, and spotted Perry standing with his back to her at the corner of a shed about twenty feet away. He was talking to someone, but the building hid all except the man's right arm and half his booted feet. Renewed raindrops pockmarked the ground between them. Not wanting to intrude, she waited in the doorway of the factory building for Perry to finish his conversation.

As if sensing her presence, he looked over his shoulder and his eyes widened. "Joanna?"

His companion stepped back behind the wall of the shed.

Perry strolled across the yard. "This is a surprise. How did you get to town?"

Despite the increasing sprinkles, she met him halfway. "I rode the horse car."

His brows shot upward. "That's an even greater surprise. Whatever made you want to see me must be important."

"It wasn't important enough to interrupt your conversation."

"Don't worry." He glanced behind him, then gripped her elbow. "Why don't you go to my office before you're soaked to the bone? I'll meet you there in a minute, and we'll talk."

Joanna leaned sideways, expecting the man Perry had been speaking with to step out into the open. He remained unseen. Drops of rain dripped off the brim of her hat. If she stood here any longer, she'd be drenched.

While waiting in Perry's office, Joanna checked the clock on the wall at least a half dozen times. She sat in the chair across from his desk for fifteen minutes and mulled over whether or not to discuss her conflict with Rose. While it might be insightful to receive Perry's advice, she decided to keep their quarrel to herself. He would only take her side against Rose.

Needing to stretch, she stood and twisted her upper body from side-to-side, then walked to the window overlooking the factory building. The rain fell in earnest and beat against the glass. Perry leapt over puddles as he trotted to the rear door of the office building.

Another man stepped from the side of the factory building headed toward the street. Hands in his pockets, his long, quick, and determined strides ate up the yards until he vanished from her line of sight.

Even through the rain and keeping his cap-covered head down, she would have known him anywhere. She had focused on his shoes, imagining they were the same ones she'd seen on the man at the shed earlier, though it was hard to tell from this distance. They looked like the normal footwear of a working man. If he was the same person, what business did he have with Perry?

The office door opened. Perry brushed the dampness from the material of his suit coat and smoothed his wet hair. "I'm sorry to leave you for so long."

Joanna spun and her body tensed. The man she'd seen in the yard had more nerve than was good for him. "What was Liam doing here?"

Perry frowned as he entered his office and shut the door. The thump of his footsteps ended at the edge of the oriental carpet where he removed his shoes. "I hope you don't mind, Joanna. I don't want to get mud on the carpet."

She couldn't wait any longer. "You haven't answered me. Why was Liam here?"

He gestured for her to sit. After she returned to the seat she'd previously occupied, he eased into the chair behind his desk. "Liam came to me looking for a Joanna."

"A Joanna?" Why would he bother to seek work when she would soon pay him the money he demanded?

A violent clap of thunder shook the walls, but the rain had slowed.

"What did you tell him?"

"I told him no, of course." Perry's chair squeaked as he leaned across the desk. A drop of water fell from a lock of his wavy hair onto the polished wood. He grimaced and brushed it away. "Look, Joanna, I know how you feel about him and for good reason. I won't tolerate a man who mistreats a woman. I told him to look for work elsewhere."

"Thank you, Perry." Her jaw relaxed, but she couldn't rid her memory of seeing Liam sneaking out of sight as he'd done. "Why didn't he ask to meet you in your office?"

Perry shrugged. "I happened to be walking past the shed, and he called to me. Why invite him up here when I had no intention of talking to him for long?"

That made sense. "Yes, of course."

He gave the desktop a soft rap with the flat of his hand and grinned. "Now that's settled, maybe you'll put my curiosity to rest and tell me why you hopped aboard a horse car to come see me. Naturally, you can't go long without my witty and charming personality, but ..." He waggled his eyebrows, and Joanna laughed at his silliness.

She forced her troubles from her mind, pulled three photographs from her purse, and laid them in front of him on the desk. "I know you chose the sentimental items you wanted when you moved out of your father's house several years ago, but I've been going through his things and found these. You should have them."

He picked up the top photograph of his mother and caressed the cardboard-backed, paper image with his thumb. "I remember the day this was taken."

"She was very pretty."

"Yes." Perry glanced up. "Whatever one may have thought of him, there's no denying that my father had excellent taste in women."

At the compliment, a burst of heat set fire to Joanna's face. Or was it ignited by the intensity of the devotion that flared in Perry's eyes? On days like today, she wished she felt that same devotion for him.

"I won't give up on us." He dropped the photograph onto the desk. "Stay in Banesville, Joanna. Marry me."

She was as accustomed to his proposals as he was to her refusals. They came every six months as if he wrote the dates on the calendar. This one had come early. Clearly, he loved her. Which was the greater wrong, marrying Perry, which would subject him to the contempt of his peers, or wounding his sense of worth in an effort to protect him?

As if he heard her thoughts, he asked, "Why do you allow the opinions of a group of gossips to rule your life?"

Yes, his welfare made her reluctant to marry him, but in all honesty, it wasn't the complete reason she continued to say no. Marriage required too much honesty from her. It meant revealing her past to him as she had done with his father—with disastrous results. What if Perry turned on her in a like manner . . . or worse? What if, out of hurt and spite, he revealed her secret to Kit?

"I can't. Choose someone better than me, Perry."

From the other side of the desk, his long exhalation of breath spoke his frustration. He pushed up from the chair and glanced out the window. "The rain is passing, and I'm hungry. If you won't agree to marry me, at least agree to have lunch with me."

Joanna hadn't entered a crowded restaurant since Clayton died and the talk began. The idea of it stifled her reply.

"You rode the horse car here, Joanna. You can do this, too."

Again, he knew her thoughts, but could she really do what he asked of her?

Chapter Sixteen

Perry's hand at her back as he ushered her into Hardiman's Restaurant provided Joanna an ounce of comfort, even as a pound of anxiety rushed through her veins. She hadn't the courage to look around for the privacy of a corner table. Her eyes guided her feet straight to the empty one near the front door.

He pulled a chair out for her and took his place across the table. "Don't look now, but Kit is seated in the back corner of the room."

Joanna paused in the process of laying her gloves across her lap. "Really?" She spread her napkin over the gloves, determined not to look, but her gaze betrayed her and drifted in Kit's direction. Their stares locked, forbidding either of them to pretend they hadn't seen the other.

He rose from his seat and ambled toward them down the

center aisle of the crowded restaurant. Her heart thundered with each step that brought him closer. *Please, walk past and out the door.* Joanna had been worried about meeting an old friend of Clayton's and being snubbed. This was worse.

"Good afternoon, Mrs. Stewart. Perry."

Perry shook his hand. "Are you eating alone, Kit?"

"I came in for a quick meal."

"Why not join us?" Perry smiled down at Joanna. "You don't mind, do you?"

Joanna peered around the room. Actually, Kit's presence might work to her advantage. If any of Clayton's friends saw them together, they couldn't assume the luncheon was a social engagement between her and Perry. Moreover, she needn't converse with Kit. "Not at all."

From Kit's hesitation, she guessed he searched for an excuse to decline. "Are you sure I wouldn't be intruding?" His gaze bounced between her and Perry. Did Kit believe she preferred to be alone with Perry?

"I don't mind." Regardless of her best attempt, her answer sounded more a hiss than a cordial invitation.

They ordered, and Kit returned to their table with his meal. Even though they encouraged him to eat his food while it was hot, he waited until they received theirs.

Kit jabbed a piece of meatloaf with his fork. "Is Annie well?"

With Rose's censure fresh in her mind, Joanna replied with a simple "Yes" and cut into her veal cutlet.

"How are your plans progressing, Kit?" Perry sampled the steak on his plate and nodded his approval.

"Coming along."

"May I ask how you and Mr. Greer became involved in your cause?"

Kit darted an uneasy glance in Joanna's direction. When she said nothing, he turned to Perry. "To put it bluntly, I was a drunkard myself."

Perry eyed him but didn't appear surprised. "Then you have empathy with the men you help."

"Yes."

"It must be rewarding and difficult work. Aren't those matters best left to physicians? It's my understanding that many of them believe it's too dangerous to try to cure alcoholism through the instant cessation of drink."

Kit lowered his fork. "It's not an uncommon practice to wean drunkards off liquor a bit at a time or use opium, cocaine, even strychnine, to ease the body's cravings. While we give our men a choice of treatment based on a physician's opinion, Ben and I have established a regimen that promotes a healthy body, peaceful home life, and spiritual growth."

Joanna focused on her meal, hoping to give the impression she paid no attention to the conversation between the men. In truth, she listened to every word.

When Kit spoke of finding God and claimed he'd been forgiven for the wrongs he committed in the past, the fork slipped from Joanna's hand and clattered onto her plate. Kit stopped talking. Perry lifted an indulgent smile that grated on her.

"Pardon me." Picking up her fork worked as a cue for Kit to continue his story.

Was it possible for a person to change as much as he led them to believe?

The first time she saw him at the Everspring Ball, he'd captured the interest of many an empty-headed woman, including her. In the months that followed, she watched as Kit bewitched young woman after young woman. She was content with snatching moments here and there in his company while Hugh grew ever more determined to win her hand.

Joanna had admired the older brother, but his staid personality competed with Kit's magnetism and carefree attitude. Too young and immature to seriously consider his flaws, she allowed herself to be swayed by an attractive face, pretty words, and temporary relief from the constricting and joyless environment at home.

How stupid she had been to fall for the rogue instead of the stable, dependable brother—the one who loved her. Now, in listening to Kit's enthusiasm and his plans for the Spencer Brockhurst House, she found herself in danger of becoming stupid again.

Joanna set her fork on the plate. "If you don't mind, Perry, I should return home."

"You haven't finished eating."

"I'm not hungry." As she stood, so did the men.

Perry set his napkin on the table. "I have a meeting in half an hour. Why don't you wait at the office until I'm finished, and I'll drive you."

"Rose and I have a number of tasks to complete before the house is sold." To relieve his concern, she forced a smile. "It's not necessary to drive me. I'm capable of riding the horse car now."

"As proud as I am of your daring, I'd rather you not travel alone."

Kit dug into a pocket and threw various coins on the table to cover the cost of all their meals. "I'll be happy to escort Joanna home."

She frowned. "It's not—"

"Necessary. I know. Are you ready?"

No. At Kit's grin, her refusal evaporated.

***

Kit and Joanna exited the restaurant into sunshine. Gone was the heaviness in the air. It was replaced by a tension hanging between them that threatened to rain on their trip.

Food aromas mixed with the odors of manure in the street. When a woman wearing too much perfume or a man with a strong cologne passed by, Kit inhaled the fragrance to take his mind off Joanna and her pleasing lilac scent.

He twiddled his thumbs as they waited at the curb for the streetcar to arrive. *Why did You impress upon me to volunteer, Lord? I have better things to do and better company to keep.*

Do you?

Over the nearby shout of a shopkeeper and the wail of a toddler, the two words were a soft whisper to Kit's soul. He stiffened. The last time he'd heard God's voice so clearly, he'd been instructed to open the Pittsburgh home.

Why is it important that I escort Joanna home today? He waited, but no further enlightenment came.

From around the corner, a bell jangled and signaled the approach of the streetcar. When it arrived, Joanna climbed the steps to the platform and slipped Mr. Rainer a coin before Kit could hand the conductor two nickels to pay for both their fares.

William Rainer tipped his hat. "Pleasure to see you again, Mr. Barnes."

"You, too." Kit leaned closer and lowered his voice. "I haven't heard from your brother-in-law."

The conductor shook his head. "I reckon, if I have anything to say about it, you will. The man isn't worth a plugged nickel as he is now."

Joanna advanced toward the front of the car until she reached a pair of empty seats on either side. She settled in the center of one, leaving Kit no option but to sit across the aisle from her.

He frowned in her direction. During the past seven years, he had lived a chaste life. Still, he could name at least a dozen women who would urge him with playful smiles to sit next to them on a short bench such as this. He wasn't accustomed to one who wanted nothing to do with him.

Joanna sat with her back straight and stiff as he studied her profile—the prominent cheekbones, strong chin, and fair complexion. She had matured into an exquisite beauty. No wonder Perry wanted her.

The horses plodded forward, pulling the car down the rails. Along with the *clip-clop* of their hooves and the occasional ding of the transport's bell, the drawl of conversation pulsed around them. Repeatedly, people hopped aboard the car or departed to walk the rest of the way to their destinations. He and Joanna remained silent, their attentions focused on the street ahead.

Kit had learned through his own experiences, as well as his mother's mistake in marrying his father, that physical attraction was not the equivalent to long-lasting love—not the kind he craved these days. He wanted what his brother had found, a woman who sacrificed for others and whose inner strength and compassion outshone the beauty of her face. Joanna possessed a beauty that failed to go more than skin deep.

Ben's advice to take it easy on her until he got to know her better rolled through Kit's mind. He glanced her way again, this time with open curiosity. Just as on the day he agreed to buy the Stewart house, fragility encircled her like a giant soap bubble. If he poked her, would she pop?

As far as he could see, she was no longer the Joanna he'd known. Had motherhood provided the motivation she needed to change? Annie displayed an unspoiled and lovable personality. Was it the child's own inherent character or due to Joanna's guidance?

Realizing his thoughts carried him toward a more sympathetic view of the woman responsible for his problems with Hugh, Kit jerked his gaze away to stare out the open window of the car. Pine, hickory, and walnut trees grew thick along the edge of town. Multi-storied oaks on both sides of the street cast a continuous swathe of shade to cool them.

Squirrels darted along the ground and up the trees, their tails swishing with agitation at the intrusion into their territory. He grinned. Almost like Joanna when he announced his intention to escort her home.

"Such a shame that Clayton Stewart isn't here to ride one of these contraptions." A deep male voice from across the aisle broke into Kit's thoughts. The gentleman and the woman with him had boarded at the last stop and occupied the seat behind Joanna.

Kit lowered his chin and tilted his head to hide his glimpse of her. Other than the sudden, white-knuckled clench of her hands in her lap, she showed no reaction to the man's comment.

"Yes. Bless his heart, he died too soon. So unexpected. So . . . suspicious." The man's seat mate glared at the back of Joanna's head.

So these were the types of rumors Mrs. Brockhurst alluded to a week ago, rumors that accused Joanna of being responsible for her husband's death. No matter her behavior in the past, Kit couldn't believe her capable of causing anyone physical harm.

"Unfortunately, we may never know the truth of his passing."

Kit turned around in his seat to face the couple. "Pardon me, but are you familiar with James 1:26?"

The gray-haired woman clicked her tongue with a *tsk-tsk.* "I've read the entire Bible, young man. More than once."

"I'm glad to hear it, madam. Then you know God's opinion of those who can't bridle their tongues."

The woman's jaw dropped, and indignation colored her husband's face. Joanna shot Kit a wide-eyed look.

Though the barb surprised even Kit, it didn't deter him from speaking his piece. "James goes on to say that part of religion is to visit the fatherless and widows in their affliction. I'm sure you've been diligent in seeing to Mrs. Stewart's welfare since her husband's untimely death." He smiled to soften the sting of his words.

At his last comment, Joanna jumped from her seat. She pushed past the driver, bumping him into the dash guard and earning an earful of criticism when he tugged the horses to a stop. As she hurried down the steps, Kit tipped his hat to the couple he'd dressed down and followed as she crossed the street.

"Joanna, wait."

Mumbling his displeasure, he chased after her as she hiked through the sun-dried, calf-high grass of Fairview Park toward Town Lake, a small, man-made body of water created for the leisure hours of Banesville's citizens. Why was she running away?

She stopped midway down the slope leading to the shore. Kit slowed his pursuit and joined her. Her chest rose and fell with the need to catch her breath.

Muddy, green water lapped against moss-covered stones laid along the edge. Ducks swam by or sunned themselves in the grass. A pair of rowboats skimmed the surface of the water on what had turned out to be a pleasant afternoon. Inside each of the boats, men showed off their rowing muscles to well-dressed women shaded by parasols. The garbled sounds of conversation echoed across the water.

A soft titter escaped from Joanna. She compressed her lips, evidently to keep from laughing outright.

His brow crinkled. "You were amused by what happened back there?"

She glanced at him, and a mischievous light shone from her eyes. "Bridle their tongues?"

"I thought it an appropriate analogy after the way they bullied you. But in hindsight, I guess I'm every bit as guilty for letting mine run away with me."

Joanna sputtered into uninhibited laughter that Kit found contagious. It was the first time since meeting her again that he noticed true pleasure in her features. No, there was another time—the moments he watched and listened as she skipped rope the day of Annie's birthday. But she hadn't known of his presence then.

As the lighthearted moment faded for both of them, Joanna stared out across the water. "Do you know the identity of your sermon's beneficiaries?"

"No."

"Mr. Weedon is a former mayor of Banesville and a friend to my husband. Mrs. Weedon is every bit as dogmatic in her temperance opinions as Mrs. Brockhurst."

Kit groaned. Had he offended another financial backer?

Chapter Seventeen

Joanna faced Kit, the desire to understand what happened on the horse car like an itch she had to scratch, even if it caused the opening of an old wound. She crossed her arms. "Why defend me?"

By the confusion contorting his face, Joanna doubted Kit even knew why he chose to stand up to the Weedons for her. "Was I wrong to do so? Is there any truth to the talk about your husband's death?"

After almost three years, the question lacked any power to anger her, not even when it came from Kit. Had he questioned her with a sneer in his voice, she would have declined to answer. Instead, the quiet inquiry prodded her to reply with an equal softness. "No."

With his gaze probing hers, she didn't dare look away. "I

believe you."

She scanned the ground for a dry spot to rest her wobbling legs while she sorted out her feelings of relief. Why should she care if he believed her?

Kit jerked off his coat, spread it on the ground, and gestured for her to sit.

"The ground is still damp."

"The coat will clean. I want to know what happened. Why do people blame you?"

Joanna hesitated a moment, then sat. Though Kit stood over her, waiting for an answer, she sensed no attempt at intimidation and impatience, only calm and self-control. The Christopher Barnes of her past was a stranger to self-control, and he'd never think to quote the Bible. In fact, if it weren't for the familiar freckle near the hairline at his left temple, she might suspect she was in the presence of a different person—a person she could confide in.

"Clayton suffered from pneumonia. When his health improved, the doctor assured me he would recover. Two days later, I went to his room and discovered him . . . dead." She had tried to relate the experience in an impassive manner, but her voice caught on the last word.

Silence stretched between them as Kit stared out across the water. Finally, he said, "I'm sorry for the loss you suffered, but it's not unusual for an ill person to take a turn for the worse. It doesn't tell me why people hold you responsible."

"I was young enough to be his daughter and a stranger, not from the South. Perry's open admiration didn't help."

Her husband had denied ever telling anyone of their troubled marriage, not even Perry, but she suspected Clayton hadn't been as close-lipped as he'd claimed. Obviously, his friends, especially the banker, David Murray, guessed a problem existed between them. Even though, in public, they pretended to be a couple who admired one another, in the privacy of their home, they spoke only when necessary.

"From the day I arrived, Clayton's friends rarely masked their distrust of me. His death intensified their hostility. For one thing, they claimed they saw no grief after his death." She plucked a piece of grass from his coat and tossed it aside. "After the funeral, someone began spreading rumors of a relationship between Perry and me while Clayton lived."

Kit settled on the flat surface of a rock far enough away from her for two people to fit between them. He drew his right knee up and draped his arm over it. His relaxed pose failed to ease the strain of the muscles running from her neck to her shoulders. Had her explanation destroyed what little harmony existed between them these past minutes?

At his stony silence, she said, "I know what you think of me, but there was no truth to any of those rumors."

"You can't deny that Perry loves you."

"And that makes *me* guilty of adultery?" She slapped her chest in frustration.

Joanna scrambled to her feet and tramped the rest of the way down the slope to the water's edge. Why was she telling Kit all this? She let her guard down for a short time and turned into a chatterbox.

God, please don't let Kit follow me this time.

She fought the temptation to roll her eyes. What good had it ever done her to ask God for anything? Since she was a child, He had ignored her pleas—first, to bring her mother home, then to make her a good enough daughter to gain the approval of her father.

By the time Kit came along, she'd learned not to count on God's help or try to live up to Edward Cranston's pious notions. To her shame, she had proven her father's assumptions about her correct.

Would the punishment never end?

Miniature waves bounced off the rocks at her feet. Not far from shore, a man rowed his young sweetheart past the spot where she stood. The movement of the oars added gentle ripples to the otherwise smooth surface of the water.

The scene calmed her. She imagined sitting at one end of the boat, shaded by a lacy, white parasol. At the other end, Kit controlled the oars with robust strokes that sent them gliding through the water, a gentle breeze ruffling the pleats of her shirtwaist. While she had longed for such a romantic outing with him, romance never entered into the time they spent together— at least not on his part.

At the continued silence behind her, Joanna twisted, sure to discover Kit had walked away, disgusted with her. He remained seated in the same position in which she'd left him, with an arm hooked around his knee and shoulders relaxed. If not for his rapt stare, one would think him casual and serene, even a bit lazy. She'd found that same stare hard to resist in the past. It beckoned to her, cajoling until she answered the invitation to return to him.

Kit looked up. "Has Perry proposed marriage?"

Before she could catch it, a wry chuckle escaped from Joanna's throat. "Like clockwork."

"Then why haven't you married him?"

"And ruin his life?"

He angled his head. "What makes you think you'll ruin Perry's life?"

Was Kit that obtuse or did he have no conception of people's judgments? "After the things I've just told you and what you already know about me, how can you even ask that?"

His grimace answered for him.

"Perry is a friend. He will always be a friend, but nothing more." Joanna shook out his coat and handed it to him. "I should return home."

"I'll walk you the rest of the way."

"That's not necessary."

"It is."

They strolled toward her house in silence. She had pleaded her case. In the end, his sullenness spoke volumes. When it came to her association with Perry, Kit didn't believe her.

As they reached the drive to her home, he grasped her elbow and tugged her to a stop. "Was your husband a good father?"

Confused at the abrupt change in subject, she said, "He and Perry put up a front, but I wouldn't call them close. From what I gather, Perry was the light of his mother's eyes, and she spoiled him terribly. Clayton leaned toward being too demanding."

"What about Annie?"

"My husband rarely acknowledged her." She stepped away from his hold. "Why are you interested in Annie?"

His lips flattened in a crimped line. "She's six years old, Joanna."

"I know how old she is, Kit." Her lips quirked. "I was at the birthday celebration, remember?"

"You weren't married to Clayton Stewart for six years." Her attempt at lightening his sudden somber mood had failed. His voice ranged lower with each word until he whispered the last. "Who is your daughter's real father?"

Her breath caught. "My daughter? Annie is Rose's child."

"Rose?" He blinked several times before confusion formed

creases between his eyes. "But she called you Mama the day I came to see the house."

Joanna recalled rushing into the foyer after Annie's distressed shout. "When you frightened her, she cried out for her mother. I heard and came running."

Kit cleared his throat and stared at his shoes. "Then you never bore a child?"

Joanna's skin turned cold as a corpse. She imagined her face to be as bloodless as one. She had come full circle today. First accused of acting like Annie's mother. Now, accused of being her mother.

Did Kit believe her to be relentlessly immoral, carrying on as if he weren't the only man—as if she were the seducer instead of the other way around? The answer was clear by his red-faced shame. In his estimation of her, Annie could have been the child of any number of men.

Kit blew out a shaky breath. A normally self-assured man, he was anything but one at the moment. "I ... uh ... I muffed this whole thing in high fashion, Joanna. I apologize if I've embarrassed you even half as much as I have myself."

Her anger lessened. How could she blame him for thinking her no better than a prostitute? She deserved his condemnation. Conscience, guilt, fear—whatever one wanted to call it—all combined to silence a response to his apology.

Rose would urge her to answer his question with the truth, but what good would it do them to grapple over the past? What was done was done. Neither of them could change it.

She looked Kit in the eye though everything inside her urged her to turn away and rush down the drive to hide inside the house. "Given our past association, I suppose I shouldn't blame you for thinking the worst about me."

Chapter Eighteen

Joanna smoothed the periwinkle blue skirt over the tiny waist and the curve of her hips. On her way to the bedroom door, she passed the mirror on the dressing table, and her reflection called to her. She stopped to sweep a stray tendril of hair upward, out of her eyes, and leaned forward for a better look in the glass. She pinched her cheeks, adding a light pink to her fair complexion, then stilled in the midst of catching her bottom lip between her teeth.

What was she thinking? Honestly, what did she care for Kit's opinion regarding the rosiness of her cheeks and lips? Years ago, yes, but not today.

With deft movements, Joanna removed the porcelain brooch pinned to the collar of the white shirtwaist and tossed it on the dressing table. It slid across the surface and hit the wooden back with a soft *clink*. She stopped short of mussing her hair for good measure.

Yesterday, Kit turned her world upside down for a second time in her life. After informing her he would return this morning with the carpenter to fix the loose spindles, he'd left her at the end of the drive, pretending all was well between them. Why had she dropped her guard simply because he defended her to those nasty Weedons?

She pressed a hand to her abdomen. How could one man cause her so much inner turmoil and emotional torture and not realize it?

Joanna walked out of the room at the same time Rose reached the top of the stairs. At least the relationship between the two of them was on firm footing again. Kit's assumption that Joanna was Annie's mother helped convince her she had taken her affection for the girl too far, and she admitted as much to Rose.

"The contractor is here with Mr. Greer. They're waiting for you downstairs."

"Kit sent his partner?"

"Yes." Rose eyed Joanna up and down, from the perfect curls she'd spent too much time creating to the form-accentuating ensemble. Her lips twitched. "Is that a problem?"

"Why should it be?" There were any number of reasons why Kit arranged for his partner to accompany Mr. Culbertson. "I'm sure he's too busy with less mundane projects to consider this one worth his time."

Joanna cocked her chin higher and flashed her best saucy grin to cover the hurt. "It's a good thing. Now I won't have to avoid him." She paused on the bottom step. Evidently, the way in which she'd opened up to Kit about her marriage and Clayton's death discouraged him from wanting to see her again so soon.

She turned the overdone grin into a full, welcoming smile for the men standing in the entry hall. After greeting her, the contractor clomped past with one of his men and climbed the stairs. Rose retreated down the hall toward the kitchen. Only Ben Greer remained at her side, watchful to the point of fraying her nerves. She strolled into the cozy parlor and settled on the settee, not at all surprised when he followed.

"I enjoyed listening to your music the last time I was here. Do you ever play the piano for the congregation of your church, Mrs. Stewart?"

Her church? Her last entry into a sanctuary was to attend Clayton's funeral. Rose used to ask her to Sunday services but grew weary of hearing excuses.

"I play only for myself."

"Ah, I hate to contradict you, ma'am, but be assured you do have an audience. Even when you're alone, God hears you."

She almost laughed at the notion that God would stop all He was doing to listen to her play. The humor evaporated with the realization that the man was serious.

"He gave you the ability to create a beautiful sound, Mrs. Stewart, and He's happy when you use it. Each time you sit down at that fine instrument in the music room, I hope you consider every melody to be an offering to the Lord."

Consider her music as an offering? "I beg your pardon?"

"Dedicate your talent to God and please Him with your music."

"God has not been pleased by anything I've done in quite a while, Mr. Greer." Feeling like a helpless rabbit caught in the trap of his steadfast gaze, she looked away and endeavored to regain her composure.

"I'd welcome it if you'd call me Ben." His soft smile eased her tension—a bit. "I'll admit, God has the right to complain about things I've done, too. Fortunately, the bounds of His grace and mercy far exceed what we offer others ... or what we too often fail to allow ourselves to accept."

The hands resting on her lap curled into fists, and her fingernails dug into the flesh of her palms. This man spoke as if he knew her guilt. There was only one reason that could be. "Kit must have provided you an earful of my sins, Mr. Greer. It's a wonder you choose to speak to me at all."

A flush stained the area above his thick beard. "I'm aware that the two of you experienced a troubling incident in the past, but I can assure you, Kit has shared nothing specific with me. What happened between you is God's concern, not mine."

Joanna's flesh burned with mortification.

His expression softened. "I'd like you to understand that nothing you've done makes you irredeemable when you place your faith in the Source of that redemption. Jesus waits to welcome you with open arms, Joanna."

This man spoke with such confidence and sincerity. "Did Kit tell you that my father is Reverend Edward Cranston of Philadelphia? I'm all too familiar with God's expectations . . . and His judgments."

"I've been a pastor, too, Mrs. Stewart. At one time, I was a good one." Ben Greer manhandled the back of the chair across from her. "When my wife and child died of typhoid ten years ago, I allowed sorrow and drink to come between me and my faith. As a result, I lost my congregation, people who had treated me like family. I also lost my self-respect."

Joanna's throat tightened at the pain in his quiet voice and her own memories of sorrow and loss.

He leaned over the chair back. "God taught me that my faith was like the house built on sand. When trouble came, it washed away. But through His grace and mercy, I've rebuilt my faith on a firmer foundation. It will take a lifetime, but I'm growing into the type of man God had in mind for me to be."

Joanna turned her head toward the soot-covered bricks lining the cold fireplace. She had allowed her father's constant diatribes to erode her trust in a loving and merciful God. Could that faith she proclaimed in her childhood be restored?

"Nowadays, Mrs. Stewart, I serve a God who forgives and accepts broken and contrite sinners, ever imperfect human beings . . . people such as me and Kit."

Broken? Contrite? Ever imperfect? When Ben smiled, his brown eyes sparkled, but in searching his face, she found no sign of deceit or piousness. He actually believed God had forgiven him . . . and Kit.

What if she trusted in that forgiveness and discovered—too late—that her father had been right all along? "My father says God extends His mercy only to those He chooses." And never to sinners such as her.

"I don't know your father or your past. However, I sense you believe God is too small-minded and dispassionate to forgive whoever calls upon Him in faith. My Bible tells me He's too righteous and loving not to forgive when we approach His throne of grace in boldness."

Bewildered by his confidence, she walked to the doorway, then paused and turned. "You and my father serve two different gods, Mr. Greer. How am I to know which one to believe?"

"Don't depend on what I say or what your father says. All men will disappoint you at some point. Seek God's mercy and grab hold of His grace, Joanna. Lean on Him through all your trials and fears." Ben's long legs ate up the space between them in three strides. He reached into his pocket and withdrew a black book about the size of a postal card. "I'd like to give you this

Bible."

Her lips parted, but no words came forth. What was it about this man that halted the sharp retort on her tongue. The gentleness of his voice or, perhaps, the compassion in his eyes? She shook her head. "I can't take your Bible, Mr. Greer . . . Ben."

"Of course, you can." He folded her fingers around it. "All I ask is that you read it, Joanna."

When was the last time she had picked up a Bible, much less read it? Her father always insisted God appointed him to explain everything she was required to know. When she was a child, she believed each word that came from Papa's mouth. As the Almighty's anointed, he told her he spoke for God. After her mother ran off, God's words grew harsh and too demanding for Joanna to ever please Him or her father.

She pressed the soft, leather-bound book to her body. "I make you no promises."

Chapter Nineteen

Resting his palms on the windowsill of his hotel room, Kit looked down on the people and vehicles. Their bustling activity barely registered. For most of the past twenty-four hours, Joanna occupied his thoughts. Not only when he'd shown himself a fool yesterday, but from the first moment he saw her kneeling at Annie's side almost two weeks ago. Desperation. Anger. Goading. Laughter. The impish grin before he insulted her with his belief that she bore a child out of wedlock.

He pressed splayed fingers to his forehead as images of her from seven years ago were magnified in his memory like pictures in a stereoscope. They were interspersed with visions of a mature Joanna Stewart, a woman capable of slaying every opinion he'd ever had of her with one look into her pain-filled, gray-green eyes.

God, what's happening to me? Why can't I push these

thoughts of the woman from my mind?

A hand clamped his shoulder. "Are you still among the living?" Kit's arms dropped to his sides. He glanced at Ben and away. "Just thinking."

"Powerful thoughts. I knocked and called out several times, but you never answered, so I let myself in. Let's talk about this morning."

Kit had asked Ben to accompany Mr. Culbertson to the house. How could he face Joanna in the midst of this mystifying turbulence? Nonetheless, he suspected Ben had guessed his history with Joanna, which meant his friend might provide insight into the strange emotions swirling inside him.

The metal frame groaned and the bedspread crinkled as Ben reclined across Kit's bed. "First, tell me what's on your mind."

"I was hoping you could tell me, Preacher."

Kit recounted the trip on the streetcar, the Weedons' comments, and his own response to the couple. He talked of sitting with Joanna by the lake but refrained from saying he'd watched her every move, even when she didn't realize it. "Are you aware that there are those who think she's responsible for her husband's death?"

"I've heard the talk."

Kit dropped onto the rocking chair in the corner and set the runners in motion. It was that or pace a rut in the floor. "They're wrong."

Ben's brows dipped. "Then what's bothering you?"

Seeking his friend's counsel meant being honest, a characteristic Kit had come to value in others but wasn't sure he'd received from Joanna yesterday. "I asked about Annie. I . . . It was important to me to discover whether or not the girl is my daughter." At Ben's understanding nod, Kit said, "You aren't surprised."

"After all I've seen and done in this life, it will take more than that to surprise me. It saddens me, yes. But shock? No."

Kit halted the motion of the rocker and scoured his face with his hands. "Joanna told me Annie is Rose's daughter. She said I misunderstood when I heard the child call out 'Mama' and she came running."

"You think she lied to you." Leave it to Ben to get down to the heart of a matter.

"Whenever I've seen them together, she's been as attentive to Annie as any mother." Kit pushed a hand through his hair. "What if I am the father of that girl? What if Joanna agreed to sell us her home in order to take her away before I discovered the truth?"

"Those are mighty big what-ifs."

"You didn't see the fear on Joanna's face as we talked about Annie yesterday. She looked as if I'd threatened her. She's hiding something from me, Ben, and I can't get out of my mind that it involves that child."

Ben sat up straight. "How many people were privy to what happened years back?"

"Hugh insisted we keep it quiet. As far as I'm aware, only the three of us know . . . now you, of course." Ben never asked a question without a purpose. "Did she say anything to you while you were there this morning?"

The iron frame squeaked when Ben left the bed and walked to the window. He propped a shoulder against the wall. "We talked of spiritual matters. Thanks to her father, she's a confused woman. After Mr. Culbertson left, I sought out Mrs. McCall and asked her about the Reverend Cranston."

Kit grunted. "I remember him. Hard. Self-righteous. Not a man most people held in as high esteem as he held himself."

"While careful not to say too much, it was clear Mrs. McCall agreed." Ben's gaze drifted out the window as he peered up at the partially gray sky that warned of another rainy afternoon. "Did you know Mrs. Stewart and her father have been estranged for the past six years?"

Though it wasn't astounding news, Kit hadn't heard. "Joanna told you that?"

"It came from Mrs. McCall. The two women have been friends almost as long as you and me." Ben twisted, his stare darker than Kit had seen it in a long while. "Her father turned her out of his house. While Mrs. McCall refused to say why, my guess is he learned about your dalliance with his daughter and condemned her to the street."

Kit bolted to his feet. As he paced to the bed and back, he muttered, "I had no idea, no idea at all."

Was his brother aware of Cranston's action? Hugh had warned he'd beat Kit black and blue if ever a rumor began that hinted at Joanna's ruin. Coming from his peace-loving and chivalrous brother, Kit took the warning seriously and never said anything, not even under the influence of liquor. He'd never thought so, anyway. Could he have been responsible for Edward Cranston learning of his daughter's transgression? Then again, the natural course of a pregnancy may have informed him. "Why did I never consider it?"

"Maybe because you never considered her."

The truth hit Kit with the power of a blacksmith's hammer. "I was angry with Hugh and wanted to get back at him. Unlike my brother, I suspected how Joanna felt about me and took advantage of it. Once I got what I went after, I tossed her away like moldy bread, then went on the worst drinking binge ever." His insides cringed at how thoughtless, arrogant, and cruel he'd been in those days.

Telling his friend about that night made it all the more disgusting, but Kit forced himself to continue. "Joanna was a means to an end. I despised her for believing my lies every bit as much as I despised myself for lying to her. For years, I convinced myself she was nothing more than a childish and obliging young siren and eased my remorse by blaming her for the break with my brother. It's taken only twenty-four hours to recognize how I failed both of us."

Kit gripped his hair and tugged until he thought he'd rip it from his head. After leaving Philadelphia, his drinking had increased. Now he understood how he'd used the alcohol to quench his guilt rather than a thirst. The physical pain in his scalp fell short of dulling the emotional pain of his shame.

"No wonder she hid her identity that day in Perry's office and refused to sell the property to me. But if I'm wrong about Annie, why did she change her mind about selling?"

"I don't know."

Kit dropped his arms to his sides and released a mirthless chuckle. "She's leaving town after I sign those papers on Thursday. I can't let her go until I've learned the truth and redeemed myself in her eyes."

Ben glared at him. "We're not talking about you and your redemption, Kit. You can discuss that with God. Our conversation is about a woman who fell for your dishonesty, made a mistake, and, by all accounts, continues to pay for it."

Chastened, Kit said, "You're right, of course."

"My concern lies with the hogwash her father apparently fed her. From what I gathered from my conversations with both women this morning, he convinced Joanna that there is no forgiveness for her actions. If you can't help her see the truth, Kit, her guilt will not allow her to find eternal deliverance."

Kit swallowed hard. "Me? You're the preacher."

"But you're the one to convince her. Let her see the change God made in your heart." A spark of humor crinkled the skin around Ben's mouth. "Show her that it's possible for the worst rogue and sinner to reform."

Kit huffed at Ben's description of him and mumbled, "The worst sinner, huh? I wasn't that bad." Yes, he was.

Deep down, Kit recognized that more than Joanna's lack of candor and his guilt prodded his unsettled feelings. He must discuss it with Ben before it drove him crazy.

"There's more to my wish for her to stay."

Ben's expression sobered. "What is it?"

"Since meeting her again, I've come to recognize that my feelings for Joanna . . . somehow, they've changed."

Ben's tight lips relaxed. "Have they changed so much, Kit, or are you finally ready to declare them?"

"Declare them?" Kit thought to protest, then dispatched the denial with the remembrance of his first glimpse of Joanna in Philadelphia. "You think I cared for her back then?"

She had caught his eye at the Everspring Ball shortly before his brother claimed her. Captivated by her beauty and infectious laughter, Kit had lingered in place to admire her graceful movements. How he had wished to hold her in his arms and lead her across the dance floor. He'd waited too long.

Over the following months, he'd envied Hugh his choice in women as he envied all his brother's choices. Wasn't that what drove him to betray both of them in the first place?

Kit sank back onto the rocking chair. "Whether or not I cared for Joanna then, I need more time to discover the depth of my feelings for her now. How do I convince her to stay, Ben? How do I win her trust?"

"You managed to influence her before through deception. This time, try honesty."

***

"Mr. Barnes, hold up."

Kit spun on the wet walkway lining Commerce Street to face the man he'd met coming out of the Moondog Saloon with Donovan.

A light mist pelted Kit's umbrella and dotted his shoes. He had not seen nor heard from Donovan since speaking with him outside the saloon, but he refused to give up on the former fighter.

When Liam reached him, Kit tilted the umbrella in an attempt to cover both their heads as much as possible. In doing so, a droplet slipped between his collar and neck. "What can I do for you?"

The burly man wiped the excess water from his hands onto his wrinkled suit coat, then stuffed them in his trouser pockets as if he were cold, even though the summer air remained warm. In the daylight, Liam appeared more worn than he had in Saturday night's darkness. "Well, sir, I was thinking it might be what I could do for you."

"And what's that?"

"You offered O'Connor a job. I was figuring, if you still needed workers, you might be open to hiring me, too."

Kit clutched the umbrella handle a bit tighter. As Ben said, they never gave up on anyone. They were both living proof that people could repent and change. Wasn't it their calling to help men like Liam?

Gesturing to a cafe across the street, he said, "Why don't we talk where it's dry, Mr. . . .?" He had never asked the man's last name.

"McCall."

McCall? "Are you related to Rose McCall?"

A smirk lined Liam's scruffy face. "She's my wife."

"I wasn't aware." Rose lived in the cottage behind the Stewart house; however, Kit's inspection the day he agreed to purchase the property hadn't suggested a man lived there, too. "Let's get out of the rain."

After leading the way across the muddy street and entering the cafe, Kit found a table near the back wall and pulled out two chairs. Once they were seated, he ordered coffee. Liam swallowed a third of his drink in a large gulp, then added two heaping teaspoons of sugar and enough milk to fill the cup to the brim.

Kit leaned back in the chair and crossed one leg over the other. The day of Annie's birthday party, Joanna corrected his presumption that Rose was unmarried. He hadn't given it much thought since, assuming she was widowed. "I met your wife at the Stewart house. She's a fine woman."

His companion grunted. "Yeah."

That was all he had to say about Rose? Upon his second meeting with Joanna's housekeeper, she had shown a kinder, less protective side, and he had enjoyed conversing with her. "I didn't realize you lived on the property."

McCall's eyes narrowed with hostility, then quickly turned docile. "Used to."

"You worked for Mrs. Stewart?"

"I worked for Mr. Stewart when he was alive and Mrs. Stewart after he died. You might say I'm between jobs now."

Kit decided not to shy away from his next question. "She

fired you?"

Liam ducked his head. "As you saw the other night, I like to have a drink now and then. Once in a while, I overdo it." He shrugged. "Guess Rose and Miz Stewart got their fill of me."

Kit studied Liam's bowed head and slumped shoulders. "Why do you want to work for me, Liam?"

The man raised his head. "I need a job. I've looked other places, but no one will hire me 'cause of my drinking."

Once a man had a reputation as a drunkard, it followed him. Kit thrived on trying to turn those reputations around. "You do realize I can't pay much, and the work wouldn't be permanent?"

"Yes, sir."

"You also realize I won't tolerate drinking whether it's during working hours or on your own time?"

"Donovan told me your purpose. That's the real reason I want to work for you. I'm thinking maybe you can help me quit the liquor."

"Why do you want to quit?"

Liam pursed his lips as if the question required a good deal of thought on his part. Finally, he said, "I want my wife back."

Kit tented his fingers and studied the man across the table. Part of his responsibility was reuniting families where possible. If he and Ben succeeded in helping Liam abstain from alcohol and win back his loved ones, it would help establish the House in Banesville and secure the continued support of Mrs. Brockhurst and her peers.

"You must want this more than anything else, Liam. Do you?" The man answered with a curt nod. Time would tell. "The sale is final Thursday. We'll start work in the afternoon. In the meantime, report to me at seven a.m. the next two mornings."

In the past, Kit had used every trick available to cover his drinking. He knew the signs to look for and the questions to ask. Seeing McCall at that early hour would provide a certain amount of assurance that he meant what he said about wanting to turn his life around. He could hardly drink until late at night without it showing, though that still left all day.

"One more thing, Mr. Barnes."

"What is it?"

"I'd be obliged if you'd find work at your place for my Rose. She's a good cook and housekeeper."

Kit straightened in his chair. A reunion between Liam and Rose would keep her in Banesville with her husband. If Rose stayed, would Joanna? Was this God's answer to his prayer?

Chapter Twenty

Joanna stood at the kitchen sink and pumped water into a glass. As she tipped the glass back to swallow the cool liquid, she spotted movement from the corner of her eye. She peered through the kitchen window toward the cottage. The glass slipped through her hand. Catching it before it hit the floor, she slammed it on the counter and stared out the window again.

Liam. What was he doing here? She wouldn't collect Kit's check until tomorrow.

Joanna marched to the door and flung it open. With one foot on the veranda, she halted at the sight of Rose approaching Liam. He reached out and pulled his wife closer, enfolding her in an embrace. The sight beat the air from Joanna's lungs.

When he dipped his head to kiss his wife, Joanna stepped back inside the kitchen and shut the door, unable to stomach seeing them together again.

Ben Greer believed in a forgiving, merciful Savior and insisted she discover the truth for herself. If that scene was an indication of God's truth, His grace and mercy, she wanted no part of it.

***

Kit and Ben ate breakfast in the dining room of the hotel, checked out of their rooms and, carrying their bags with them, walked out the front door into blazing sunshine.

To alleviate the burn in his dry, tired eyes, Kit blinked several times. In an hour, he'd sign the papers to purchase Joanna's house and the work in Banesville would officially begin. Less than two months remained until the deadline given them by Mrs. Brockhurst and her temperance friends. That and other concerns had hampered his sleep.

"So what is your plan to win Joanna back?"

At the abrupt interruption of Ben's voice, or possibly the question itself, Kit stumbled over a loose brick in the walkway. He snatched at his partner's coat sleeve to catch his balance. "I never said for certain I wanted to win her back, just get to know her better. You told me yourself I should do that, remember?"

"What you need is a plan"—Ben elbowed him—"or maybe a brain."

Kit glowered up at the grinning giant. Try as hard as he might, in and out of sleep, he couldn't erase from his mind Ben's suggestion that he had cared more for Joanna in the past than he realized.

Ben had visited an old friend in Greensboro during the past two days, and there were things, besides his relationship with Joanna, that they hadn't discussed. "I met Liam on the street the other day. He'll be working for us for a while and suggested I hire Rose as our housekeeper and cook."

"Why would he do that?"

"He's her husband."

Ben's lips parted with the drop of his jaw.

"I finally surprised you."

His friend batted away the teasing. "That must ease your mind about Joanna being Annie's mother."

Did it? "My gut continues to scream that she avoided telling me something the other day—something I should know. What if, in order to protect herself and the girl, she allowed Rose, a married woman, to raise Annie as her own?"

Ben groaned. "More what-ifs? Believe her, Kit. Believe Joanna is a compassionate woman who loves the child."

Was it that simple? "I hired Rose to cook and clean."

Ben blew a soft whistle between his teeth. "Are you sure that was a good idea? She's a lovely lady, but remember the trouble we had finding a woman in Pittsburgh who wasn't annoyed daily by improper advances from the men?"

"We need a cook who serves healthy meals. We'll be there to watch over her, and I figure a man would be a fool to risk Liam's ire by bothering Rose."

Ben halted, forcing Kit to backtrack a couple feet. "Why do I think this has more to do with you and Joanna than Rose and Liam?"

Kit scuffed a clod of orange dirt under his shoe. "It occurred to me that God provided the perfect answer to the problem of keeping Joanna in town."

"How so?"

"Even if she isn't Annie's mother, Joanna will think twice about running off who knows where alone and without the people she considers family. That will give the two of us time to get better acquainted and you more time to work your spiritual expertise with her."

Ben rolled his eyes. "Me? I assigned you the task."

Kit laughed. "You are the preacher."

"I hope you aren't making a mistake by getting involved in all this, Christopher. Joanna may not take kindly to your interference."

"I didn't approach Liam or Rose with the idea of working for us. He came to me. We're helping them save their marriage, Ben. I'm sure Joanna supports their happiness. Besides, since the McCalls have reconciled, Rose has no reason to leave Banesville. How can it be wrong to help two people mend their marriage rather than encourage their separation?"

"For what it's worth, I think you did the right thing for the McCalls. For your sake, I hope Joanna sees it that way."

Kit ambled toward their destination. Had he made a mistake by interfering in Joanna's life? One she wouldn't forgive?

Ben tapped his arm. "Furniture store's on the way. While you're in the attorney's office, I'll check on that order I placed last week."

They approached a break in the buildings and waited until an empty freight wagon left the alley for the street. Once it rattled past, a slouched figure stepped from the shadow of the nearest building. "Mr. Barnes."

Kit tugged Ben to a stop. "Donovan. Good morning."

The fighter shoved his hands into the front pockets of the tired-out trousers he wore and nodded to Ben before returning his attention to Kit. "I heard you hired McCall to work for you."

"I did."

Was that a scowl on Donovan's face? If so, he covered it quickly. "Is that offer of a job still good for me, too?"

Kit contained the smile of satisfaction fighting to break free.

"It is if you're interested."

He drew in a deep breath. "I am."

Kit detailed what would be expected of Donovan and how they planned to help him. "Now that you know what it means, do you still want to join us?"

Donovan's Adam's apple rippled. "I do."

"It won't be easy, but Ben and I have walked in your shoes. You're not in this fight alone. We'll provide as much assistance as we can, but the bulk of the responsibility is yours." Kit paused to let him think about it. If Donovan had an urge to run, he hid it well.

"All I'm looking for is the chance at a better future."

So am I, Dynamite.

***

After dropping a stack of petticoats into the trunk, Joanna reached for the folded skirts. Soon this room and everything other than what covered the surface of the bed—her clothes and the mementos she'd carried with her from childhood—would belong to Kit and his mission to the inebriated. The thought made her wish for a decanter of brandy for herself.

"Jo?"

She glanced at Rose standing in the doorway of her bedroom, then turned away and let go of the skirts. They fell inside the trunk in a multi-colored pile of cotton, silk, linen, and wool. "Yes?"

"I'd like to talk to you."

"Has Liam moved back into the cottage?" Behind her, Rose sucked in a breath, obviously not aware of Joanna having seen them together.

"I-I told him it'd be best to wait until . . ."

"Until I no longer hold any influence over you? I hope he realizes he'll not get a penny from me now."

"I wouldn't let him take one."

What was Liam up to? Why would he exchange thousands of dollars for Rose and Annie—a family for whom he'd shown no respect or concern?

Rose entered the room. "I'm sorry, but this separation from him has weighed on my mind for weeks. I can't break marriage vows spoken before God without good cause."

"And being hit by your husband is not good cause? Annie's safety is not good cause?" Disappointment and anger sharpened Joanna's voice. "How can God expect you to keep a promise to a man who, given half a chance, will hurt you again?"

"Liam promises to change. He says he no longer drinks." Was Rose trying to convince Joanna or herself?

Joanna tossed a corset that had seen better days on top of the skirts. "And you believe him?"

"I'm willing to give him the benefit of the doubt . . . for now." To her credit, Rose didn't try to feign unquestionable faith in her husband's proclamation. "Sobriety is a condition he agreed to meet when Mr. Barnes hired him."

Those last words battered the inner wall of Joanna's chest. She swiveled to face Rose. "Kit hired Liam?"

Rose ducked her head. "Liam wants to change, Jo. He wants his family back, and Mr. Barnes agreed to give him a chance. He plans to hire men like my husband—"

"Drunkards, you mean?"

Rose straightened and shook her finger at Joanna. "You know yourself, there's a good bit of work to be done before the ministry opens. I came to tell you that Liam asked him to hire me, too. I'm to be the head housekeeper and cook for the Spencer Brockhurst House. So you see, Annie and I can't go with you." With that final statement, her voice fell along with the chastising finger.

Joanna's eyes burned and her throat ached with the effort to ward off the tears brought on by Kit's treachery. The moment she saw Liam kiss his wife, she anticipated leaving Banesville alone. Based on the way in which her friend grieved over the failure of her marriage, it had been certain she would jump at the chance to reconcile with her husband if things were different—if Liam were different.

But the fact that Kit would plunge a knife into Joanna's back once more by hiring a wife beater, placing her best friend in danger, and pulling Rose and Annie away from her . . . She never anticipated that move from him.

She erred when thinking that, after their time together in the park, they might part in a civil manner. He'd broken her trust at every turn. Why should she have expected anything else of him?

Joanna grabbed her friend—her rock through times in which she could barely think, let alone act rationally—enfolding her in a breath-stealing hug. The idea of leaving her to deal with Liam alone produced a cold sweat that rolled down her backbone. Yet there was nothing she could do. "I know your marriage is important to you. I won't try to talk you out of going back to Liam."

Rose pulled back. Her eyes sparkled with tears similar to those that threatened to spill down Joanna's cheeks. "He'll need to prove himself to me. I'm not so foolish as to just accept his word."

"Good." Joanna hadn't received another note from the man since the day Annie took sick. Perhaps he had changed, but it would be a miracle. She tossed more clothes in the trunk. "When I'm settled, I'll send my address. If you ever need me or you want to come—"

"We'll keep in touch."

"Please be careful."

"I will, and I'll pray for you." Rose dabbed her eyes with the apron she wore. Her grin wobbled. "We must be a sight."

Joanna chuckled, her mood anything but lighthearted. "It isn't the first time we've cried together over men."

"I hope it's the last." Rose backed out the door. "I'd best mind the stew pot before the meat burns."

Once she'd left the room, Joanna dropped onto the bed, her stomach in knots too tight to eat the chicken she'd smelled earlier. She dug the heels of her palms into her eyes to ease the sting.

"Why are you putting your clothes in there, Aunt Jo? Mama says we won't go away now."

Joanna rubbed the moisture from her cheeks and smiled. "That's true for you, sweetheart. Did you know that today, your friend, Mr. Barnes, will move in here?"

Annie ran a hand along the edge of the trunk. "But where will you go?"

Joanna picked her up and cradled her on her lap. With her chin resting on the top of the child's head, she said, "I'm taking the train to Chicago."

"What's in Chi . . . Chi . . ."

"Chi-ca-go. It's a big city on a lake with tall buildings, lots of people, and exciting things to do."

"I don't think I'd like it. Neither would Jelly."

Joanna grew up in a city, but Annie knew nothing more than the Stewart property and the shops in town.

Annie snuggled closer. "Don't go away."

The appeal of moving with the purpose of becoming lost in a crowd of people—a place where no one had an inkling of her history—faded with the comfort of holding this sweet child in her arms. "I must."

"Papa is coming home."

The words Joanna should have kept to herself burst forth. "Are you happy about it?"

Annie's bony shoulder rose and fell. A faint quiver ran through her body. "Mama says it's for the best. She says we'll be a family again and that's the way it should be."

Could Liam change and grow into the husband and father Rose and Annie required—a man who nurtured his family and didn't frighten them? Joanna's stomach sank as if she'd swallowed a cannonball. She doubted it.

Annie squiggled off her lap. "I forgot something." She ran out of the room and returned a short time later, waving a drawing. The sun shining through the paper revealed writing on the other side. Taught not to be wasteful, Annie must have employed correspondence Joanna had sorted into a pile to be thrown away. "I drew this for you."

Joanna smiled at the crude but endearing images of a girl playing with her kitten. An extra-large sun beamed on them from the sky. "It's perfect, sweetheart. I'll keep this al-always." A sudden whimper escaped her throat.

Annie caught Joanna's cheeks between her hands and gazed into her eyes. "Don't cry, Aunt Jo. You'll be back." It was the confident pronouncement of a child unaware of the complexities of adult lives. Her lower lip protruded. "I don't like Mr. Barnes anymore."

Fighting the urge to say "Me, too," she gently tapped Annie's pouting lip. "It's not his fault that I'm going away for a while. Will you be a good girl and be nice to him?"

"Do you think he'll bring me another kitten?"

Despite her sadness, Joanna laughed. Children tended to see the good in most situations. For the first two years after her mother fled, she expected to see her walk back through the door and greet her with a hug and kiss. It wasn't until she began to understand the vile comments of others that she understood how unlikely that was to happen.

"I hope he brings you a whole litter." She'd leave Kit one more thing—the yarrow salve—and hope he was able to make good use of it.

After Annie skipped out of the room, Joanna packed the rest of her belongings. She smoothed the folds in the drawing and laid the sheet flat inside the trunk, picture side up, on top of Ben's Bible. She closed the lid and locked it. In an hour, Perry would send one of his men to cart her things to the railroad station.

With nothing left to do, she slogged down the stairs to the music room and settled on the piano stool for the final time.

No one had responded to the advertisement she had placed in the newspaper. She ran a light hand over the polished and sleek surface of the Honduras mahogany cabinet. No one wanted her beloved instrument. She had no choice but to leave the piano in this room for Kit to possess, contrary to her claim never to do so.

Everything Joanna held dear would remain with Kit, including Rose and Annie.

After placing unsteady fingers on the cool ivory, she waited, but no melody flowed through them to the keyboard. It was probably best. Why upset Rose and Annie with what could only be a dirge?

What would become of them after Liam re-entered their lives?

Chapter Twenty-one

Kit opened the door of the office and backed into the second-floor hallway while bidding the attorney farewell. "Thank you, Mr. Elliott."

He bumped into a soft, but solid object, spun around, and reached out to steady the woman who winced when he stepped on her foot. "I apologize, Joanna. I didn't see you."

"Hard to do without eyes in the back of your head." She shook off his hold and assessed him with a cool detachment. "Mr. Elliott has the money?"

"Not even a 'Hello, Kit, how are you?'" He cracked a smile and earned a glare in return. "Yes. He has the money."

She stepped forward, ready to enter the attorney's office.

Kit leaned against the door frame. With his feet crossed and his body diagonal in the doorway, he blocked her entrance.

"Excuse me. I'd like to go inside." When he remained in her

path, she crossed her arms and tapped her foot—the same one he'd stepped on—in an agitated rhythm. Her chest rose and fell with impatience. "What are you doing?"

Good question. If hiring Rose hadn't influenced Joanna to remain in Banesville once she signed the papers, she would board a train and depart from his life. "You never told me where you'll go from here."

"I wasn't aware that was a requirement of the sale."

What was wrong with her this morning? The air swirling around her threatened a late June blizzard. "Give me a few minutes of your time first. Please."

She leaned back, and her eyes narrowed. "Why?"

"Well . . ."

In a nearby office, someone whistled a tune, and the answer hit him. Without stopping to reason through his plan, Kit reached out and wrapped an arm around her shoulders. She sputtered a protest as he propelled her to an alcove at the end of the hall and gently pushed her into a chair. "Did you sell your piano?"

A spark of pain tightened her jaw before she relaxed it and regained her cool distance. "I'm sure you'll discover a use for it."

Kit crouched in front of her and grasped her hand. Her back stiffened, but to his amazement, she didn't pull away.

The warmth from her palm and long fingers seeped through the lacy material of the glove she wore and worked on his emotions like a match put to kerosene. Memories exploded in his head, creating fireworks in the form of moments they had spent together in Philadelphia, both alone and in the company of others—the looks that passed between them, the subtle flirtations, the jealousy when he watched her with Hugh—all feelings he'd deliberately suppressed over the years. Ben was right.

He had cared more than he ever let on ... more than his guilt ever allowed him to admit.

The tug of her hand snapped him back to the present. "I remember how much music means to you, Joanna."

"I doubt you remember anything about me." Her voice reached barely above a whisper. "Nothing good, anyway."

If she'd had the power to see into his mind a moment ago, she would realize the truth. How could he ever make up for the way he'd mistreated her? He exhaled a long, low sigh. Apologizing for his most recent insult was a start.

"Joanna, about the other day . . . I'm sorry if I suggested—"

"Please, release my hand."

He should, shouldn't he? Then why did his fingers remain wrapped around hers, unable to move? His pulse drummed in his ears. If he let go, she would bolt. The lines around her pinched mouth and between her eyes shouted the fact. "Just give me another minute."

After a momentary pause, her head bobbed, giving guarded consent. He figured curiosity overcame the desire to quit his company.

"Several nights a week, Ben holds after-supper talks. They're informal, but include the singing of hymns. Have you ever heard a group of off-key male voices croaking out "Amazing Grace" without any accompaniment?"

She ignored the weak attempt to lighten the mood between them and glanced over his shoulder. "Mr. Elliott is waiting for me."

Kit ground his teeth. Impatience was not a shortcoming he remembered. "My musical abilities can't match yours. Will you consider playing *your* piano for us during those times?" He dangled the pronoun like bait on a hook.

After a brief silence, her lips parted and her expression grew pensive. Confidence surged inside him. "The men would even enjoy an occasional evening of entertainment, Joanna. Beautiful music will take their minds off their struggles." As a final incentive, he added, "You'll be paid, of course."

"You mean I'll be an employee?" Her wide smile indicated genuine interest in his offer, but her voice held a false note that raised the hairs on the back of his neck. "Like Liam and Rose?"

Uh-oh. "Yes."

The smile mutated into a sneer. "Absolutely not." Crimson stained her cheeks and fire lit her eyes. She worked to pry her hand loose, jabbing his skin with knife-like fingernails. He thanked God she had no axe to do the job.

Kit tightened his hold. "Why not?"

"As soon as I sign the papers and Mr. Elliott hands me your check, I'm boarding the first train chugging away from Banesville's station."

"You're determined to leave knowing Annie will remain here with Rose and Liam?"

She broke eye contact and mumbled, "As she should."

What was she hiding? "Joanna—"

She recovered her obstinacy and swatted his hand. "Let go of me."

A portly gentleman paused on the landing, panting and trying to catch his breath. He eyed them, tipped his hat, and grinned as if amused by what he perceived as a lover's quarrel taking place in the alcove. He continued down the hall, his shoulders bouncing on a chuckle.

"Kit," she leaned close enough to tickle his ear with the breath of her whisper, "let go of my hand, or I'll scream until they hear it inside the sheriff's office in the next block."

What else could he do other than kidnap her? He dropped her hand, stood, and swept his arm out. "All right, go. I won't stop you. But the piano belongs to you. Whenever you want it, it will be there."

"All I want is a new life."

"Running won't provide it, Joanna. That new life isn't fifty, a hundred, or a thousand miles away from Banesville." He jabbed a thumb at his chest. "It's in here."

Joanna gazed at him and opened her mouth as if to reply, then closed it and walked away. She stopped outside the law office and looked back, her brow crinkled. "Do you have any idea what you've done?"

Before he marshaled a response to the vague question, she entered the attorney's office. The door closed behind her with a click that hit Kit's ears like a gunshot.

***

Joanna walked out of the attorney's office, clutching her purse in a tight grip. Stuffed inside was the largest check she had held in her lifetime. The largest check she'd probably ever hold, and one that tempted her to hold it again.

After drawing it from her purse, she removed her glove and rubbed the smooth paper between her fingers. She breathed in the scent of it—the scent of freedom and a new beginning.

Her name, written in flowing script by Kit, was at the same time satisfying and heartbreaking to see. Part of her believed the amount he paid above the property's worth had been her due—a pittance in comparison to the agony she'd experienced at his hand. Yet, after falling so far, she still had a conscience that nagged her over her failure to tell him the truth.

Joanna shook away the guilt. Kit owed her so much more than mere money. He owed her respect. He owed her the safety of Rose and Annie. She wanted to believe that if he'd known of Liam's tendencies to violence, he wouldn't have hired the man, but her trust in him didn't rise that high.

She should have told him, but even if Kit fired Liam, what good would it do? Rose had made her decision and deserved the opportunity to try to save her marriage. If Joanna had possessed half the determination of her friend, perhaps she would have found a way to save her own.

Drawing to a halt at the top of the staircase, she saw herself descending the steps and walking out the front door, straight to the railroad station. With a fortune in her purse, she'd take the first train leaving the depot. Whether it went north, south, east, or west, she wouldn't care as long as it carried her far from Banesville—away from the people who looked at her with disdain and away from any further connection with Kit.

Once she reached the outer door, Joanna glanced up and down the street, expecting Liam to be waiting for her. She ignored the strong instinct to run and turned in the direction of the Farmer's Bank.

"Good afternoon, ma'am." The teller punctuated his greeting with a genuine smile that spread under an ample mustache. Joanna supposed he grew it to disguise an otherwise youthful face. He was a stranger to her, but not necessarily a new employee of the bank. She hadn't stepped inside the building in at least two years. "What may I do for you?"

She pulled the check from her purse and slid it across the marble surface, under the iron bars that separated the teller from the customer. "I'd like to cash this."

His eyes widened. He leaned forward to whisper, "Cash? Are

you sure you wouldn't prefer to deposit at least a portion of it?"

"No, thank you. I'll also be closing my account."

"I'll need to speak with the manager. Excuse me."

The young teller walked away from his cage and into a room off the lobby. When he marched back out, David Murray, a vice president of the bank, beckoned her inside his office with the crook of his finger. He held her check in his other hand and produced a smile that barely made a dent on either side of his mouth.

The banker was the closest her husband came to having a best friend and confidant. He'd taken Clayton's death harder than most, certainly harder than she had. It only added fuel to his dislike, one stoked, no doubt, by whatever her husband told him. Like the Weedons, he had either sensed a problem in their marriage or Clayton had lied to her about keeping their business private.

Once the rumors surrounding her husband's death began to swirl, Joanna had suspected David Murray as the source. By that time, Clayton had been in the ground for three weeks. She had been questioned, but after a session with Perry, the sheriff refused to proceed further on such insignificant evidence as disapproval of the widow.

Rather than being a blessing, it turned into a curse, as nothing could be proved one way or the other. People in Clayton's circle believed what they wanted—that she had hastened his death in an undetectable manner, most likely poison. After all, she grew numerous resources in her garden. And they wanted to believe the well-respected banker over the "greedy, too-young, Yankee" wife.

Joanna raised her chin and followed Mr. Murray inside the room. He snapped the door shut, and she flinched with the ludicrous notion that the door of a prison locked behind her.

After gesturing for her to sit, he eased into the chair behind his desk. "I understand you've sold your house, Mrs. Stewart."

It came as no surprise to her that he was privy to that tidbit of information. "Yes. Now I would like to exchange that check in your hand for cash."

He laid the paper on his desk. "I also hear you want to withdraw the rest of the funds in your account. May I ask if you've found our services lacking?"

"No. I find your services no longer needed." At his raised eyebrows, she said, "You'll be happy to know I'm leaving town shortly."

"Is that so?" With his elbows resting on the arms of his chair, he leaned back and tapped his fingers together. "That's a great deal of money for a woman to carry on her person while traveling. Perhaps you'll consider waiting to cash it until you reach wherever you're going, or is Perry accompanying you to act as bodyguard?"

Joanna pointed to the check. "After you cash that and close my account, I won't trouble you again."

A smug grin lined his face. "If Clayton still lived, you wouldn't go anywhere with any of his money."

Heat flooded Joanna's cheeks. Anger and humiliation coursed through her like rotting debris carried along by swift waters. "Mr. Murray, either cash my check or I'll take it straight to your employer."

He lowered his arms and pinned her with a harsh stare. "As you wish. Frankly, I'm happy to know the property will benefit by your absence."

After their meeting, Joanna rushed from the bank with her head down and her hands crushing the purse to her chest. She couldn't leave this town fast enough.

***

Joanna exited the bank across the street and rushed down the steps. Kit pushed away from the brick wall at the side of the butcher's where he'd waited for fifteen minutes.

He had credited her with more sense than to travel hours or days on a train with thousands of dollars in cash. But when he saw her enter the bank, he suspected he had been wrong, a suspicion proved correct based on the bulge in the handbag pressed against her body.

Telling himself his objective was to be sure she remained safe, Kit dodged a carriage and crossed the street. He followed at a discreet distance. As long as she kept her head bent and shoulders hunched, he needn't worry about being spotted by her. The only time he ducked out of sight was when she looked up and down the street before crossing it.

Joanna employed long strides in her haste to reach the railroad station. She passed the businesses along Fourth Street. In case she decided to look back, Kit expanded the distance between them and dipped his head in an imitation of her own walk.

They entered the stark warehouse district near the depot. Wagons rolled up and down the street, pulled by plodding horses and mules. Their heads drooped and hooves kicked up dust.

Kit's hope of exploring these feelings that churned inside dwindled with each yard that brought them closer to the depot.

After Joanna walked inside the long, wooden, one-story building that housed the ticket counter and waiting room, he leaned against a telegraph pole several yards away. As time passed, defeat hovered over him like the black cloud drifting over the train chugging through the rail yard. He peered through the

170

windows of the cars, but couldn't see her. He inhaled the smell of machine oil and hot steam and winced at the whistle that blasted his ears as the cars picked up speed.

Where was she headed? He had studied the departure schedule in the newspaper. The next train didn't leave until late afternoon. There were too many stops and points at which she could change trains for him to determine her destination. The one place he felt certain she would not go was Philadelphia.

Kit could ask Joanna outright to stay, but why should she? He had nothing more to propose than paying her to do what she most enjoyed and a desire to know if his feelings for her were based on more than a guilty conscience. The former offer she soundly rejected. He had no doubt the latter would produce either a slap to his face or hearty laughter.

Nonetheless, how could he let her leave without one more try? Kit approached the building without a hint of what he might say to convince her. He pulled on the lapels of his coat and straightened his tie.

"Are you here for the same reason I am?"

Kit released a frustrated sigh and turned to address Perry. "I want to be sure she knows what she's doing."

"I want to keep her from leaving."

Of course he did.

Perry opened the door. "After you."

Both of them stepped inside. They were too late. The room was empty. Perry marched to the ticket clerk. "Was there a young woman in here earlier?"

"I've seen several. They're all gone."

Kit walked back out the door. Joanna had boarded the train heading south while he'd stood by the telegraph pole and watched it roll away from the depot.

Sandra Ardoin

Chapter Twenty-two

Rather than wait tedious hours on a bench inside the ticket office, Joanna had slipped out a side door. As she strolled down residential streets, she passed homes where children of various ages played in the yards or ran up and down the dirt lane. Their laughter competed with her heavy heart.

For weeks, leaving Banesville had been uppermost in her mind. Now, a dread of returning to board the train destined for Chicago's Union Depot weighted her shoes until she dragged them down the dirt path running alongside the street.

Joanna's index finger rose to touch the side of her mouth, the area on Rose's face marred by Liam. Was it only two weeks ago? Her qualms about the man multiplied with each thought of the damage he was capable of doing. Once she reached her journey's end, would she sleep at night knowing she had deserted Rose and

Annie when they needed her, as Joanna's mother had deserted her?

A familiar fear clutched her in its icy grip. How could she stay here? Even in her anger over his hiring of Liam, she had nearly come undone when Kit reached for her hand that morning and stared at her as if he saw her for the first time.

And nothing had changed with Clayton's friends. The sooner she left, the sooner Perry would look elsewhere for love, and no one would think poorly of him. He'd be considered another unfortunate victim of a Delilah.

What made her think anything would be different somewhere else, somewhere like Chicago? She would still be Joanna Cranston Stewart with the same past and regrets—with the same fears.

To take her mind off her quandary, she turned her attention to the houses along First Street. Although not a wealthy neighborhood, the homes were neat. White, yellow, blue. They adorned the street with a rainbow of color. Several of the facades were plain. Others sported porches and gables decorated with fancy scroll work and arches.

Joanna's steps slowed as she neared a lovely apricot-colored house with a porch to her front right and a bay window to the left. A rental sign had been propped against one of the interior glass panes. Her heart thumped in a triple-time tempo.

She ambled up the path to the porch and peeked through the window in the door. Then she walked around to explore the outside of the whole house, standing on her toes in order to see through the windows into each vacant room.

After a complete circuit, Joanna climbed the porch steps again, her beaded purse pressed to her chest with both hands. Her gaze traveled over the simple white railing and slender posts. It was a comfortable house with a porch meant for sitting outside and visiting with neighbors.

She started down the path to the street and turned for one last look. A house for friendly people. Not for her.

The sun had dropped to graze the tops of the lofty oaks that dotted nearby yards. She should return to the station or risk missing her train.

"I saw you from my front window."

Joanna turned to face a plump, middle-aged woman who smiled at her, her ruddy cheeks like mountain apples. "The house is lovely."

"Belongs to my son. He moved his family to Asheville a short time ago and decided not to sell for now. Are you interested in renting?" She hobbled forward, her gait awkward as she favored her left leg or perhaps her hip. "I'm Greta Samuels from across the way. I reckon I could do you and your groom a good deal on the rent."

"I'm not married." Joanna squeezed the material of her purse. "I'm a widow."

"Bless your heart, honey. You got any young'uns?"

A tiny face filled Joanna's vision and snatched her breath. "No."

Mrs. Samuels pointed to the house behind Joanna. "It's not big—perfect size for a widow woman—clean and sound. Nothin' to fear."

Nothing to fear? Why would the woman add that? Fear in one sense or another had haunted Joanna all her life, no matter where she lived.

"All men will disappoint you at some point. Seek God's mercy and grab hold of His grace, Joanna. Lean on Him through all your trials and fears."

Her experience over the years had proved the first portion of Ben Greer's advice sound. After all, where had trusting any man ever gotten her? Any man, but Perry. He'd never disappointed her. Then again, he didn't know the worst about her, either.

But to trust God? Where had the Almighty been through the darkest times of her life? According to her father, He had washed His holy hands of her.

If that were true, why would Kit and Ben believe so strongly in their redemption and forgiveness? Why would Ben insist she seek God's mercy if he didn't think it was possible for her to find it?

Joanna looked west toward her house—now Kit's house—almost a mile away. Tonight, Liam would move back into the cottage. How could Rose want him again when she'd lived through his drunken tantrums for too long to expect anything different? Was it truly possible that God could redeem men like Liam McCall and Kit Barnes?

"Got good neighbors." The woman's smile grew more encouraging with the pronouncement of each of the home's assets.

"Actually, I was on my way to . . ." Her voice faded.

The weight of indecision bore down on Joanna. She could board the next train and start over in a place where no one knew her, or she could remain here until assured her friend was safe.

Joanna shut her eyes as if that would help her think more clearly. "Mrs. Samuels, tell me about that good deal on the rent."

***

For the past four days, Joanna had made do with a secondhand bed, linens, and several other items Mrs. Samuels loaned her until she either bought her own things or decided to purchase another train ticket to Chicago.

In the gray light of early morning, she removed her robe and laid it across the borrowed bed, then grabbed one of the three dresses hanging from metal hooks on the wall. The rest of her clothing remained folded in the trunk she used as a bedside table.

With nothing to do but feed her curiosity, Joanna had spent hours with Ben's Bible sitting open across her lap. Not knowing where to start in her quest to learn the truth about the God she had grown up fearing, she'd read a random chapter here and another there, alternating between the Old and New Testaments.

Too much of what she read perplexed her. When one passage of scripture proved her father's version of a judgmental and harsh deity true, another spoke of the loving and forgiving God Ben Greer said he served.

Joanna fastened the buttons running down the front of her dress and propped a hand mirror against the pillow. She did her best to arrange her hair in a neat fashion and pin her hat on straight while craning her neck to see her reflection. Though the weather had been cooler than normal, it was far too warm to add a scarf to hide her face.

She set the mirror on the trunk. What was missing? With hands propped on her hips, Joanna stared at the items on the flat top where she had set an oil lamp, Annie's drawing, and Ben's Bible.

Annie's drawing. Where was it?

She sank to her knees and peered under the bed. There it was, in the middle and out of easy reach—naturally. The paper must have fluttered to the floor in a breeze from the open window.

Joanna crawled closer to the bed and stretched her arm until her fingertips touched the paper. She inched it toward her, then slapped her hand on it and dragged it clear of its hiding place. The sheet had fallen with the artwork facing the floorboards and exposed a letter she'd ignored before—one that bore Clayton's handwriting but no recipient's name.

She read the short missive through—once, then a second time. Over and over, her focus returned to the last paragraph. She finally read it out loud to let the words sink in.

"In regard to your inquiry, be assured, your business holdings will profit by the addition of the Stewart Broom Factory. If you are free on Monday, 23 September, I shall take pleasure in meeting with you to discuss the details of a sale."

Under his signature, at the bottom of the paper, Clayton had dated the letter 17 September, 1889—the day before his death.

Perry never mentioned that his father planned to sell the company. For his sake, she was glad the sale never materialized. If Clayton were still alive, he would be proud of his son's competency in business.

***

For the second time, Joanna hiked the side streets to her former home. No one knew she remained in town, not even Perry, and she wanted to keep it that way for now.

She concealed herself within the woods on the north side of the property and waited for Rose and Annie to leave the cottage. Seeing them both without a physical sign of suffering would ease her mind . . . a little.

They emerged from the cottage in Liam's company and traversed the rear yard to the house. Annie chased Jelly through the grass. At the door to the kitchen, Liam pulled Rose against him and kissed her. Joanna's empty stomach lurched. When Liam walked away, Rose brushed her hand across her mouth. The subtle motion spoke volumes. Joanna sagged against the trunk of an oak tree. Her friend wasn't as happy to have her husband back as she'd pretended.

A short time later, Mr. Culbertson arrived with three of his workmen. Liam and two others joined them. She recognized the man with the crooked nose as the one she'd provided a meal the day Kit arrived at Perry's office. She wished him well in seeking help for his problem.

The contractor pointed to various sections of the structure as he assigned the jobs to be done to repair and remodel the house. Kit stepped outside holding a cup of coffee. He laughed at whatever Mr. Culbertson said, and her heart seized at the sound.

Joanna backed away and turned to leave. A sense of abandonment washed over her like a storm-fed wave. It threatened to carry her down to despair deeper than a pit in the ocean.

Everyone carried on with their lives. No one missed her.

Chapter Twenty-three

You look like you're walking in your sleep." Ben picked up a board, carried it to the sawhorses spread four feet apart, and cut into the wood.

Kit straightened his shoulders and moved with more speed in a wordless effort to deny the truth. "If Perry shows up again today, grousing and pestering Rose, we may have to put your big foot down on the situation. Better yet, let's apply it to his posterior and send him packing."

Ben clicked his tongue with a *tsk, tsk,* then laughed. "According to those low-hanging clouds, it will rain again today. If he has any sense, he'll stay home. Depending on where Joanna chose to go, she may not have arrived yet."

According to Perry, she had promised to send a telegram when she reached her destination. It had been a week, and no one had heard from her. In the meantime, Rose wrung her hands, and Annie whined about missing "Aunt Jo."

"I don't understand why she told Annie she was going to Chicago, but she boarded a southbound train."

"Women are at the top of the list of life's mysteries, my friend."

Kit eased closer to Ben and lowered his voice. "I can't say I blame Perry for being anxious. Over and over, I see that bulging purse filled with the money I paid her for this property. Who knows how much else she added from her bank account. I see visions of her lying beside a railroad track or behind a vacant building, both her savings and her life taken by a violent thief."

This burden over her safety gnawed at Kit. How did he soothe the worry that interfered with his work? Now he understood with better clarity how his brother felt knowing Violet roamed the streets in the middle of the night while delivering sacks of food to the poor. Unlike Hugh, Kit had no way to follow Joanna to protect her.

The apprehension had sent him to Medford's Ice Cream Parlor twice in the last week. On Saturday, he had taken Annie with him after sensing the child's desire to escape Liam. Was her nervousness around the man due in part to his neglect of her? He treated her as if she were a stranger living in his house.

Liam's attitude toward Annie irritated Kit, but what right did he have to say anything about the situation? With Joanna's departure, he acknowledged the probability he wasn't the child's father. After all these years, if Joanna were Annie's mother, how could she find it easy to leave? Even if she lied to him, Kit's absence from Annie's life didn't place him much higher on a reliability scale than Liam.

Ben stood between the sawhorses, poised to cut the wood

into smaller lengths. "We pray for Joanna daily, Kit. It's all we can do."

"I suppose." For once, prayer didn't seem enough. After less than a half-dozen meetings with her during his weeks in town, Kit felt as though he'd lost a part of himself when she left. How could that be when, before coming here, he had learned to live without her?

After slicing through the board with the hand saw, Ben straightened. "If it's any consolation, every time I pray for Joanna, I get a sense of peace. I think God has a special plan for that woman's life."

Kit shut his eyes. Lord, can you let me in on Your plan and give me that same peace?

"You two fixin' to waste all day jawin'? It's gonna rain and we got work to do."

At the raspy and bad-tempered voice, Kit opened his eyes. A brown stream of tobacco juice splashed in the grass near his shoe.

The struggle for sobriety affected people in various ways. Some, like Donovan, dealt with shakes and nausea. Some hallucinated, suffered from headaches or despondency. For William Rainer's brother-in-law, it worsened his already vulgar temperament. It was no wonder the streetcar conductor had wanted the man out from under his roof. In the three days since Howard Cox moved into the house, he'd been caught with a jug of a powerful moonshine once and managed to alienate everyone but Liam McCall.

The thought reminded Kit to keep a better eye on Rose's husband. Two nights ago, he had seen him prowling the property at one a.m. Liam claimed he'd been unable to sleep, not an uncommon problem when a body fought the craving for alcohol, so he couldn't contradict the man's excuse. Kit smelled no liquor on Liam and told him to return to the cottage, then went back to his own bed to toss and turn until daylight.

In the back of his mind, Kit continued to hear Joanna's final words to him. In her absence, he determined to watch over Rose and Annie. It was the least he could do.

If she would inform someone, anyone, of her safe arrival, maybe he would lose this emptiness that overwhelmed him at odd times of the day and night. Maybe he could stop shuffling around the property half asleep and focus on his duty to all the men in his care.

Then again, maybe he'd only miss her more.

***

Joanna searched through the canned goods and staples on the shelves of the general store. The days when Rose and Liam shopped for her were over and to eat meant venturing out in public.

Located on the northeast side of town, Franklin's Store catered to people who were strangers to her. Still, she tucked her chin in a pointless pretense of invisibility as she added a number of supplies to the basket dangling from her arm.

Despite the dread of leaving her house, she'd gained a sense of satisfaction in doing things for herself. She was learning to face her fear of rude comments and condemnation without the urge to run back to a sanctuary of walls.

Joanna paused to scan the pages of a catalog. During her marriage, she had lived with the decor chosen by the first Mrs. Stewart. Clayton saw no reason to waste money on "frippery" reflecting his second wife's taste. After he died, the lack of funds kept her from buying furniture, dinnerware patterns, and knickknacks in her own style.

Several minutes passed while she dreamed of placing an order for the things in the catalog that caught her eye. She saw herself cutting maroon chrysanthemums and pink roses to add to a colorful Majolica jardinière. In her imagination, she set it on a round table in front of the bay window of the house on First Street, then stood back to admire the beauty as the sun shone on the velvety flower petals.

A woman's cackle behind her broke the spell. In real life, Joanna had no table to display a jardinière. She shut the book and finished her shopping without another thought given to dreams.

She arranged for the delivery of the food and household supplies and paid her bill with money she'd stashed in the secret compartment inside her trunk.

Once she'd decided to rent the house, Joanna snuck back into the bank after seeing David Murray leave. She exchanged two of the one-hundred-dollar notes for much lesser denominations that wouldn't raise eyebrows when presented to merchants. She still couldn't bring herself to open another account.

Joanna turned the corner at the next block and breathed a sigh of relief after escaping the store unrecognized.

As she passed a vacant and decrepit building hardly larger than a tool shed, a whimper drifted from one of the broken windows and slowed her steps. She cocked her head to listen. The sound intensified. Drawn to the distress, she crept toward the structure with its rotting gray boards. Her common sense shouted to mind her own business. Her heart responded differently.

Inside the building with its old wood and earthy smell, she almost tripped over a hindrance at her feet. Sitting on the dirt floor with her head and upper body bent forward, the woman's arms covered wavy hair partially pinned. The remainder hung down her back in damp, tangled strands. Continued sobs wrenched her shoulders.

Joanna reached down and touched her arm. "Excuse me."

Except for a strangled sniffle, the weeping ceased. With sluggish movements, the woman lowered her arms and raised her head. Veins of tears zig-zagged down a puffy face, splotched from crying. Though she looked familiar, Joanna struggled to place where she'd seen her before. "I don't mean to pry, but may I assist you?"

The spontaneous gesture of a hand rubbing the protruding belly prodded a recollection. What was the woman's name? "Darcy Baird?"

Darcy nodded and used her hands to push to her feet. She poked greasy, wayward hair behind both ears. Her muddy palms brushed the dampness from her cheeks and left behind pumpkin-colored streaks. "Yes, ma'am. It's me."

The day she turned up on Joanna's doorstep, Darcy had been neat and clean, dressed in a manner that bespoke an upper-middle-class upbringing. After glancing around the dirty space, littered with crates and rubbish, Joanna asked, "What are you doing here?"

"I . . . I . . ." The tears in those green-brown eyes revived.

"You never found the work you sought?"

"No, ma'am." The woman shifted her weight from one foot to the other.

Don't get involved. Joanna rubbed her hands together. "Where are you staying?"

"Here and there."

"Here?" Joanna observed the holes in the roof and imagined how the recent rains poured through each one. "You may as well have slept outside."

Darcy's chin dipped. "Yes, ma'am."

Without permitting herself time to reason away her reaction, Joanna slipped her arm around the woman's waist and steered her out the door toward the street. "Come with me."

"Where"—Darcy sucked in a shaky breath—"are we going?"

"To my house."

Darcy started to pull away. "What will people say when they see you with me?"

Sardonic laughter bubbled up from Joanna's chest. "Nothing they haven't said at one time or another, I'm sure."

The two of them traveled the remainder of the way in silence. Joanna stood aside after opening the front door of her house. Darcy peeked in and looked around the empty front room.

"I've recently moved here and have nothing yet. I ordered two wooden chairs from Mr. Franklin, but they won't be delivered until later today." Joanna needed so much more to live in comfort, but why waste the money when she'd be here a short while? She stifled a grunt. Somewhere along the line, she'd picked up Clayton's frugal ways.

Darcy chuckled. It was the first time humor overtook the sadness. "You found me sitting on the ground. A clean floor that won't leave stains on my dress is an improvement." She glanced at her hands and clothing and winced. "Your floor won't stay clean if I sit on it."

"We can fix that problem."

Joanna led her down a hall to the nearest of two bedrooms. She snatched necessary items of clothing from the trunk and laid them on the bed. "You can take your dirty things off. Give me time to heat fresh water, then come into the kitchen and wash."

"I don't know how to thank you for your kindness, ma'am."

Joanna paused at the door and turned. "Most people call me

Joanna."

Darcy tilted her head. "I know you, don't I?"

"You came to me looking for work once."

"I remember now. You're from the old house on the edge of town. Mrs. Stewart. I thought you were moving away."

"There's been a temporary change in my plans." Joanna walked to the bedroom doorway. "I'll call out when I'm ready for you."

Her steps faltered. Dare she leave the woman alone in the bedroom with her trunk—with all the money she had in this world? She was foolish to keep such a large amount of cash in the house. What if the place burned?

Until now, she hadn't been concerned about being robbed. The recent burglaries reported in the newspaper happened in a wealthier neighborhood. But with a stranger here, a homeless and desperate woman, was she taking a reckless chance with her future?

Joanna brushed away the concern. The money was hidden, and she would risk the loss rather than turn Darcy out on the street without helping her.

She heated a large pot of water. When it steamed, she took it off the stove. "All right, you can come in."

Darcy walked into the kitchen wearing nothing but a yellowed chemise with seams stretched to their limits and a pair of drawers. Her cheeks flushed a pleasing pink, and she rubbed her stomach in a nervous manner. "Before I take further advantage of your kindness, I must be honest with you, Mrs. Stewart." She raised her chin. "I am not a married woman. I never have been."

Joanna kept her expression neutral while Darcy studied her reaction. It wasn't hard to accomplish since she'd already guessed the truth.

"I'm carrying the child of a man who tossed me aside when I told him about it. He has a wife already and wants nothing to do with me or my baby. When my condition was discovered, I lost my job and my room in a boardinghouse."

A crescendo of anger and resentment swelled inside Joanna. She wasn't sure where to aim the bulk of her ire—at Darcy for her gullibility, the man for his deceit, or herself for understanding so well the fear and guilt this young woman suffered.

"He said nothing about being married. How could I have been so dim-witted as to throw away every bit of my upbringing and cause a scandal for my family? Should I return home, life will never be the same for them." Darcy's tears threatened again. "If you want me to leave, Mrs. Stewart, I will."

Barely able to retain her composure, Joanna managed a tight smile. "It's Joanna, and why waste the water I heated for you?"

She added cool water from the pump into the wash bowl Mrs. Samuels had supplied, then poured in hot water from the pot and tested the temperature with her finger. She handed Darcy a rag, a towel, and a bar of Pears soap. "It's almost as fragrant as the lotion you asked me to smell last time."

Darcy's eyes bulged. "I didn't lie about that. All my things were stolen a week ago."

"I wasn't accusing you of a fabrication." Joanna pointed to the bowl of water. "I'll be in the sitting room when you're finished dressing."

As she waited, Joanna sat on the built-in seat under the bay window and stared out the glass. What was she doing? She had trouble to spare and didn't need to complicate her life even more by taking in a woman whose predicament brought back memories she'd as soon forget.

Among Papa's favorite Bible passages had been the first twenty verses of Ezekiel 18. He'd sit her down in the parlor and glory in reading all the ways in which she could sin and suffer spiritual death while reminding her that, just because he was her father, God did not hold him responsible for her actions. What would he think of her taking in a woman like Darcy—like herself?

Last night, Joanna had worked up the courage to read the verses, every last disheartening one of them. Then she went on to read the whole chapter, verses of promise to those who turned away from sin. She had turned away from her worst sin long ago. Did that mean God would forgive her if she asked?

Why would her father fail to mention the hope that glowed from the pages of Ben's Bible to shine on her with the light of mercy?

Bare feet padded across the floor behind her. Gone were the dirty hands and face and the strong odor. Darcy wore Joanna's loose-fitting wrapper and had used her brush to arrange her rebellious hair into a neat bun at the back of her head. "Thank you for the clean clothes. After I've washed my own, I'll give these back."

"No hurry."

A time of silence stretched between them.

Joanna asked, "What happens when the baby arrives? I'd guess it won't be long now."

"About a month, I think."

A month. Joanna hadn't planned on remaining in Banesville much more than that—only until she felt certain Rose and Annie were safe.

Maintaining her anger with Kit had proved too big a strain on her nerves, so she'd chosen to believe he knew nothing of Liam's past violence toward his family and had hired the man with good intentions. From what she had gleaned from her furtive visits, Liam behaved himself, but there had to be a way to know for certain. Hiding in the bushes didn't provide that assurance, especially after witnessing Rose's aversion to her husband's kiss.

Besides, she hadn't fulfilled her promise to notify Perry of her safe travel. He must be worried by now. Then again, he might be like the others and not even miss her.

"I don't know what to do, Joanna."

Neither do I. "We'll think of something."

Chapter Twenty-four

Play for drunkards?

The vivid dream vanished with the fluttered opening of Joanna's eyes and left behind the unanswered question.

She blinked several times to clear her sleep-blurred vision. The gray light of dawn obscured all details but the bold flower-shaped outlines on the papered bedroom walls. Try as hard as she might, though, she couldn't conjure the murky impressions that in the realm of sleep were distinct and sensible. All that remained of the elusive fantasy was Kit's voice offering her an opportunity to play her piano for him . . . for his men.

The steady beat of raindrops danced on the roof. Every so often, a gust of wind drove the rain against the window of Joanna's room, as it had on occasion all week. Sick of dreary weather, she longed for sunshine again.

Joanna sniffed the air. Coffee. Bacon. Biscuits? A week had

passed since she'd awakened to the smell of food and fresh-brewed coffee. How she had missed the homey aromas.

Throwing off the sheet, she climbed out of bed and slipped into her robe. A star quilt from her trunk lay folded in the far corner of the second bedroom. Darcy had refused the offer of the bed, insisting that if she could fall asleep on the ground, she'd sleep even better on a wood floor cushioned with a quilt pallet. No amount of pleading changed her guest's mind.

Darcy stood at the stove in the kitchen with a spatula in her hand. Bacon grease popped and sizzled in the cast iron skillet. Gone was the nightgown Joanna provided the night before, replaced by the ample wrapper covered by a long apron. Darcy had tamed the wild hair—as much as possible—and lifted the down-turned lips of yesterday to form a bright smile. She turned an egg onto a plate purchased from the general store. "Good morning."

Joanna's mouth watered. Where did this appetite come from? She rarely ate breakfast. "Did you sleep well?"

"Very. For the first time in weeks, I felt safe."

Hoisting the coffee pot, Joanna poured a cup of coffee and refilled Darcy's. "I understand what you mean."

"You do?"

At Darcy's quizzical glance, Joanna looked away. How well she remembered that sense of security the day Rose provided her a safe haven. After being cold, destitute, fearful, and lonely, she'd wept with relief throughout those first nights and kept her new friend awake.

Joanna inhaled. "The food smells wonderful."

Lacking a table, the two of them stood at the counter while they ate and conversed. Darcy spoke freely of her background. Although her parents were not as well-to-do as Joanna's, she came from a respectable family in Charlotte and had three brothers and a sister.

"Why didn't you go home? Did they cast you out?" Joanna stopped short of adding "too."

"I thought I was so smart and able to take care of myself. Look how well I managed." The tines of Darcy's fork scraped the graniteware as she swished it through the egg yolk that spread to puddle on her plate. "The shame is more than I can face, Joanna. I can't put my family through it."

Joanna lowered her fork to the empty plate, wiped her mouth on a napkin, and sought a change of subject. "You've told me you can clean house, and I've tasted your breakfast. What about other meals?"

"Mama insisted I learn, even though we employed a cook."

"I'm not proficient in the kitchen. My father discouraged me from stepping inside the room." Joanna pushed her plate away and gathered the courage to do what she'd known she would do since bringing Darcy home with her. "I can't pay much and can't promise I'll be in town long, but I'd like to hire you to fix meals and clean. Of course, you'll have room and board for as long as I rent this house."

Darcy froze with her lips parted. She gathered her composure and asked, "Even when the baby comes?"

"Yes."

Darcy reached out and pulled Joanna into a robust embrace. "God bless you."

Once again, scenes from the elusive dream burst into her thoughts. What kind of blessing would it be to play her cherished piano again, to laugh with Rose and Annie, and . . . and to see Kit without hiding among the trees like a spy?

***

"Nice and smooth, Annie. Like this." Kit knelt with one knee on the ground and grasped the child's hand. He guided the brush left, then right, using gentle strokes as they applied a thick white layer of paint to new boards on the side of the house. He'd indulged Annie in her request to help, even though time was fleeting and much more work remained.

Thanks to Mr. Culbertson's supervision, they just might manage to meet the schedule their backers had set—despite the bad weather and difficulties presented by the three men in their care.

Donovan worried Kit most. At times, the former fighter's hands shook with such intensity, they dared not assign him anything more important than to fetch and carry supplies.

Howard's grumbles and insufferable behavior dwindled the longer he went without drink.

On the other hand, Liam gave the impression he was overcoming his dependence on liquor without much trouble. Kit wavered between satisfaction and skepticism.

When they weren't being examined by doctors, exercising in the yard, or eating Rose's good food, they all worked hard. None had deserted the House. Yet. Experience told Kit and Ben at least one would fall away in the near future, perhaps all three, but their purpose wasn't to attain numbers. They wanted to reach men one at a time.

"This is fun."

"It is, huh?" Kit laughed and ran a finger over Annie's smooth, paint-spattered cheek, then wiped the white residue on his well-used coveralls. The child giggled. What was one more splotch on the denim material if it brought a smile to Annie's face? Together, they probably had more paint on them than what the bucket held.

"It looks as though you two missed a spot."

Annie whipped around. "Aunt Jo!"

Droplets from the brush she held colored the air around Kit and rained on his hair and face. When one splashed into his eye, he jumped to his feet and stepped on Jelly's tail. The cat screeched and sprinted off.

While he rubbed the paint from his eye, Kit's feet danced in an attempt to maintain his balance. His right foot plopped inside the bucket. Kicking it free sent the container into the side of the house with a dull *thud*. It landed upside-down on the ground. What remained of the contents in the bucket coated the grass with a thick, white pool of paint.

Kit's shoe and the lower portion of his pant leg were as white as a country snowstorm. The material stuck to his skin. He crimped the stinging eye shut and feigned a glare at the two females standing a safe distance away. With their arms wrapped around one another, they howled with laughter.

Joanna covered her mouth and reined in her amusement long enough to say, "May I see that again?"

The laughter broke free once more. Kit drank in a sound of joy he had come to believe was forever lost to him. He spread his arms and stalked toward Joanna. "How would you like a welcome-back hug?"

Staring at the wet paint spattering his clothing, she sobered. Her jaw dropped, and she backed away.

Kit tried to maintain a semblance of gravity, but the sputter of a chuckle gave him away. He picked up his pace and closed the distance between them.

Annie squealed and ran in circles. "Grab her, Mr. Kit. Hug

her."

Joanna shook her finger in the air. "Christopher Barnes, you stay away from me or you'll be laundering my clothing."

Her words spawned the mental picture of a half-dressed, well-rounded beauty. Abstaining from his past indiscretions failed to remove the images from his mind. But to give in and wallow in the pig sty of his weakness would affect this fragile camaraderie with Joanna, not to mention his relationship with the Lord. He dropped his arms to his sides and stayed his approach.

"I'm gonna find Mama and tell her you're back, Aunt Jo." Annie ran around the rear corner of the house.

In her excitement and innocence, the child left Kit alone with his struggle and the woman who incited it. Once he gathered his control, he found his voice. "Everyone believes you boarded a train out of town." He stopped short of revealing he and Perry had followed her to the station.

His statement drew Joanna's attention from the path Annie had taken and back to him. "Not yet."

"Where are you staying?"

"I rented a house on First Street."

She rented a house? "You're remaining in Banesville?"

"For a while."

"Have you spoken with Perry? He's worried about you."

"It's nice to hear someone missed me."

Joanna hid away, put them all through eight days of anxiety, and had the nerve to whine that no one missed her? "Everyone missed you. We've all wondered if you were safe."

Her throat rippled as she swallowed hard. She flipped a hand as if to dismiss his claim. "Were you serious about needing a pianist? Is the offer still open?"

Kit stepped closer to be sure he'd heard correctly. "You've

changed your mind?"

"I can only agree to a temporary period."

At this point, he'd take any time she allowed. "Understood. Are you free to play in the evenings? Our men are busy during the day."

"I can arrange my schedule to accommodate yours."

The moments passed while they watched each other in silence, as if self-consciousness ran off with their tongues. Kit was afraid to move for fear Joanna would shy like a spooked mare. She showed the wild eyes of one.

"You really are back." Rose trotted across the yard with Annie following. "Where have you been for the past week? How long will you stay?"

Joanna studied Rose's face. What was she looking for?

"Oh, never mind." Rose clutched her friend's arm and began to drag her toward the house. "Let's go inside. You can tell me everything over a cup of tea."

Joanna laughed, a gentle tune Kit committed to memory. "All right, but don't jerk my arm off."

When she glanced over her shoulder, he smiled and said, "Welcome home, Jo."

***

Home? How could Kit possibly think she had come home? Like the rental of the house, this job was temporary, a perfect position to keep an eye on Rose and Annie.

Joanna's mind didn't gloss over the fact that Kit had used the shortened version of her name. Never before had he called her Joanna. Dare she read into it a message of friendship, or was it a slip of the tongue, a repetition of what he'd heard over and over from others?

She followed Rose into the kitchen and sat at the table along the wall while her friend poured hot water over the leaves in the teapot and prepared the serving set. Joanna pulled Annie onto her lap. The child squiggled close, which filled Joanna with joy. How could she ever think they hadn't missed her?

"I can't tell you how glad I am that you're here, Jo. When we never heard from you, we weren't sure what to think." Rose poured the tea into the cup in front of Joanna. "Perry has come around every day asking if we've received word yet."

"I'm sorry. I'll contact him today and let him know I'm fine."

Rose handed Annie two cookies. "Why don't you go outside and play with Jelly?"

"But I want to stay with Aunt Jo."

"You'll see her later. Now scoot."

Joanna released Annie. The girl slid off her lap and trudged out the door.

Rose asked, "Why didn't you leave Banesville as you planned?"

Joanna stirred cream into her tea. "I bought my train ticket, but turned it back in."

"You decided to stay to make sure Liam behaved himself, didn't you?"

Joanna blew on the hot liquid. "Something like that."

"Exactly like that."

"Has he behaved?" She set the spoon on the saucer and peered at Rose over the rim of the cup.

"I noticed you checking my face for bruises." Rose heaved a breath. "Liam has given me no reason to doubt him when he said he wanted us to remain together. So far, he isn't drinking, and he works hard around here." There was nothing defensive or warm in the matter-of-fact statement or the tone in which the words were spoken.

Joanna almost asked Rose if she was happy. She caught the question before it spilled from her lips, fearful it would lead to admitting she had seen Rose wipe away her husband's kiss. Those times in their friendship when she had bitten her tongue on a subject had been rare, but at least for a while, she would tread lightly with this one.

"It will take time for Annie to trust him. Right now, she's enchanted by Kit, and that doesn't help."

Joanna had trembled inside while watching him with Annie. Their clear delight in one another's company tugged at her heart—and conscience. "He tends to affect our gender that way."

Rose raised a speculative brow. "Not you, though?"

She remained silent rather than lie.

"I've gotten to know Kit and Ben over the past week. They're good men. They care about those they're trying to help. Kit isn't the same person you described to me. He's changed."

It was true that, for the most part, the man outside was a stranger to Joanna. Yes, he still charmed anyone in his path, including her at times, but she hoped she had matured sufficiently to discern between true regard and counterfeit flattery.

Had Kit seen a change for the better in her? Not according to the look on his face after she made the offhand and silly remark about laundering her clothes. He'd turned as crimson as the bow on her dress.

At times in the weeks since he arrived on her doorstep, Joanna had seen more in Kit's expression toward her than a physical desire. She had seen that true regard and longed to see it more often.

"Do you remember me telling you about the young woman

who came here last month looking for a job?"

Rose scratched her temple. "I think so. She was expecting a child?"

"Yes." Joanna explained about the rental of the house from Mrs. Samuels, then coming upon Darcy and taking her home with her. "I want to help her the way you helped me."

"If it keeps you here, I'm happy." Rose lost her grin. "Do you think it's wise?"

"Wise?"

"First, there's your reputation to consider."

"You never worried about yours."

"No one cared about mine. Second, have you considered the hardship once the baby is delivered?"

"I know it won't be easy, but don't you think it's time I stopped focusing on my own misfortune?"

"Is it possible without being honest?"

When the rear door off the back hall closed, the conversation ceased—to Joanna's relief.

Kit walked into the kitchen carrying a book. He stopped at her side, opened it, and removed a sheet of paper, then handed both to her. "You'll need these. Ben wrote down the page numbers for the songs he wants to sing in the next week. If you're agreeable, we'll start tomorrow night with the ones he's marked."

Joanna opened the hymnal, read through the titles, and frowned. She pushed away from the table. "I've never heard of most of these. I'd better practice."

"Practice?" Rose glanced from Joanna to Kit. "What is this about?"

"Joanna has agreed to play the piano for our after-supper gatherings."

"Temporarily." She mustn't let him forget that part of the

agreement.

Mischief equal in devilry to that of a naughty boy sparkled in his eyes. "We'll see." Kit's chuckle followed her from the kitchen all the way to the music room.

For the first time in years, Joanna prayed in sincerity. She prayed for the strength to maintain her guard against the pleasure such comments triggered in her.

Chapter Twenty-five

The grand piano no longer reigned as the centerpiece of the music room. It had been shoved to one end. On Saturday evening, Joanna sat on the stool with her hands in her lap while three men filed into the room and dropped onto chairs that faced a simple, handmade lectern.

The men appeared as eager for what was to come as dental patients with a toothache. Each eyed her: Liam with contempt, Mr. Cox with an unrestrained leer, and Mr. O'Connor with a keen inspection more disturbing than the stares of the others.

Kit and Ben entered behind them. Ben sat in a chair near the lectern. Kit occupied a seat on the end of the short row of chairs, next to Mr. O'Connor. When he glanced in her direction, she looked away.

At the pastor's nod, she placed her fingers on the proper keys and launched into "There Shall Be Showers of Blessing," an appropriate hymn given the rain streaming down the windows.

Musical notes were like the alphabet to Joanna. Although she had never played many of the songs on Ben's list, after a couple of times through each, her fingers swept over the ivories with expertise.

The men's dissonant voices filled the room, hitting both harmonic and sour notes. After three hymns, Ben stood behind the lectern and opened his Bible. Earlier, Kit had told her she needn't stay for the short talk unless the idea appealed to her, so Joanna rose from the piano stool and prepared to leave the room.

She'd reached the door when Ben said, "Shall we thank Mrs. Stewart for her lovely accompaniment?" He clapped his hands. All but Liam followed with more enthusiasm than her playing deserved.

Joanna dipped her head in embarrassment. What kind of service did Ben lead? Her father would never encourage his congregation to offer praise to anyone but God. When the applause died down, she stole away from the music room.

With her back pressed to the closed door, she paused. What should she do with the next twenty minutes until she was summoned to play a final hymn? A cup of tea would soothe her dry throat and ward off the temptation to turn around and open the door a crack in order to listen to Ben—to compare his style of speaking to Papa's.

She took a step toward the kitchen and stopped. The allure of the quiet, muffled voice tugged at her as she wished for those mercy drops they had sung about to fall on her.

The music room door opened. Kit slipped out and shut it behind him. "Is everything all right?"

"Yes. I was on my way to the kitchen to wait until Ben needed me again."

"If you'd like to listen to what he has to say, you're welcome to take my chair, or I'll find you another one."

"Can you find one for me to tote home? I could use somewhere comfortable to sit." Joanna cringed at the attempt to be flippant. Kit brought out every idiotic comment within her reach.

His brow crinkled. She twisted her hands and rummaged her brain for a more intelligent remark. "Ben is certainly quiet when he preaches." That was the best she could do?

Kit flashed a crooked grin that warmed her from her heels to her scalp. "He doesn't believe it's necessary to shout God's message to people who aren't hard of hearing."

Another way in which Ben and her father differed.

"Ben prefers a more subtle way to spread the guilt."

Spread the guilt? Joanna's breaths grew shallow. Maybe Ben Greer wasn't as different as she thought. Maybe his understanding of God matched her father's flawlessly. She had hoped Papa's beliefs were wrong. "Then I have no need to listen to him. I've heard it all before."

The smile on Kit's face collapsed. "What I said was meant as a joke."

"I see nothing humorous in being told that my past choices mean certain and irrevocable judgment and condemnation."

"That can't be further from the truth." He reached out, grasped her hand, and squeezed it. Experience told Joanna to pull away, but when he led her across the hall to the kitchen, she followed without a fight.

After seating her at the table, Kit slid around to sit at the other end, his warm and firm hand still holding hers. "Joanna, God is nothing like your father portrayed him. Take me, for instance. We both know my faults. I've been pardoned for every one of them."

His brash claim ignited a firestorm within her. If it hadn't been for him, her conscience would be clear. She would have no fear of God's wrath for a moral lapse.

"Why are you special? What makes you think God forgave you for the drinking and the other things you've done . . . for what you did to me? How is it right that I be punished, that I should suffer like I have while you pretend all is well?"

Joanna had kept her voice low, but at the harshness and accusation, Kit let go of her hand and turned in his chair to face the outer wall of the room. *That's right, turn away from me one more time.* Anger and hurt balled in her throat.

"Joanna, I'm . . ."

When Kit's gaze met hers once more, his glassy eyes intensified her fury. How dare he use that long face and slumped posture to heighten her guilt.

"What makes you so sure your redemption isn't a fairytale? Fool yourself all you want about God's forgiveness, Kit, but don't bother trying to fool me. I learned the hard way that I can't believe anything you say."

A cough interrupted her scolding, and they both glanced at the doorway. "Sorry. I came for a glass of water." Mr. O'Connor coughed again. "Throat's like sand."

"I'll get it for you." To escape Kit's woeful expression, Joanna pushed the chair from the table and stalked to the hand pump at the sink.

When she returned with the glass of water, Kit was gone, and Mr. O'Connor continued to stare at her with that odd interest that made her want to shrink into a corner.

"Is there anything else I can do for you?"

"No, ma'am." He gulped the water and handed her the glass.

"I thought maybe I could help you. Payback, you might say."

"Payback? I don't understand."

"You did me a good turn one day. I'd like to do one for you. May come a time when you need a way to defend yourself."

"Defend myself against what or whom?"

He stuffed his beefy hands in the pockets of his trousers. "I was figurin' a woman living alone like you can't be too careful. I can teach you useful moves in case you find yourself in a tough situation."

"Teach me moves?" Her eyes widened. "Are you talking about fisticuffs?"

"No, ma'am, just actions to fend off an unfriendly sort. There are things a lady can do that . . . uh . . . well . . ." His face turned a deeper red than the stripe in his faded shirt. "They'll leave a man crying, Mrs. Stewart."

She was no naïve maiden, but it was her turn to feel the heat of a blush.

Surely, he didn't mistake her argument with Kit for a threat? A ridiculous notion since she had been the aggressor. "It's nice of you to want to look out for my welfare, but I don't think what you have in mind will be necessary."

He stared at her as though he wanted to argue, and then said, "Suit yourself, ma'am."

As he started to leave the kitchen, she said, "Thank you for your concern."

Without turning, his head bobbed. "Yes, ma'am."

Even with his rugged exterior and gruff voice, it comforted Joanna to realize she had a protector in this house. Movements to make a man cry? She shook her head. It was tempting.

***

Kit laid his gray suit across the bed. Who was he trying to impress? Why don his best clothing for no reason? He wouldn't see Joanna at the July Fourth festivities in the park today. After Saturday, she would seek to avoid him altogether.

He should stay here and remove the stained wallpaper from the drawing room. Might as well spend his day on a useful project.

Kit glanced around. This room required work too. When they moved in, Ben gave him the choice of bedrooms to occupy since he would live here on a more regular basis. Kit had chosen the smallest room. Sleeping in Joanna's room, in her old bed, was too . . . uncomfortable. Even in here, he'd tossed and turned the past two nights.

A whistle of admiration pierced the air. "Come in, Ben."

His friend lounged against the door frame with his head canted to avoid brushing the top. He grinned like a bearded halfwit. "You'll look quite the citified dandy in that outfit, sir." Ben laughed at the abominable impression of a Southern gentleman.

Kit snarled at his friend's lighthearted mood and plucked the clothing from the bed. "Hardly. In fact, I've changed my mind. I'll stay here and work."

Ben ambled across the room. He grabbed the coat from Kit and made a show of examining the material as if he were the high-priced Philadelphia tailor who had stitched it together. "Joanna plans to be there today."

Kit paused in the midst of snatching the coat back. Joanna avoided going out in public, and it didn't get more *public* than the crowds on a July Fourth celebration. She'd stood nearby when they discussed it on Friday and said nothing about attending. "How do you know?"

"She told Rose on Saturday that Perry asked her and she accepted. Rose told me."

Frustration pressed on Kit's chest. Joanna and her stepson were close, so why should he be disturbed to find out that Perry talked her into going?

Kit removed his robe, tossed it on the bed, and slipped into the suit pants. "You and Mrs. McCall are getting chatty."

Ben laughed. "We're conspiring against the two of you."

"Well, you're wasting your time. Joanna hates me ... has hated me for years. She all but said so."

"Now, you're being petulant. She doesn't hate you."

"You weren't in the kitchen with her." Kit ran a hand down the side of his face. At least her rebuke slapped sense into him. He'd ruined her—physically, emotionally, and spiritually—as fully as liquor had ruined the men down the hall.

"Kit—"

"I tried to apologize, but Donovan interrupted."

"So now avoiding her fixes everything between you?"

"It fixes nothing. She wants nothing fixed." Kit buttoned the white dress shirt and seized the coat from Ben.

"Then why are you dressing in your best suit clothes to work on the house?"

Kit stared at his hand wrapped around the material. What was he doing? Drive leaked from him like air from a punctured bicycle tire. He sank onto the mattress. "For years, I blamed Joanna for my troubles. That mote in my eye turned into a giant beam that blinded me to how much I hurt her."

He swallowed past the fist-sized regret in his throat, then reached for the black tie and dragged it across the bedspread. As he wrapped the material around his neck, the image of Joanna's face materialized before him, her eyes smoky with outrage and something else. Heartbreak? Yearning?

He formed the large knot, straightened the tie, and tucked the excess under his vest. While Joanna was wrong about God's forgiveness, Kit understood his obligation—his desire to help her see the truth. "She doesn't trust me, Ben, and I don't know what to say to change her mind. At the least, I owe her an apology, but she won't believe me."

"Then don't say anything."

Kit balked on his way to the dresser. "Not try?"

"Apologies—words—are important, Kit, but if we only spoke encouraging platitudes to the men downstairs, how effective do you think we would be in helping them turn their lives around?"

"You're saying Joanna needs to see a change in how I treat her as well as hearing an apology—words and deeds working together."

"It's what we do."

Kit picked up the brush on the dresser and ran it through his hair, then poured a couple drops of the spicy Macassar oil on his hands and smoothed it through the longer of his locks to tame them. How might he show Joanna he was a different person these days? Even if they never moved past being associates in this house, he must atone for his actions and show her the difference the presence of Christ would make in her life.

He laid the brush down on the dresser top and examined his reflection in the mirror. The oil for his hair was practical. At the same time it added a nice scent to the air around him.

"My first act should be to help Joanna." Kit ran a finger across the smooth cherry surface of the dresser as her odd comment about the chairs spurred a question. Why hadn't it occurred to him that she might have rented a house without an adequate amount of furniture? The remainder of what she once owned occupied space in his attic.

"I know where I'll start, Ben."

Chapter Twenty-Six

Joanna stopped in the midst of pulling on her gloves to open the front door and allow Perry inside. "I don't know how you talked me into this."

He bent and pressed warm, dry lips to her cheek. "It took far less encouragement than I'd been prepared to employ."

She gave the edge of her right glove a frustrated tug. She should have put up more of a fuss and declined Perry's offer to escort her to Fairview Park for a picnic. This was the first Independence Day celebration she had attended since Clayton's death, and she expected a large crowd to be present. Large crowds provided the opportunity to meet people she'd rather not see.

Kit had told the men they could attend today's celebration—after issuing a warning to avoid liquor and those who might serve it. A short-lived hope had flared within her that he would include her in their group. She walked away disappointed.

Under the circumstances, it turned out for the best. On Saturday, Joanna had been like a firecracker—a sizzle of anger, an explosion, then nothing but burned out emotions. While she regretted the tantrum, her confrontation with Kit had the result of a cleansing spring rain and, afterward, she'd slept better than she had in weeks. Maybe all she needed over the years was an opportunity to make clear to him how much he'd hurt her.

Perry glanced around the sparse sitting room, his lips pinched in disapproval. "Honestly, Joanna, how are you living like this? I happen to know Kit stored your unused furniture in the attic. Tomorrow, I'll send Carter to retrieve various pieces. You should enjoy more appropriate furnishings than an apple crate for a table. Or is it supposed to be a chair?"

Her comfort wasn't something Kit Barnes had thought of in the past several days—another indication of his lack of consideration toward her and the difference between the two men. "Now, Perry—"

"I'm putting my foot down and will brook no argument about the matter. You say this is temporary." He exhaled a soft snort. "I certainly hope you mean living in this house."

When Perry made up his mind to have his way, nothing stopped him. Over the years, Joanna had succeeded in slowing his pursuit of her, but furniture wasn't an issue worth arguing over. At any rate, she and Darcy would be more comfortable.

"I mean it, Joanna, I won't have you living like a pauper."

Perry must have developed a skewed vision of how she lived until recently. "Very well. I'm sure Darcy will appreciate sleeping in a bed for a change."

"That's another thing. As inadvisable as it is to take in strays of any sort, whatever possessed you to choose a woman like that?"

Joanna stiffened. "A woman like what?"

"One in her condition, of course."

"Darcy is no stray, as you put it." She voiced the words in a contralto growl.

"Then where is her husband? Why isn't he providing for her?" Perry folded his arms across his chest. Her expression no doubt matched his—heated and inflexible. At that moment, he displayed too much of his father to her liking. It reinforced Joanna's determination never to disclose her own shameful history to him. "She's an unmarried woman, isn't she? She'll give birth to a—"

"Do not say it." Joanna forced a gentler note into her voice. "Darcy is a young woman who made a mistake. Now she has nowhere to go."

"At least you didn't invite her to join us today."

"Actually, I left the decision to her, and she chose to stay here."

"No wonder, given the circumstances." He entrapped her within the circle of his arms. "While I question your wisdom, Joanna, your kindness is a commendable virtue, so let's not bicker. I'm just happy to have you to myself."

Perry's gaze burned into hers as he leaned forward. When he raised his hands and cradled her face, time and motion stopped for Joanna. She had never allowed him to go this far. A kiss to her forehead or cheek, yes, but the intention reflected in his eyes left no room for guesswork on her part. Her breath caught as a whirlwind of reasons she should let him kiss her swept up and carried away all the reasons she shouldn't.

Yet the storm raging inside her missed one.

She twisted sideways, away from his hold. "Perry, don't waste any more of your time with me. I can't give you the kind of love you want."

His nostrils flared and his jaw hardened. Then his features relaxed, and with words soft as his kiss of greeting, he said, "I'm sure you'll change your mind, Joanna. One day."

Would she? Perry sounded positive. Would he get his way when it came to marrying her?

Not while Kit Barnes still occupied that space in her heart reserved for the ever-after kind of love poets praised.

***

Joanna wrapped her arm around Perry's. As they strolled through the grass toward the crowds surrounding the lake, her grip tightened. Over and over, she glanced around her, seeking familiar faces among the scattered multitude. Contrary to her better judgment, she sought one face in particular, a handsome face with pale blue eyes.

Despite the gray sky and recent rains, throngs turned out to commemorate the birth of the nation. Patriotic ribbons bedecked every costume from dresses to top hats.

The organized games would occur later. In the meantime, toward one end of the lake, town officials had set up lawn tennis nets, croquet wickets, and horseshoe pits. At the other end, a group of men played baseball while onlookers cheered. Couples rented rowboats that skimmed the water, and children ran to and fro, playing games of tag and hide and seek. Red, white, and blue bunting draped a stage and decorated several carriages. A brass band on the stage filled the park with the lively strains of John Philip Sousa's *The Washington Post*.

Choosing a relatively private spot a sufficient distance from the band, Perry set the picnic basket he carried on the ground and spread a blanket on the grass. He helped Joanna into a sitting position and held her hand a bit longer than necessary. She pulled free, and his mouth turned down. "Are you still upset with my remarks regarding Darcy?"

"You know I can't stay angry with you, no matter how vehemently we disagree." Joanna added a smile to emphasize her remark.

"Good. As to the other subject we discussed," Perry grinned, and handed her a plate with a fried chicken leg and potato salad, "I'll never give up on us, Joanna."

She picked at the breading on the meat. "Why can't we enjoy ourselves today and leave the future for another time?"

His gaze held hers. "Because there are only two things in this world I care about—you and my business."

"Then I'm glad your father didn't sell the broom factory."

Perry stilled, his focus on the plate in his lap. "What makes you think he wanted to sell the factory?"

"Annie drew me a picture on a sheet of paper she found in an old wooden box belonging to Clayton. On the other side of the paper is a letter he wrote the day before he died. He was arranging to meet with someone to talk about an agreement for a purchase of the company. He never told you?"

"No." Perry frowned, then dug into the picnic basket and pulled out a jar of tea. "I guess it doesn't matter now, does it?"

How it must hurt him to think his father sought to sell the business he labored to build. "I'm sorry. I shouldn't have brought it up."

"He's long gone, Joanna, and I've proven my ability to run the company. Let's forget it."

They ate the cold chicken and potato salad, entertained by the activity around them. Just as Joanna was beginning to enjoy the outing, a teen employed at the factory coaxed Perry to be his partner in the three-legged race near the ball field.

Perry jumped to his feet. "Do you mind, Joanna?"

"Not at all. Go ahead."

"Why don't you join the others and watch?"

Joanna glanced around and found a tree on a knoll not far from where the competition would take place, but away from the crowd. She pointed it out. "I'll watch from over there."

She stood next to the tree while Perry and the boy prepared for the race. Both laughed as they tied their legs together and stumbled toward the starting line.

Grass rustled behind her.

"Afternoon, Miz Stewart."

Joanna refused to turn around. The momentary sense of peace abandoned her. "What do you want, Liam?"

"Now is that any way to speak to the loving husband of your best friend?"

"Go away."

His breath, overwhelming with the scent of mint, blew across the back of her neck. Somewhere, he had gotten hold of liquor and tried to cover up the odor. It had been one of Kit's favorite tricks in the past but hadn't quite worked for Liam. "You owe me."

"You failed to keep your end of our agreement. I owe you nothing." The tremble running through her negated the bravado of her speech.

Liam ran his blunt forefinger along the back of her ear and down the side of her neck in a seductive, yet covert, fashion. She shivered with disgust. He leaned over her shoulder and whispered, "I'm thinking you wouldn't want me to tell Kit why you left your papa's house, would you?"

Joanna took a step forward and whipped around so fast she

shut her eyes to allow her vision a moment to catch up. When she opened them, she lashed out with her left hand, striking Liam's cheek with such force her palm stung from the impact. He jerked away and rubbed the side of his face.

"What's going on?" Kit sprinted to her side and barged in between them. He eyed the reddened skin where her hand imprinted a mark on the right side of Liam's face. "Are you all right, Joanna?"

A pistol shot rang out. She turned toward the three-legged race as the entrants, a blur of men and children, hopped and shuffled across the grass. "Get him away from me."

Liam chuckled. "She misunderstood is all."

Joanna whirled to refute Liam's statement, but nothing in Kit's fiery expression said he believed the lout.

"You heard Mrs. Stewart. Ben is near the bandstand. I'm sure he'll be happy for you to join him."

Joanna stood her ground when everything in her wanted to flee from the low, rolling thunder in Kit's voice.

Liam glared from one to the other of them, muttered under his breath, and walked away.

Kit looked her over. "He didn't hurt you?"

"No." Joanna's ear and the skin along her neck still prickled from the trace of Liam's finger. Repulsed over the man's touch, she let Kit believe there was nothing more to Liam's purpose than an unwelcome overture.

He glanced around. "I wish I knew where he got the liquor."

"I'm sure any number of men here are willing to share."

"Unfortunately, you're right." Kit's gaze changed from inquisitive to cold. "What did he say to upset you?"

Liam wouldn't tell Kit anything if he still hoped to extort money from her, so why should she? "He has no need to say much. We don't get along. Forget this incident happened, because I will."

Kit opened his mouth as if to argue, but she intervened. "Please."

"All right, but if he ever gives you a problem again, I want to hear about it." Kit reached out. She stepped back, and he dropped his arm to his side.

Shed of his third leg, Perry approached them, panting and wiping perspiration from his face. "I discovered I'm not in the proper physical condition for strenuous competition. I suppose I should start doing more calisthenics." He frowned. "Joanna?"

She quelled the inner bedlam and assumed a relaxed expression. "I'm sorry, Perry. I'm afraid my attention drifted. Did you win?"

"We were a close second . . . from last." He hesitated, then stuck a hand out. "Welcome to Banesville's Fourth celebration, Kit."

Indecision passed over Kit's face. Would he tell Perry what transpired before he arrived? Joanna waited. Finally, he shook Perry's hand and said, "Quite a gathering."

She released her curbed breath.

Kit removed his hat and smiled as though he spoke to her for the first time that day. "It's good to see you taking part in the festivities."

Her stomach tumbled each time the nickname rolled off his tongue with such ease. Did he use it because the turmoil it caused showed on her face? Or was he indicating a desire for peace between them, despite the fact that, two days earlier, she'd poured her resentment over him like hot grease from a skillet?

Feeling Perry's watchful gaze, she pretended to search the park. "Have you seen Rose and Annie?"

"Ever the entrepreneur, Mr. Medford brought an ice cream maker." Kit spun the hat in his hands. "Annie and I have visited his shop on occasion. She's developed a taste for the treat, especially the chocolate flavor."

First a cat, then ice cream and teaching her to paint a house. Kit was becoming the type of father Annie had never known. He gave the impression of being fit for the role.

Kit pointed to a spot not far from a gazebo. "I'm not sure how Medford will keep up with the demand. Right now, the two of them are standing in line with at least a dozen other children and their parents."

Joanna craned her neck to glimpse the girl laughing with a boy around her age. Poor Annie. Between Joanna's fear and Rose's busyness, she rarely left the house and had made no good friends in her short lifetime.

"I'll find Ben"—Kit tipped his head in the direction Liam had gone—"before another of our men discovers a temptation."

"One of them is drunk? Why did you allow them to attend?" Perry followed Kit's stare though Liam was nowhere to be seen. "You've risked your hard work for no reason."

"They're not prisoners. It's their choice to change their lives or continue in their old ways."

When Kit turned to her, Joanna retreated a step under his piercing stare, and her back brushed the trunk of the tree. His indulgent smile held a hint of sadness. "We all make poor choices at times, choices that hurt others. I know I have, and I'm more sorry than I can ever express in words."

Was that supposed to be an apology aimed at her, or had she read a more personal message into the statement than he meant to imply? And what was he apologizing for—Liam's behavior today or his own years ago?

Joanna struggled to retain her skepticism toward Kit, but that hang-dog look threatened to thaw the ice encasing her resolve until it puddled at his feet.

Chapter Twenty-seven

Kit rode beside Donovan in one of the wagons he'd rented from a livery. He should have driven and kept his mind occupied. Instead, he sat on the hard bench with nothing to do but think, and those thoughts invariably turned to Joanna.

Why did she slap Liam yesterday? What occurred between them that neither wanted to talk about? Once they returned to the house, Liam retired to the cottage, and Kit didn't see him again until breakfast this morning.

He'd looked for Joanna yesterday, intending to apologize, but the incident with Liam and Perry's arrival forced him to couch the message in vague words. Had she understood his veiled request for forgiveness, and would she see a sign of his regret in this delivery? Words and deeds—both were important.

Donovan pulled up the horses in front of a neatly kept house. The man had recovered from the worst symptoms of withdrawal from alcohol, though his fight against inebriation was far from over. His spiritual progress was another matter. Donovan's dry mouth attacked him with each mention of God.

He set the brake on the wagon and glanced at Kit. "According to Mrs. McCall, this is the one."

Kit jumped to the ground and walked to the second wagon driven by Howard Cox. Both beds were loaded with bits and pieces of Joanna's old furniture. "I'll tell Mrs. Stewart we're here."

"You're too late." Cox nodded toward the house and then spit a wad of tobacco into the street.

Kit glanced over his shoulder. Joanna stood at the porch rail with her arm wrapped around a post and her expression a study in confusion. "Good morning. We brought your things."

She descended the steps and strolled across the yard wearing a day dress of a light gray material that highlighted the gray in her eyes. Those eyes darted from one wagon to the other. "Where is Carter?"

"Carter who?"

"Didn't Perry send you?"

His enthusiasm fell with the mention of Perry Stewart. Her dependence on the man was beginning to get his goat. "No. This was my idea."

Her eyes ballooned and her lips parted. "Your idea?"

Was it so unbelievable that he *might* show her some consideration?

Joanna repeated the curious glance from one wagon to the other but said nothing. Would she reject his attempt to make up for a portion of the harm he'd done her and send everything back out of spite?

Donovan walked around the horses, impatience displayed in the set of his jaw. "Do we have your permission to unload, ma'am?"

More moments of hesitation passed, before she said, "Yes. Thank you, Mr. O'Connor."

As they unloaded the furniture, Joanna directed them where to put it. It was clear she had expected this delivery and, in her mind, had arranged each piece beforehand.

***

Joanna instructed the men in the placement of the furniture, all the while striving to avoid focusing on Kit.

How was she to dismiss him if he continued to come to her aid? An inward groan sapped her breath. When had she been able to keep him from her thoughts? Even during times of despising his very name, it was still lashed to her memories.

"I can't believe we'll actually have furniture." Darcy ran her fingers over the worn damask material of the settee Donovan and Kit had carried into the sitting room. A sheepish grin flickered, and she rubbed her stomach in the familiar sign of nervousness. "Of course, I'm simply thankful for a roof over my head."

"The place did appear bigger when it was empty." Stationed in the middle of the crowded room with her arms crossed, Joanna grinned. "Mind you, I'm not complaining. A roof is good, but comfort is better."

"The men must be thirsty after working in the heat. I think we have a lemon or two left. I'll make a pitcher of lemonade for them." Darcy waddled off to the kitchen.

Joanna dodged the furniture to peek out the front window. The beds of both wagons were now empty of the large pieces, and the three men each carried a box or crate toward the house.

Kit had abandoned his coat and hat upon his arrival and

rolled up the sleeves of his shirt. The muscles in his arms and between his shoulders swelled with the weight of the contents he held, and sweat dampened his hairline.

No matter how hard she fought it, warmth oozed through her at the sight. He could have sent his men to deliver everything, like Perry had planned, but he had come himself and worked as hard as the others to see to her comfort.

Boots clumped up the porch steps. She rushed to the front door to open it. Working on the house had provided Kit with sun-golden skin, but his face was flushed from the exertion of unloading the wagons. "Rose sent you kitchen items . . . dishes, pans . . . whatever she could spare. I think you'll also find various frills."

Joanna dug through the box, pleased with Rose's choices. She pulled out a feather duster. "Darcy has made do with what I've purchased, but the lack of what you call frills hampers her work."

Kit led the way to the kitchen and set the box on the table he'd brought from the veranda of her old home. "If you want, we can help you unpack."

"Thank you, but it won't be necessary. We can manage."

The other men settled their loads next to Kit's and propped their backs against the wall. Mr. Cox's gaze wandered up and down Darcy's frame. After getting his fill of her condition, he turned away. His lip curled with disgust as though he had a right to judge her.

Mr. O'Connor wiped his damp brow with a handkerchief. One corner of the cotton cloth hung in an awkward manner, torn from overuse. Joanna studied the man with the crooked nose and facial scars. Despite his rough looks, crusty demeanor, and proclivity for alcohol, she sensed a lonely man who wanted respect but didn't believe it possible to attain. She sensed a kindred spirit.

What motivated his offer to teach her techniques of self-protection? Given the incident with Liam yesterday, perhaps it wasn't a bad idea to learn ways to defend herself. At the same time, it would provide Mr. O'Connor a purpose in line with his former profession.

Kit rubbed his hands together. "Well, we're done. I suppose we should head back." He continued to stand in the middle of the room looking like he'd misplaced the location of the front door.

"You men must be thirsty. Darcy made lemonade." Joanna grabbed the pitcher to fill glasses before Kit declined the offer. "I think we still have some of her peach pie. You'll like it. She's a wonderful cook."

For some reason, Joanna was as hesitant to let Kit leave as he seemed to be to go. Maybe she wasn't sure how to say thank you without believing it a form of self-betrayal.

The men each swigged a glass of Darcy's lemonade, then Mr. O'Connor and Mr. Cox prepared to leave the house to return the two wagons to the livery. They got as far as the front door before Joanna stopped them. "Mr. O'Connor, may I speak with you?"

He glanced at Howard Cox. "I'll see you later."

Once the other man had gone, Joanna stepped closer and lowered her voice. "The other day, you offered to show me how to defend myself. Are you still willing?"

For the first time, he grinned. "Yes, ma'am."

"Then I'm willing to learn."

They arranged a private place and time to meet, and Joanna returned to the kitchen. If Liam ever bothered her again, she'd make him bawl like a baby.

Kit watched Darcy as she toddled out of the kitchen. Joanna followed him to the sitting room. He perched on the edge of the settee while she sat in a nearby chair. An awkward silence filled the space between them. Since he'd glanced at Darcy several times while downing the pie and lemonade, Joanna waited for the same criticism she'd heard from Perry.

"Is she unmarried?"

"Yes."

He leaned forward. "Not many people would take an expectant, unmarried woman into their home, Joanna. Your compassion toward her is admirable."

"But?"

One eyebrow arched slightly above the other. "But what?"

"But it's not wise or responsible? It will hurt my reputation?" She almost laughed at the second question.

His lips flattened, and he rubbed his forehead. "I meant only to relay my admiration for your courage. She's in a difficult spot right now and needs a friend on her side. There was no other motive for my comment."

Joanna ducked her chin. Her over-sensitivity to the opinions of others had spoiled their amiable morning.

Kit rose from the settee and crossed the room. "I should go."

She followed at a sedate pace. If he knew the root of her concern for Darcy, would he still admire her? This ascending harmony between them, if one could call it harmony, was still too brittle for her to want to find out.

Someone pounded on the front door, and Joanna flinched. She passed Kit and opened the door.

Perry stomped into the house. "Joanna, I came to see if Carter's story is true."

She winced at the deafening statement. In light of Kit's unexpected benevolence, she had forgotten Mr. Carter's mission and Perry's generosity. "If you're talking about the delivery of my furniture, Kit brought everything this morning."

Perry sneered at the suit coat hanging from a hook on the wall near the door where Kit had left it earlier. His face hardened into a flesh-and-blood semblance of the carved granite blocks lining the curb along the street in front of his house. "Where is he?"

Joanna shut her eyes and rubbed the bridge of her nose. This promised to be one long morning.

Chapter Twenty-eight

Joanna shut the hymnal and rose from the piano stool, gratified by the opportunity she had been given to play her cherished instrument again.

For three weeks, with the exception of Sunday, she had walked into the music room to practice. On Monday, Wednesday, and Saturday, she played the selections Ben chose that accompanied the theme of his short talk that night. On Tuesday, Thursday, and Friday, she played for the entire household the classical selections she loved.

At first, Joanna played the required hymns and left the room until needed again. Ben's reasonable volume and the gentleness in his voice eventually persuaded her to stand outside the door and listen.

It wasn't long before she remained in the room while Ben talked to his congregants. He didn't shout. He didn't accuse them of vile transgressions. He conversed with them in a non-threatening manner that relayed his belief in God's grace and mercy. Maybe the struggling inebriates would never be accepted by society, but they were accepted here, and so was she.

On occasion, Joanna would approach Ben during the day and ask for an explanation of a passage she had read in the Bible he'd given her. He would clarify the scripture and then point her to various other verses that confirmed his answers.

More and more, she felt in her soul that her father either lied to her about God's refusal to forgive certain sins, or he was mistaken.

Kit peeked inside the music room. "Ready?"

"Let me get my hat and gloves." In a jovial mood, Joanna tapped out a high C and smiled as she passed him on her way to the parlor.

A month and a half earlier, Joanna would have berated anyone who suggested her heart rate would quicken with pleasure at the thought of a social outing with Kit Barnes. But since the morning Kit and Perry eyed one another in her sitting room like warriors prepared to battle, hardly a day passed when she and Kit had not spent leisurely time together. They strolled through the garden or sat on the veranda. They watched bursts of light from fireflies and listened to squirrels as they rustled through the underbrush. When he walked her home in the evenings, their minutes together felt like the honorable courtship she had dreamed of long ago.

She pinned her hat on her head and met Kit in the foyer. He opened the front door for her. "Annie's waiting outside with all the patience of a six-year-old."

Joanna stopped under the porte-cochere. "How do you do that?"

"What?"

"Talk Rose into allowing Annie to go for ice cream so close to suppertime." Joanna still hadn't figured out how he had talked *her* into going with them today.

"We bring ice cream back for Rose. Of course, by then, it's usually melted."

Kit's silver tongue had gotten Joanna into trouble once before. She shouldn't give him a second chance, but where he was concerned, she had no more control over her response than ice cream had against the summer heat.

Outside, Liam passed a scythe back and forth over the grass and gave the impression he paid no attention to them, but her experience said he knew every move she made. So far, the intensity of Kit's watch over both of them kept him at a distance. She dreaded the next time Liam found her alone.

Kit made no secret of the fact he no longer trusted Liam, but to question why he allowed the man to stay might lead her to reveal the blackmail and, worse yet, the reason for it.

"What's wrong?"

Joanna raised her gaze to Kit's. "Nothing. Why do you ask?"

He grinned. "Oh, I don't know. Maybe it's the fact that, if you get any closer, you'll walk in my shoes."

She sidestepped. "Sorry."

"I wasn't complaining."

Annie slipped into the space between them and grabbed each of their hands, pumping them up and down as she skipped down the drive with her freshly-brushed hair bouncing against her back.

Kit glanced over his shoulder toward Liam. "One day, I hope you'll trust me enough to tell me what happened on the Fourth."

Joanna had paid close attention to both Kit and Ben lately. In particular, she watched and listened to the things Kit said. For her, his actions spoke with more power than his words, but she wasn't ready to bare her soul.

As they reached the street, a surge of melancholy washed over her. To anyone watching, they could be mistaken for a happy family.

***

The clock in the foyer struck with seven bongs. Kit waited in the front hall while Joanna, Annie, and Rose went through their nightly routine, hugging goodbye and acting as though Joanna planned a trip across the sea.

Let her take her time. Every day she lingered in Banesville blessed him with another chance to prove himself trustworthy. Every day she lingered, his feelings for her grew deeper.

He'd tried to show her the difference in his life and believed he was making headway. Too often, though, she held back both her feelings and whatever secrets she protected. Did they involve her relationship with Perry?

A barrage of regrets assailed Kit. Resentment, envy, and anger had cost him dearly during his Philadelphia days. He couldn't allow himself to be carried away with jealousy this time and let it exact its price while Perry accelerated his pursuit of Joanna.

After their encounter at her house the day he delivered the furniture, Kit resolved to be more affable and less challenging when it came to Perry. The man didn't make it easy, especially on days when he treated Joanna to lunch in town then delivered her to Kit's door. One good thing happened. Between the two men, her reclusive tendencies were falling by the wayside.

Once they were outdoors, she said, "You don't need to walk me home every night, you know."

"If that's the way you feel . . ." He turned and took two steps back toward the house.

Joanna grabbed his coat sleeve and yanked him to a stop. "Where are you going?" Her voice wavered with amusement. She slipped her arm around his and held on tight. She was different from the young, coy woman who made it easy for him betray his brother, but she still possessed the ability to dazzle him with an engaging smile. "You can't leave me alone in the darkness."

"Never again, Joanna. Never again."

They ambled past the park. A narrow sliver of moon cast a yellow glow across the water. Kit paused to stare at the pinpoints of light that dotted the blackness above his head.

"'When I consider thy heavens, the work of thy fingers, the moon and the stars, which thou hast ordained; What is man that thou art mindful of him? and the son of man, that thou visitest him? For thou hast made him a little lower than the angels, and hast crowned him with glory and honour. . . . O Lord our Lord, how excellent is thy name in all the earth.'" Kit shut his eyes and whispered the final words, his throat tight with thanksgiving.

"At times, I wonder why God bothered." Joanna's soft voice complemented the peaceful surroundings and contradicted the troubling words she spoke.

"Because He loves us."

"Even when we're not worthy of that love?"

Kit's heart may as well have been made of paper. She'd torn it in two with her question and his responsibility for its cause. He covered the hand she'd placed on his arm and issued a silent appeal for the Creator's wisdom.

"The death and resurrection of Christ makes us worthy. God's grace is a gift, Joanna. With our acceptance, the old sins— *all* the old sins—cease to exist in His eyes. We're new creations."

"Redemption?"

"Yes."

"My father teaches that certain transgressions cannot be forgiven."

Kit vacillated between loathing the spiritual perversion that deceived Joanna and loathing the physical perversion he'd committed that held her faith prisoner to that deception. "From what I've heard of your father, I think he distorts scripture to fit his own outlook on life."

She nodded. "You and Ben offer imperfect men the opportunity to change. They come to you in all physical and moral conditions, yet you don't demand they be sober and respectable first."

"If that were the case, we'd be useless, and the house would be empty. God doesn't demand perfection from us first, Joanna. He perfects us through our faith in Christ."

She squeezed Kit's arm in a way that communicated more than words. It spoke of her understanding.

They rambled along the residential streets, carrying on frivolous conversation. For Kit, it hid an anticipation coiled inside, prepared to spring at the right time.

Once they reached her porch, she pulled away, ready to leave him at the bottom of the steps. He stayed her with the clasp of his hand over hers and inhaled a fortifying breath, never this unsure of himself around a woman. "Joanna."

"Yes?"

Kit untangled a thread of courage from the fear balled in his stomach. "May I kiss you?"

She said nothing for several agonizing moments, and he let her hand go. Was there a chance, or was she looking for a nicer way to reject him than he had once shown her?

Her chin dropped. "I need more time, Kit." She reached the porch in three heavy steps.

Kit waited until she went inside and lit a lamp in the front room. Time. Even though she hadn't agreed to a simple kiss, she hadn't rejected the idea. She hadn't shamed him for asking. He would give her whatever time she needed to see him as worthy of her affection—maybe her love.

He turned and journeyed halfway down the front path when she screamed his name.

Chapter Twenty-nine

Joanna dashed to the front hall from one direction and Kit burst into the house from another. He gripped her arms, and her neck jolted with the sudden stop.

"What's wrong?" Worry etched lines between his eyes, the kind of concern for her that she had longed to see on his face years ago.

Joanna slapped a hand against her chest, which ached with the swift pace of her heartbeat. "It-it's Darcy. Back there." She pointed in the direction of the bedrooms.

Kit paused in the midst of rushing around her when he caught sight of the sitting room. His hold loosened and his jaw slackened. "What happened here?"

Joanna pushed away. No need to look at the upset chairs and toppled table or the papers and books strewn across the floor. The scene was imprinted in her mind. The bedrooms were worse. She pressed her hands together to control the shaking.

He stared at the shambles in the sitting room. After another two-beat pause, he blinked away the dismay. Holding a lamp, Joanna picked her way through the mess to the second bedroom. Kit followed so close to her his warm breath fanned the sliver of skin at the back of her neck between her collar and hairline. His nearness provided the conflicting senses of security and anxiety.

They found Darcy propped against the wall next to her bed. Her chin touched her chest, and her unruly hair covered her face. With the tip of his finger, Kit raised her chin and tucked the hair behind her ears to examine her face. Though both eyes were shut, the reddened area around the left eye bulged with swelling. He held his hand under her nose. "She's breathing."

Joanna sighed with relief. "Will you fetch Mrs. Samuels? She lives across the street. Then, please find a doctor."

The low light from the lamp created shadowed hollows under his cheekbones. "I'm not leaving until I'm sure whoever did this is long gone."

Joanna waited with Darcy while he searched the five rooms in swift order.

"I'm still not comfortable with leaving you here unprotected."

"I'll be fine. It's Darcy and the baby who should concern us. We can worry about what happened here later."

Kit cupped the side of her face and ran his thumb over her cheek. "Be careful."

His reassuring touch tempted Joanna to close her eyes and enjoy the sensation, to beg for the kiss he'd wanted to bestow and let it soothe her fear. Instead, she forced her eyelids to remain open like those of a china doll, refusing to even blink. The feel of his fingers lingered well after he ran out the door.

Now alone with an injured woman and a house torn apart by an intruder, Joanna pulled a handkerchief from her pocket and dabbed at the trickle of blood running from a minor gash over Darcy's left cheekbone. She felt along the back of the woman's scalp and stopped at a penny-sized bump. Her index finger came away sticky with a spot of blood. "Who did this?"

Could it have been the child's father? Darcy had never mentioned a tendency for violence in the man. In fact, she'd said nothing but that he was married. Joanna hadn't asked for more. If she had, could she have prevented what happened?

While it unnerved her to think a stranger entered her house and produced this damage, her greatest concern was with Darcy's baby. The woman wasn't due to give birth for another week or so. What impact would the attack have on the child?

A groan pierced the quiet of the room. Darcy's eyelids fluttered open, and she stared at the wall behind Joanna.

The *clump-clump* of uneven footfalls echoed in the hall. Mrs. Samuels hobbled into the room and gasped. "Oh, the poor girl."

Darcy bent over, grasping the bulge in her midsection. She squealed and began to pant. "Hurts." As the pain faded, she relaxed against the wall.

Joanna glanced at Mrs. Samuels. "What do we do?"

"I'm guessing it's her time. Let's try to move her to the bed."

Joanna grabbed one arm and Mrs. Samuels the other. Together, they lifted Darcy with cautious movements and helped her to the mattress.

"Your young fella went to fetch Doc Hazard. He lives the closest." Mrs. Samuels caressed Darcy's hand before limping toward the door. "Reckon I oughta heat a kettle of water to clean her up ... and for whatever else'll be necessary. Better make coffee, too. I think we got us a long night a-comin'."

Joanna held Darcy's hand as the poor woman writhed on the bed and moaned. At intervals, she settled into a period of restfulness. During that time of calm, Joanna removed Darcy's skirt and petticoat. She caught her breath at the sight of blood on the cotton material. Had they made things worse in moving her?

Oh, God, no. Nausea churned in her stomach as memories beset her. "I can't do this," Joanna whispered. She backed away, ready to run from the room, and would have if Mrs. Samuels hadn't blocked the doorway when she returned.

With a tender touch, the older woman bathed Darcy's battered face. "I don't suppose you know nothin' about midwifery? Silly question. I can tell from that scared look on your face you're no midwife, and you never had young'uns, so you got no experience that way." Heat rushed to Joanna's face, but Mrs. Samuels spared her an answer. "Doc Hazard oughta be here in a shake."

With those prophetic words, Kit called out, "Joanna?"

"Back here." Thankful for the opportunity to escape, she trotted to the bedroom door and waved Kit and the bearded, middle-aged man behind him down the hall.

Joanna stood aside as Dr. Hazard's long strides carried him past her and into the room. With the doctor and Mrs. Samuels to care for Darcy, she turned and scurried to the kitchen where she could breathe.

***

The muscles in Joanna's legs were as rigid as fence posts and her fingers like ice.

Kit brushed aside a lock of hair hanging over her right eye.

"You're pale."

"Am I?"

"Go sit down. I'll get this." He removed the coffee pot from her hold.

She reached out to take it back. "That's not—"

"I know. That's not necessary."

At her scowl, his mouth slanted with a lackluster grin. "It's your favorite phrase. I've come to expect it."

Kit poured two cups of coffee, handed her one as she sat at the table, then backed against the counter to drink his. The warmth of the coffee cup warmed Joanna's hands. Strange how, on such a balmy night, she could be chilled.

With each sip from his cup, Kit watched her over the rim. "Did Miss Baird say what happened?"

"No. When she woke, she was in too much pain. I'm afraid for her . . . for the baby."

He set his cup on the counter, crossed the space between them, and crouched next to her chair. "Let's pray for her."

Kit closed his eyes. "Dear Lord, we come asking for Your mercy and healing for our friend, Darcy Baird."

Open-eyed, Joanna observed his calm. She listened to the low voice and conversational tone—the same style of prayer used by Ben—and compared it to her father's twisted features, loud voice, and stilted speech.

Kit's past was far from lily-white, yet his prayer reflected a confidence that God would answer. "We pray for the health of the child and ask that you give Darcy strength through this ordeal. Heal her, Lord, and bring a healthy baby into this world."

While he spoke, a dozen questions galloped through Joanna's mind, but one made the circuit over and over. What if God waited for her to pray along with Kit for Darcy's sake and she refused?

She might be held responsible for another's life—or death.

Joanna pressed her eyes closed. Father in heaven, I don't deserve any favors, but I want to believe that you'll answer this request and see past the sins Darcy and I have committed. Please, do not hold them against the child. Hear my cry for the baby's safety and well-being. *She recalled a verse quoted by Ben.* Help my unbelief.

When she opened her eyes, Kit was staring at her. His beaming smile left her lightheaded. "How long since you stopped praying?"

"Long enough to be affected by the earnestness of your own prayer."

"How did you know?"

"Your mouth moved. Don't worry. I'm not a lip reader." His smile evaporated. "Why would anyone hurt Darcy and ransack your house?"

"I've asked myself the same question."

"Joanna, I saw you leave the bank the day of the sale. When you decided to stay, did you re-deposit the money from the check I issued?"

The money. Why hadn't she considered it earlier? Joanna vaulted from the chair and ran to her room. The trunk was open and the items from the top scattered as if the culprit lashed out with his arm in impatience and sent them flying. Brushing aside shards of glass from the globe of the broken, bedside lamp, she knelt and dug through the jumbled contents until she reached the false bottom of the trunk. After raising the thin, paper-covered wood, she sank to the floor. The bills were still there. He hadn't found them.

"I see the answer to my question is no."

Kit had followed her inside her bedroom? Had he any idea

how terrifying it was for her to be alone with him in such a setting, especially after he'd asked to kiss her not two hours ago?

The last time Kit kissed her, he hadn't asked. He took, and she let him. She let him take everything. Then he cast her away as if she were a week-old fish polluting the air he breathed.

The urge to flee from his question and the temptation to say yes had warred inside Joanna. She had reason not to trust him, but mostly, she didn't trust herself.

"You shouldn't be in here."

"You're changing the subject."

Through the closed door of the room across the hall, Darcy's cry reminded her they weren't alone. Nothing would happen. No need for concern. She forced herself to relax. "It's safe."

"Who else is aware you're keeping that much money here?"

"Anyone who knows I sold my house and closed my account at the bank."

Though she didn't like David Murray, she doubted he would commit such a crime, and the teller knew nothing about her, so it was unlikely he was involved. That left one person at the top of her list of suspects. Liam.

Joanna studied Kit. Perhaps it was time to tell him of her agreement with Rose's husband. Maybe Kit should learn the reason she sold him the house, and why he should never have hired Liam McCall in the first place. She could tell him the barest of versions, one that stressed the safety of Rose and Annie and ignored the rest of his threat.

But if she did, how would Kit respond? Would he go to Liam and learn the whole sordid story anyway? Blackmail. It was an ugly term, and she couldn't afford for him to question her in depth about it.

No. She would deal with Liam on her own.

A loud screech from Darcy's room introduced the shrill cry of new life. Joanna lifted one more plea for the child's good health . . . and another for her good sense.

Chapter Thirty

Clothing and other personal items covered Joanna's bed. One by one, she folded the clothes and placed them in the trunk and the dresser Kit had delivered.

Across the hall, Jamie Baird slept in Darcy's arms, his stomach full and his mother resting to regain her strength. Before he left, Dr. Hazard assured them the injuries Darcy suffered were not serious, though bed rest was required for the next four or five days. Mrs. Samuels volunteered to stay with Darcy whenever Joanna was gone. What would she have done without her landlady last night?

What would she have done without Kit? She shut the trunk and locked it. He had coaxed a promise from her to open a new bank account this morning, but she was not to go without him to accompany her.

How easily he had wheedled his way into her life again. At the same time, she had been given a second chance to win his heart. Hadn't he said as much when he *asked* to kiss her? Then again, he hadn't asked to court her. Shouldn't that have come first?

She covered her face with her hands. How could she consider kissing Kit when the courage to tell him the truth fled from her at every opportunity?

Joanna lowered her hands and straightened her back. She peeked into the bedroom across the hall. God had extended His grace and mercy toward Darcy, a remorseful sinner. What did that mean for Joanna? *Help my unbelief.*

Darcy turned her head and lifted the corners of her mouth in a tired grin.

Joanna stepped inside the room. "How are you feeling?"

"My head hurts." Darcy ran a hand over the light fuzz covering the sleeping baby's head. "Nothing will ruin this time for me. Isn't he beautiful?"

"Yes." Joanna's heart lurched. Over the last hours, gratitude for Jamie's healthy body and lungs had overcome the bittersweet announcement of his arrival.

She tore her gaze from the child. "Kit notified the sheriff, but you were in no condition to speak with him. He'll be by this morning. Will you feel up to answering questions?"

"I don't expect to be of much help. My back ached, so I crawled into bed early. Not long after, I heard a loud noise in the house and saw a light. When the noises continued, I left the bed, thinking it was you. I saw a man near your trunk."

"You saw his face?"

"No. He must have sensed me behind him because he blew out the lantern he carried and came after me. It happened so quickly. I didn't see much of anything."

"Did he speak?"

Darcy shook her head. "Just cursed, then hit me and knocked me against the wall. I don't remember much else." She tightened her grip on the baby.

Whoever broke into Joanna's house knew about the money. It was the only thing she had left of value. With the lamps dark, he must have thought both women were gone, and it was safe to search.

A thundercloud of guilt hung over Joanna's head. How would she forgive herself if Darcy, or worse her child, had perished because she'd been too afraid of David Murray to do a simple thing, such as open a bank account?

The blame for the housebreaking pointed to Liam, but with no proof, she would keep her suspicion to herself for now. If she told the sheriff, he would ask her to explain.

"I'm sorry for what you went through, Darcy." Joanna caressed the baby's plump cheek. "You should follow Jamie's example and rest."

She lumbered back to her room, stricken by her conscience. Life was becoming more complicated with each secret she kept.

***

Kit checked his pocket watch and suppressed a yawn. He had returned home around three-thirty in the morning. Unable to sleep, he'd spent most of the past four hours seated in a wicker chair on the rear veranda. Eventually, the sun poked its rays above the horizon.

The House would officially open in a month with a tour for town officials and a reception at Mrs. Brockhurst's home. Kit scanned the list of tasks in front of him but found it hard to concentrate on anything other than last night's events.

Even though the attack caused her to deliver her baby early, Kit was thankful Miss Baird suffered nothing more serious than a cut and a bump on the back of the head.

Joanna concerned him most. What if she had been the one home alone? His heart had nearly stopped when she screamed and ran into him, ashen with fear. Then to see the condition of the sitting room . . .

Kit scratched the stubble on the side of his face and shut his eyes. He should have questioned Joanna about the money from the house sale last month and insisted she deposit it in a bank account. Who was aware that the money was in the house?

"It's going to be a hot one." Ben shuffled to another chair and fell into it. He yawned. "You're up early."

"Never went to bed."

"What's wrong?" After Kit explained, Ben leaned forward. "Any idea who did it?"

"Given the situation, we couldn't question Miss Baird."

If Darcy's child hadn't chosen that moment to be born, Kit would have asked Joanna the reason for the sudden, contemplative expression on her face when they discussed the closed account. Later, she discouraged his questions with vague responses. The maddening woman hugged her innermost confidences closer to the vest than a gambler.

At the same time, he had witnessed Joanna's love and loyalty for Rose and Annie, the sympathy and benevolence toward Darcy, and the kindness in a simple gift to Donovan. Kit wouldn't have known about the latter if he hadn't caught the gruff fighter staring with admiration at three fine linen handkerchief squares. Using a different colored thread for each, Joanna had embroidered his initials in the corners.

Only one person here never benefited from her generosity.

Kit glanced at the cottage. Over the past hours, while he sat here in the dark, he'd made a mental list of everyone who might prove guilty of invading Joanna's house. Like oil in water, Liam's name rose to the top each time.

Was the man aware she kept her money in the house? "Rose knows everything Joanna does and doesn't do."

"Are you thinking Rose would steal from her? They're tight as ticks, Kit."

"No, but we can't be sure she didn't say something to someone in innocence. What if that person knows Joanna kept her money in the house?"

"Someone like Liam?" Ben raised an eyebrow. "You don't trust him, and I understand why, but are you sure you're not letting what happened at the park color your reasoning?"

"Yes, I suspect him because of what happened then." Kit relived the memory of the confrontation with Liam. "We found out last year that a man isn't above seeking our help in order to cover his crimes. Where Joanna's safety is concerned, I'm willing to consider every possibility."

"I think you've settled on one. It's been a month since that incident. If you're right, why has he waited so long?"

It was a good question. Kit had no answer to it.

Jelly jumped onto Ben's lap. Ben ran his hand along the cat's arched back and received a noisy purr in gratitude. "I looked for Liam after you left to walk Joanna home last night. I couldn't find him."

"Did Rose know where he was?"

"She'd already gone to the cottage, so I assumed Liam accompanied her. What I wanted wasn't important enough to bother them." Ben shooed Jelly off his lap and stood. "It probably means nothing, but I figured I'd make you aware of it."

Kit dug out his pocket watch. Almost eight. He needed to get to the livery, pick up the buggy, and drive to Joanna's house. When he returned, he'd question Liam regarding his whereabouts last night.

Chapter Thirty-one

Kit had helped Joanna straighten the sitting room in the middle of the night. Now, she undertook the task of putting the bedroom in order.

She swept up the shards of glass scattered on the floor. After the trip to the bank, she would stop at the mercantile and purchase a new globe for the lamp. Ben's Bible had been flung halfway across the room, so she retrieved it and placed it back on the top of the trunk, along with her hair brush and mirror.

"Joanna!" As usual Perry had burst into Joanna's house without knocking.

She set the broom against the wall near the bedroom door and met him in the sitting room. "Hello, Perry."

After tossing his hat on an empty chair, he reached for her hands. "You weren't hurt, were you?"

She squeezed his fingers in reassurance. "I wasn't home when it happened, but thank you for being concerned. How did you find out this early in the morning?"

"I met the constable in town. Do you know who did it?"

Joanna considered telling him of her suspicion about Liam but thrust aside the idea. What if she was wrong and Liam was innocent? Without proof, bandying Liam's name about could harm her relationship with Rose. "No."

Perry eased Joanna onto the settee beside him, still holding her hands. "I understand Miss Baird met the man."

"She's the one who was hurt, and I feel awful about it."

"Did she recognize him?"

"It was dark."

At Jamie's cry, Perry glanced over her shoulder in the direction of the bedrooms. His face lost its color. "She had her baby?"

"Yes. A boy."

He recovered from his surprise in quick measure. "It wouldn't surprise me to learn the child's father was responsible. Women like that attract an equally sordid man."

"Don't make me ask you to leave, Perry."

"Joanna, what makes you protect Miss Baird? Is she a relative who landed on your doorstep, or a stranger who means to take advantage of your kind heart?"

"Neither. She's a woman experiencing a difficult time, and I want to help her. It was my decision to ask her to stay here."

"Risking your own reputation."

His superiority was the reason Perry wouldn't understand how she could have let herself be duped by a bitter and merciless drunkard—how she could have done the unthinkable with Kit.

But Kit wasn't the same man, just as she wasn't the same woman. In the past days, she'd taken that to heart. She'd begun to trust in his reformation. And if God forgave Kit Barnes, surely He would forgive her, too.

"Please, keep your voice down."

Perry bobbed his head. "Fine. Are you sure she has no idea who molested her?"

"I don't think he was after Darcy. I think he intended to rob us. Kit thinks so, too."

"Kit? When was he here?"

Leave it to Perry to focus on the least important information if it involved the man he imagined as his rival. "He walked me home last night, as he does every night."

Perry flicked a smile he clearly didn't feel and looked around the room. His brows drew together. "Why would a thief believe you have anything worth stealing?"

It embarrassed Joanna to admit her foolishness, but he would learn of it sooner or later. "I failed to open a new account once I decided to stay in Banesville."

Perry dropped her hands. "You mean to tell me you've had the money from the property sale in this house the whole time?"

Joanna winced at the rise in his voice. "Yes, but don't worry. I've learned my lesson, and Kit insisted I put it in the bank. He'll be here shortly to escort me."

Perry scowled, withdrew his pocket watch from his vest, and popped it open. "It's almost eight-forty. I don't want that money to put you in danger one more minute. Get it, and I'll drive you to the bank myself."

"Kit will arrive at any moment, Perry. If I'm not here, he'll be concerned. I won't repay his kindness to me last night by worrying him needlessly."

"Get the money, Joanna."

She bristled at the order. "It isn't like you to be overbearing."

"Neither is it like you to be irrational." Perry's shoulders fell. "I don't like the authority Kit Barnes wields over you."

"He wields no authority." Or does he? Maybe not so much authority as temptation. Right now, she wanted nothing more than to be in his company, to have him comfort her and pray with her as he'd done last night, even if it meant suffering through a humiliating trip to the bank. It was a dangerous longing, and she couldn't afford to repeat their history.

"Let me get my purse and tell Darcy I'm leaving."

Before they reached the front door, someone knocked. "That may be Mrs. Samuels to stay with Darcy." Joanna opened the door. Kit was early.

He smiled, then looked past her. The smile withered. "Good morning, Perry. I didn't expect to see you here."

"Joanna and I were about to leave for the bank." Perry rested his hands on her shoulders in a possessive manner. "I want to thank you for seeing to her safety last night, but we don't want to trouble you further."

"No trouble." Kit turned to Joanna. "I brought a buggy."

Perry's fingers bit into the muscles on both sides of Joanna's neck. She grimaced and squiggled from his hold, then brushed past Kit and onto the porch. "We'll all go."

At nineteen, Joanna thrilled at being the bone fought over by two snarling dogs. At twenty-six, "tawdry" best defined the way the competition made her feel.

Two one-horse buggies awaited them at the curb. She marched down the path without looking back, expecting both men to follow, and climbed onto the seat of the nearest vehicle.

With the top down, they looked ridiculous squeezed together as Kit drove down Broad Street. He parked the buggy as close as possible to the bank. After Perry climbed down, Joanna scooted across the leather seat and allowed him to help her to the bricks. Pressed between Kit and Perry, she climbed the steps leading to the door of the bank.

Kit ushered her inside, then eased into a chair by the door. "I'll wait here and drive you back home."

"That's . . ." Joanna sealed her lips and swallowed the rest of her standard reply.

The corners of Kit's eyes crinkled with amusement. Then they smoothed with seriousness. "Until we discover who ransacked your house, it isn't a good idea for you to wander around alone."

"I agree." Perry walked her to David Murray's office without stopping to be announced.

As much as Joanna hated to admit it, the support of the two men provided the confidence she needed to face people like Mr. Murray without shrinking into the wallpaper.

***

To walk off his burgeoning irritation with Perry, Kit prowled the trails that wound through Joanna's garden. He would always think of this place as her garden. Every ornamental blossom and herbal leaf reminded him of a side of her personality he'd discovered or rediscovered in the past weeks.

She had broken the quarter-acre into sections with various themes ranging from fragrant, colorful blooms that overwhelmed him with their beauty and warmth, hidden spots of shaded privacy meant for rest, hedges trimmed to display formality and prudence, and parcels left wild to swell with passion and subtle humor. Encompassed by this diverse creation, Kit had immersed himself in thoughts of *her.*

It was one thing to entertain wistful dreams, another to assume they would come true. Joanna needed more time. How much more?

Her answer to his request to kiss her was another way to say she didn't trust him. How could he blame her? Getting past her reservations would not be easy, but no matter what it took or how long, Kit would repair his image in her eyes.

Once he departed the garden, he shook off the romantic musing of the previous half hour and started for the house. Assuring Joanna's safety came before mooning over her, and he hadn't spoken to Liam yet.

Preoccupied with his thoughts, Kit shied away before bumping into Rose as she crossed the yard. He fell in alongside her. "Sorry. I wasn't watching where I was going."

Rose climbed the steps to the veranda and stopped outside the kitchen door. "I heard what happened. How is Joanna?"

"Shaken, but strong. Darcy and the baby are well, too."

"Ben said it was a boy."

"Jamie."

"He's healthy?"

Kit grinned. "And loud."

Rose heaved an excessive sigh of relief, then kneaded her left wrist in a gentle, but nervous manner. "You're sure Joanna is fine?"

"Positive. Is your husband around? I haven't seen him since I returned from town."

Her darting glance landed on a potted fern behind Kit and stalled there. "He's in the cottage."

"When did he retire last night?"

"I don't remember." She refused to look Kit in the eye and didn't ask why he questioned her about Liam. What did she know that she wasn't telling? She glanced over his shoulder and opened the door to the kitchen. "I should prepare lunch."

"Rose—"

"I was already in bed when she came in, and I stayed there all night." Liam stomped up the steps of the veranda. "Isn't that right, dear?"

Rose eyed her husband, rubbing her wrist at the same time. "Yes. I remember now." Even as she spoke, a look of defiance tightened her features and replaced the nervousness. Rose's stiff pose and Liam's too-pleasant smile laid bare their lies.

Kit turned his attention to Liam. "I'll ask again. Where were you last evening?"

"I told you. I went to bed early."

The man's cockiness and Rose's behavior brought to mind an ugly notion. Too often, drinking led to violence. Kit had witnessed his share of men who, under the influence of alcohol, lost control over their anger and frustrations. He could never abide bullying and abuse, particularly from a sober man.

A fuse lit inside Kit. It burned and sizzled its way to an impending explosion. As long as Rose and Annie remained on his property, he owed them his protection.

"I think you intimidated your wife into saying she was with you." Kit stepped forward and waited to see if Liam would retreat. The man held his ground, suggesting a lack of fear—not a good sign. Mere inches remained between them. "Maybe you do more than just terrorize females with words. Did you hurt Rose? Is that why she's rubbing her wrist? Did you beat Darcy last night and ransack Joanna's house?" With each question, the timbre of Kit's voice heightened until it reverberated in his ears.

One side of Liam's mouth lifted in a smirk. "Now how could I do that when I was in bed?"

Kit had no proof to trigger a confession, only suspicion based on the Independence Day incident, Rose's odd behavior, and a dislike of Liam. "Why did Joanna slap you?"

This time, Liam backed a step and started to turn. "I don't have to answer to you."

Kit grabbed his arm and swung him around. "As long as you remain on this property, you will answer to me."

"Hey, what's going on?" Howard Cox loped toward them, followed by Ben.

Kit seized a fist full of Liam's shirt and jerked him closer. "Don't ever lay a hand on Rose or Annie. And stay away from Joanna."

"Or what?" Liam tried to shove Kit away, but Kit held onto the shirt.

"Or I'll—"

"That's enough, Kit." Ben yanked him backward, tearing Liam's shirt in the process.

As Howard pulled Liam into the yard, Kit raked an unsteady hand through his hair. Every nerve tingled with the horror of what he'd done. What was he thinking getting into a shouting match with the man?

Liam stumbled backward through the grass. "You don't know nothin', Barnes. Nothin'. Why don't you ask Miz Stewart to educate you, 'specially since she's taken up with her kind?"

At the muffled shriek behind him, Kit turned. Rose stood outside the kitchen door with a damp towel pressed against her mouth. Her eyes were round as the blue buttons on her dress. With her sleeves rolled halfway to her elbow, a bruise on her left wrist stuck out like a sailor's tattoo.

She lowered the towel. In a voice as calm as a lazy summer day, she said to her husband, "Gather your things from the cottage and get out of my life."

"You got no say in this, Rose." Liam tried to break free of Cox, but the other man held fast.

"She doesn't need any, McCall." For the first time since he began his work with inebriates, Kit ordered a man to leave the premises and not return.

Chapter Thirty-two

Kit sat behind his desk in what had been the family parlor before the carpenters built a wall that divided the space into an office and a private meeting room.

The new walls had been plastered and painted but remained free of paper. With the closeness of each room, Kit preferred the light color of the cream paint. It provided a sense of space as opposed to the bold, and often suffocating, patterns of wallpaper.

Ben returned to Pittsburgh on Monday, so one of the local pastors had filled his shoes this evening with a rousing sermon meant to keep the men's attention. Now he'd left, and on the other side of the wall, Joanna played her piano for pleasure, if that was what one called it.

She had arrived early this afternoon to console Rose, who still mourned the finality of her marriage though not the departure of her husband. Almost a week had passed since Kit had tossed Liam out in a fit of temper. After being ordered off the property, the man packed his things and, without a word to Rose or Annie, left the cottage. As far as Kit knew, no one from the Spencer Brockhurst House had been in contact with Liam since.

Between the housebreaking, caring for Darcy, and worry over Rose, Joanna's frame of mind showed in the discordant notes issuing from the music room.

Kit winced at another exasperated clash between pianist and instrument. Then, he was struck by blissful silence.

"What are you working on?"

He glanced up. The glow from the lamp shimmered over Joanna's hair and sparkled in her eyes. Even with the frown that tugged the sides of her mouth downward, the sight of her captivated him.

He reminded himself to breathe and answer her question. "I'm reviewing Mrs. Brockhurst's list." He held up the papers. "This morning, she sent me two full sheets of paper with confirmed responses to the reception on the twenty-second of next month. It's pretty much a directory of the area's privileged class."

"I'm sure you read my name at the top."

Kit chuckled when she rolled her eyes. He pulled out a sheet of paper from underneath the others and held it up for her to read. "Joanna Stewart is written at the top of my list. See?"

She pressed a hand against her throat. "Are you . . . are you asking me to attend the reception with you?"

"Yes."

Based on the bemused expression and her budding comfort with social excursions in town, he half expected her to accept.

Instead, she crossed her arms in a demonstration of stubbornness. "Don't be silly. You know they would welcome a case of typhoid before they would welcome me. I'll only ruin your chance to impress future supporters."

"No, you won't." Kit tossed the papers onto the desk. With her sigh, he sensed a change in subject. Fine. He wouldn't push it. Plenty of time remained to convince her to accompany him.

"I understand you and Ben plan to conduct a tour of the home for non-temperance-minded politicians."

"They may not want to see alcohol prohibited, but they're interested in reducing the number of inebriates. In turn, they believe it will reduce crime, thereby saving Banesville money."

"Are they right? Will it work?"

"Statistics back the theory. For instance, arrests for drunkenness in the area around the Pittsburgh home have lessened."

"What about women? Aren't they worth saving?"

"Of course they are." Kit kneaded the tight muscles in his neck. "Decent women don't enter drinking establishments, so they hide their weakness behind the walls of their homes. It makes it more difficult to reach them."

Kit bent forward to stretch the screaming muscles at the back of his neck and between his aching shoulder blades. He had high hopes for success in Banesville, but it demanded time, and the teaching of a different way of life, a different way of handling daily trials. He and Ben sought to pass on the key to their victory over alcohol—a faith in the God who created both men and women to be more than slaves to drink. They—he—had failed with Liam McCall and it continued to eat at him.

The one man who surprised Kit with a strong resolve to turn his life around was Donovan. Though he had yet to express an interest in embracing that soul-saving faith, he'd come a long way in his struggle.

Often lately, Joanna and Donovan wandered off for half an hour or an hour during the day. Neither one would tell Kit why, but they returned red-faced and perspiring. Once again, he rubbed the back of his neck and grimaced. Not long ago, he would have talked himself into believing the worst about the two of them. Now, he was curious rather than critical.

"You've made quite an impact on Donovan. I'll admit, when he first asked to come here, I wasn't confident he would stay. I appreciate the way you've encouraged him, Joanna."

"Under that crotchety exterior, he's a nice man."

Joanna maneuvered around the desk and behind his chair. She brushed his hands away and worked her fingers under his collar and on either side of his exposed neck, then pressed her thumbs to the taut muscles—up and down and in tiny circles that set his nerve endings on fire.

Kit wrestled an urge to drag her in front of him and take that kiss he'd asked for, and she'd never given. Since the night of the housebreaking, neither of them had raised the subject of turning their growing companionship into a deeper, more romantic bond. Each time he looked at her, though, he wished for more than a walk in the garden together.

"You two are spending quite a bit of time together. Where do you run off to?" He shut his eyes and released a groan of bliss. At the sound of his pleasure, her fingers halted, then withdrew.

Before he realized she'd moved, Joanna stood in the doorway again. She twisted her hands in front of her as though the chafe would rid her fingertips of the feel of him. "I'm ready to leave."

"Joanna . . ."

"I'm not the same woman, Kit." Like a dove on the verge of taking flight, she perched in the doorway, one foot on each side of the threshold. "I thought you were in pain, and I wanted to help."

"I know." Kit eased from the desk with unhurried movements and stopped, leaving almost a yard between them. "Joanna, since meeting you again, God has shown me things about myself I tried to deny. All these years, I've blamed you for my failings. It's been a humbling experience to realize I have no one to blame but myself.

"What happened before—what I did to you—was wrong in too many ways to count. If you can forgive me, it's my wish to do things right, to court you properly like you've always deserved." He risked closing the space between them but kept his arms at his sides and his voice low. "I ran from you once, Joanna. I won't do so this time. Please, don't run from me."

Motionless, Kit waited as her eyes grew large and glassy. Finally, she whispered, "I don't want to."

Never had he wanted to kiss a woman as much as he wanted to kiss Joanna at that instant. He longed to sweep her off her feet and demonstrate to her his joy, his devotion, his thanksgiving.

Not now. Not until that lingering doubt in her expression vanished.

***

Dead leaves and twigs crunched and snapped as Joanna's feet danced on the path that wound through the trees. Even in the cool shade of the woods behind her old house, sweat beaded on her brow and upper lip. It rolled down her back and stuck her chemise to her damp skin.

The attack had caught her by surprise. Her arms were pinned behind her with a firm and aching hold. She wheezed a ragged breath and scrambled to get away.

The gravelly voice whispered in her ear. "Remember all I told you."

Her mind raced for a solution to her predicament. She stopped struggling and stomped her heel on his toes. Without waiting for a reaction, she swung her leg forward and back, connecting with his shin. He grunted and loosened his hold—not by much, but enough to let her jab her elbow into his abdomen. She smiled at the *whoosh* of his expelled breath though he still held her arms.

"Thunderation!" The cry came from Joanna's left.

Before they could stop him, Kit bolted through the brush and yanked her captor away from her. He spun Mr. O'Connor, not a trivial feat, and pushed him to the ground. Joanna suspected the man's fall was due more to the surprise of the shove than the power behind it. Kit had the muscle to do the job, but the fighter had the training to withstand almost anything but this unexpected assault from a friend.

When Mr. O'Connor's nostrils flared, and he leapt to his feet, Joanna grabbed his arm and tried to tug him backward. "Stop it, both of you."

Kit planted his right foot several inches in front of the left and raised his fists in a fair imitation of a pugilist. "Explain yourself, Donovan."

Joanna jumped in front of her teacher, and her role shifted from his student to his shield. She glowered at Kit. "What do you think you're doing?"

Kit's chest pumped in and out. "I heard you scream."

"He caught me by surprise."

With one fist still in the air, he brushed her behind him. "And I'm protecting you. Now move away."

He was protecting her? Against his friend? In the course of

seconds, a range of emotions flitted through Joanna. Should she try out her new self-defense moves on Kit, laugh over his misunderstanding, or weep over the sweetness in his desire to rescue her?

"There's no need for your protection. He isn't trying to hurt me."

With his attention glued to Mr. O'Connor, Kit turned his head halfway toward her. "I saw what I saw, Joanna. His arms were locked around you, and you were struggling."

"True, but like you, his purpose was to save me from harm."

He frowned at her. "Save you from what kind of harm?"

Joanna placed a hand on Mr. O'Connor's arm. "Thank you. We'll finish another time."

"Whatever you say, Mrs. Stewart." With a final glare at Kit, he stomped through the wooded area toward the house.

He barely cleared the tree line before Kit rounded on her. "Finish what? What's going on, Joanna?"

***

"In the event I ever need it, Donovan is teaching me to defend myself."

Since the attack on Darcy, Kit had been more vigilant, escorting Joanna to the house in the afternoon and back at night—except on those occasions when Perry interceded.

Kit had no idea she had taken the matter of her safety into her own hands. He merely knew his delivery of rotted wood slats to the trash heap was interrupted by her scream, a sound that plunged him into action. Unnecessary action, as it turned out.

Joanna brushed dirt and bits of dead foliage from the hem of her skirt. "Please don't scold him. I asked him not to tell anyone."

"So with another of your secrets, I've struck a friend. Why couldn't you just tell me?"

The day they moved the furniture into her house, she took the fighter aside. Had her plan for this instruction begun then? Kit stood stock-still. That was the day after her altercation with Liam. Was Joanna hiding a secret more sinister than lessons in protecting herself?

"Who are you afraid of?"

She lowered her gaze and gasped. "Oh, you cut your hand."

He hadn't noticed the sting from the broken skin on his finger until she mentioned the cut. "I must have scraped it when I tossed the wood aside to come to your rescue."

"We should put something on that." Joanna started past him, but Kit latched on to her arm and dragged her back. He had no intention of letting her brush this episode aside without an explanation. She had felt sufficiently threatened to ask Donovan to teach her self-defense. Though Kit believed he knew the answer to his last question, it was high time she told him why.

"I don't need yarrow salve. I need the truth. Who frightens you?"

Her attention traveled to the toe of her boot as it kicked the pine needles on the ground, then to the soaring treetops and the hawk circling above. It landed everywhere but on him.

"Liam."

Lost in his irritation, Kit almost missed the name. He released her arm but wasn't ready to let her slip away. "No one has heard from Liam in the six days he's been gone."

"He may have left the property, but as I found out a month ago, he can't be trusted to stay away."

The tic above his eye eluded Kit's struggle to maintain a semblance of self-control. Deep anger in Joanna's voice assured him she still held the hiring of Liam against him.

With her hands clasped behind her back, she paced one, two, then three feet, spun on her heel, and tramped the same number of steps in the opposite direction, as if weighing her next words to see if they would stand in a court of law. "That day in the park . . . Liam demanded I give him the money from the property sale."

"That was thousands of dollars." No wonder she'd slapped him. Kit folded and unfolded his fingers, and the sting of the cut revived. "Liam thought you would hand over money simply because he demanded it?"

"We had an agreement. He broke it when you hired him, so I refused to pay."

Like a primed pump, Joanna had begun to spew the information Kit sought, but it wasn't enough to satisfy his thirst. Was this what Liam meant when he said Kit knew nothing and Joanna could "educate" him?

"Why make such an agreement?"

"Because he knew I'd do anything to keep—" She stopped pacing and guarded her expression.

Kit's teeth clenched at the spark of indecision in her eyes. She was about to tell him—or rather *not* tell him—the truth. What more could he do to gain her trust? "To keep what, Joanna?"

"Liam hurt Rose on more than one occasion. He's a despicable man. I'd finally had enough and fired him."

"What about Annie? Did he ever . . ."

"He never laid a hand on her. His raised voice was sufficient to frighten her."

Kit relaxed over that piece of information . . . somewhat. "When did you fire Liam? Before or after we met in Perry's office?"

She hesitated before saying, "After."

"That's why you changed your mind about selling me the house, and why you negotiated such an outrageous sales price. You agreed to pay him to stay away from his wife and child."

While the explanation sounded logical to Kit, Joanna still avoided eye contact with him. "Liam knew you were interested in buying the property, but his sum was more than I could manage. You're right. I would do anything to keep Rose and Annie safe, and Liam knew it."

Kit stepped forward and cupped her face in his hands to get her to look at him. "You've deposited the money in the bank. He has no access to it now, and you've no need to worry."

"You believe that will stop him from threatening me or those I care about? Why do you think I stayed in Banesville after the house sold, Kit?"

He had asked himself that question numerous times. While he'd assumed it was for Annie, lately, he'd hoped her purpose also involved him.

She backed away from his hold. "Why did you bring him here? Couldn't you see the type of person he was?"

"Joanna, Liam asked me to help him regain the life and marriage he had before the liquor took control. It's one of the things Ben and I try to do for the men—reconcile them with their families. I didn't know about the violence."

Hadn't he suspected Liam's true character?

In his eagerness to keep Joanna in Banesville, Kit had been willing to overlook his reservations about the man. At the time, he cared about nothing more than receiving a chance to prove to her his new character. In doing so, his pride and self-interest hurt three women. How was he to make amends for that?

"I'm sure Darcy was attacked because he was looking for the money. What happened to her was my fault, Kit."

"You aren't responsible for Liam's actions, Joanna. I'm at fault." Kit rubbed the scraped skin on his finger. "We should tell the sheriff."

"No."

"We can't allow him—"

"You're right. He's gone and not likely to bother us again."

Joanna hiked the trail Donovan took while Kit followed at a slower pace. Her refusal to report what she knew nagged at him. At least Liam was gone.

Chapter Thirty-three

Joanna dressed in a hurry. She'd spent too much time cooing at Jamie, and now Perry waited for her. Over the past week, his pursuit of her had grown bolder and his jealousy of Kit more obvious. Today, she would tell him of her decision to court his rival.

Her hand quivered as she buttoned the shirtwaist. Did this tremble have to do with dread of hurting Perry, or was the cause anxiety over allowing Kit to beguile her a second time? What if Kit broke his promise and ran from her anyway?

God, please keep me from making another mistake.

She inhaled a deep breath, and her lips curved with a grateful smile meant for no one but the Lord. Little things, like receiving this sudden peace of mind, encouraged the conviction that her father preached a dangerous dogma.

God never turned his back on her but waited for her to turn to Him. In recent days, Joanna had chosen to embrace *that* truth.

After brushing her hair, she pinned it in a simple chignon and added a hat that reminded her of the day she and Rose had sifted through the items in the attic. Annie still played with the old clothes and accessories they had carried downstairs. A wistful sigh escaped. Before they knew it, the girl would grow into those items.

She eyed the top of the trunk and the empty spot where she used to keep Annie's drawing. Because it continually fluttered off the top, she had placed it inside weeks ago, planning to purchase a frame. With all that had happened lately, the errand had been forgotten. While she was in town with Perry, she would look for one and hang the drawing on her bedroom wall.

Joanna moved everything from the top of the trunk and dug through the contents inside, but the paper wasn't there. After scouring the room, she entered the kitchen. "Darcy, have you seen Annie's drawing? I thought I put it inside my trunk."

Darcy held Jamie and swayed back and forth while stirring sugar into a pitcher of tea. "Not lately. Are you sure you didn't move it elsewhere?"

Had she? For all the attention Joanna had paid to her surroundings lately, it could have been staring her in the face for weeks. Perhaps she'd misplaced it when straightening her room after the housebreaking.

"Well, I'll look for it later."

Joanna rode the horse car to the factory on the other side of town. During the ride, she'd rehearsed what she would tell Perry. Now standing outside Perry's office door, she tried to relax the muscles in her neck and shoulders, but the rigidity only reminded her of her brazenness with Kit on Wednesday night. Why was she bound and determined to sully her character around him? Amazingly, he still asked to court her. That might change once she confessed everything to him.

What if she never told him? It was in the past. Why bring it up and risk another rejection?

Perry opened the door of his office, glanced at her face, and frowned. "Is something wrong?"

She wore her emotions too visibly these days. "There's something we must discuss before we leave for the restaurant."

"What is it?"

Once inside the room, Joanna hesitated. No matter how she phrased it, he wouldn't be happy. "Kit has asked to court me."

Perry stood with his hand wrapped around the knob of the office door as if it were an orange to be wrung dry of its juice. Several seconds passed before he replied. "And your answer?"

"I agreed."

He turned away and grabbed his hat from the coat rack with a force that set the furniture piece rocking on its base.

"I'm sorry, Perry."

"I suspected from the first day I saw the two of you together that you shared more of a past than you admitted to me. He's a drunkard, Joanna. He'll never be dependable."

She simmered with the need to defend Kit. "You're wrong. He's changed."

His grunt spoke his disbelief. "It was probably one of his men who broke into your house. It wouldn't surprise me to learn he was involved, maybe even arranged it."

"He had nothing to do with what happened. We both believe we know the identity of the man."

Perry stiffened. "Who?"

Although she regretted speaking from anger, Perry's hurt

would run deeper if she continued to keep the information from him. "I told you about keeping the money from the property sale in the house."

When she related the incident at the park, his eyes darkened with a fury she felt all the way to her toes. "Why didn't you tell me this before?"

"It wasn't necessary. Why upset you over a theory I'm not one hundred percent sure about?" As she had done with Kit, she told Perry nothing more than Liam wanted to be paid to leave Rose and Annie alone.

"When it comes to you, Joanna, nothing is unnecessary. I assume Kit handled the situation while I ran that confounded race."

"Yes."

"Have you told the sheriff of your notion regarding McCall?"

"I have no proof, and Darcy is afraid of the exposure her presence will cost me after an arrest. Besides, no one has seen Liam in a week, so I hope we're rid of him."

After several seconds of hushed tension between them, the noticeable strain faded. Perry opened the door and gestured her into the hallway. Their luncheon progressed without another word about either the housebreaking or her courtship with Kit.

***

The oars sliced through the water of Town Lake without much splash. From the bow, Kit pulled the rowboat through the water as they moved farther from the shore. Joanna sat in the stern, holding fast to each side of the wooden frame. A gentle breeze fanned her face while the heat of a full sun seared the back of her shirtwaist.

Kit grinned as he rowed the boat toward the middle of the lake. "You can relax. I know what I'm doing."

With reluctance, she let go of the sides, returned his smile, and turned her attention to their surroundings.

Numerous people filled the park on this lazy Sunday afternoon. At the south end, a group of a dozen or so teens played a game of football that, from a distance, resembled nothing more than a mob brawl. To the east, a man ran across the field in an attempt to show off his kite flying skills in front of his sweetheart. The paper toy shuddered, then flipped and plummeted to the ground. The courting couple laughed.

Although she still endured moments of anxiety when preparing to venture out in public, Joanna now realized much of her fear was in her mind. Most people never gave her a second look. On occasion, she crossed paths with an old friend of Clayton's who snubbed her, but she'd ignore the insult and go about her business. Unlike the day she first rode the horse car, apprehension simply nibbled at her without trying to devour her.

Nevertheless, her stomach fluttered each time the boat rocked from side to side due to another's gentle wake, or when Kit looked at her as he did right now—as though she had emerged from his dreams into reality. Without doubt, her face displayed the same happiness because for this moment, she was living a scene from *her* dream.

"I'm glad you accepted my invitation, Joanna."

"So am I."

A sudden fit of timidity overcame her and smothered conversation. Joanna leaned sideways and ran the tips of her fingers through tepid water that smelled of fish and algae. She tilted her head back and gazed into the silky, blue sky with its smattering of wispy clouds.

Kit stopped rowing and permitted the boat to drift. "Do you mind if I ask you a question?"

Alert to the seriousness in his tone, Joanna drew her wet hand inside the boat. "I suppose it depends on what you ask."

"It's clear how Perry feels toward you. Is there any part of you that returns those feelings?"

Joanna paused to control her relief. She could answer this question with total honesty. "It's true that since his father died, Perry has sought more than friendship from me. Although I counted on his support, I never encouraged him in a romantic sense. Now he knows nothing more is possible between us."

Kit nodded. "You told him about us?"

"Yes." She added in haste, "Only of your request to court me."

"How did he react?"

"Perry is used to getting what he wants. Of course he was upset." Joanna leaned forward and clasped Kit's hand. "Yesterday, I broke his heart. Please, don't ever give me a reason to regret the need for it."

Kit's gaze held hers as he raised the back of her hand to his lips. The fire that threatened to weld them together the day of Annie's birthday celebration warmed her all over again.

Too soon, their boating adventure ended, and Kit helped her to the shore. While he pulled the boat onto the grass, an older couple trotted past them. The woman pressed a hand to her chest. The distress in both their expressions dragged Joanna's attention toward a mound of bedrock that had been removed when the lake was built a year ago. A group of ten or twelve people gathered in front of the jagged granite pieces of various sizes, from cobblestones to boulders.

She tapped Kit's shoulder and pointed in the direction of the growing crowd. "I wonder what's going on over there."

He lowered the bow of the boat and glanced toward the assembly. "They're curious about something."

Too far away to see over the heads and hats in front of them, Kit said, "Stay here, and I'll see what this is about."

He pushed through the throng, and Joanna lost sight of him. She approached the onlookers but remained on the fringe.

Once Kit re-emerged, he cupped her elbow and led her away from the gathering.

"What happened?"

"Let's get you home."

She twisted to see over her shoulder, but he was driving her forward at a pace that risked a stumble. She planted her feet and yanked to free her arm. "Why are you rushing me? What's wrong?"

He turned, but kept his hold on her. "I'm trying to protect you from a scene you shouldn't see, Joanna. A man is dead."

She shot another glance toward the rock pile. "How awful. Do they know what happened?" His mouth compressed into a grim line, and a clump of ice chilled her insides. "Is it someone you know?"

"It's Liam."

Chapter Thirty-four

Rather than allow Kit to see her home, Joanna chose to be with Rose when her friend learned of her husband's death. Now, she sat in the cottage and wished Rose didn't have to endure more sorrow due to Liam.

Once the body's identity was officially established, the sheriff and one of his deputies wasted no time in arriving at the Spencer Brockhurst House. The preliminary evidence suggested that late Saturday night or early Sunday morning, an unknown person picked up a large rock at the park and struck Liam with a force that caved his skull. At the mental image, queasiness assailed Joanna, and she was glad Kit had insisted she not follow him to the front of the crowd to witness the gruesome scene.

Sheriff Myers asked and received permission to search the entire premises, including the cottage. Kit agreed. Afterward, Joanna took him aside. "Are you sure you want to consent to it?

Sandra Ardoin

What if they find something incriminating?"

"What would they find?"

"If it pertains to Liam, it could be anything."

"There's nothing to hide, Joanna, no reason to deny the request." His mouth tipped up in a closed smile, probably meant to cheer her. It fell flat for both of them.

Oblivious to the death of her stepfather, Annie played outside until dusk when Mr. O'Connor offered to entertain her away from the other adults. Tomorrow was soon enough to tell her of the tragedy.

At the end of the search, Joanna, along with Kit and Rose, prepared to answer the questions put to them. If the lawmen found anything suspicious on the premises, they weren't saying.

While Myers conducted the inquiry, the deputy stood propped against a wall and watched them. What he hoped to see, Joanna wasn't sure, but each time he turned his black, bushy eyebrows and perpetual frown on her, she almost jumped out of her skin.

"When was the last time you saw your husband, Mrs. McCall?"

In her mind, Joanna willed that Rose not commit the same error she had done after Clayton's death. She willed her friend to show a sign of grief or regret, anything other than the stoicism that bred rumor, insinuation, and suspicion.

"A week ago." Even though Rose sat erect and unemotional, tremors ran through the hand Joanna held in comfort.

"Sunday?"

"Saturday."

"Do you know where he went when he left here?"

"No."

"Mrs. McCall, why did he leave? Was it a matter of his

276

abandonment?" Myers knew the answer. It shouted from his watchful gaze. He waited to see if Rose would lie. Joanna squeezed Rose's hand and released it, encouraging her friend to tell the truth.

"He left because I told him to go."

"Why would you do that, ma'am?"

Rose flicked an apprehensive glance at Kit, then Joanna. "Because he was a wicked man."

The two men eyed one another, and Joanna groaned inside. The interrogation of her friend lasted another half an hour before they turned on Joanna. Under their questioning, she related her history with Liam and the fact that she fired him for hitting his wife.

"You experienced a housebreaking a short time ago, isn't that correct?"

"Yes." Dread enveloped Joanna like a moldy blanket.

"Was anything taken?"

"Nothing that I know of."

"And you have no idea who did it or why?"

Joanna hesitated. Kit and Perry both knew of her suspicion, so it was best not to hedge. "I think Liam tried to steal the money I'd been paid for my property."

She may as well have said night had fallen for all the surprise her answer elicited in the man. "Why didn't you report this earlier?"

"It was an opinion with no proof."

What she chose to leave out of her account amounted to lies of omission that could cause further trouble if, during the investigation, Liam's attempt at blackmail was exposed.

"An opinion that should have been relayed to us. Are you aware that Mr. McCall was discovered with certain stolen items on his person—items missing from a recently burgled home?"

Joanna gaped at him and shook her head. Was that what they looked for in their search, more stolen goods? Did they find any here?

Rose released a tiny cry and crushed Joanna's fingers. "He robbed the people of Banesville?"

"Possibly, ma'am. We believe it's also possible he had an accomplice."

After that announcement, they focused on Kit with even more enthusiasm. Joanna avoided everyone's gaze as Myers asked about the Independence Day incident, and Kit repeated what she had told him. This time her lie of omission affected an innocent man. The guilt multiplied with each partial answer until it raked her conscience raw. She couldn't tell the whole truth, not now, not in front of Kit. She owed him a private conversation . . . a private confession that was weeks overdue.

"You threatened Mr. McCall."

The forceful accusation broke through Joanna's soul-searching.

Myers glared at Kit, whose face reddened as if all his air had been pilfered. "I ordered him to leave the property and not return."

Rose had provided Joanna with the details of Kit's argument with Liam that day. Someone else must have told the sheriff a more lurid tale.

"You assaulted him."

"I grabbed his shirt."

"We have a witness who says you grabbed him with such rage that his shirt tore, Mr. Barnes."

The "witness" must be Howard Cox. He was . . . had been a friend to Liam and a troublemaker in his own right. Now the lawman intended to twist Cox's statement to fit his own version of what happened.

Kit's outward composure deflated. "I won't deny it."

Joanna spied a smile on the face of the deputy propped against the wall, a smile that gouged her with fear for Kit. She wouldn't sit mute while he was treated in such a manner. "I am a witness, too, sir. I'm a witness to the cruelty of Liam McCall toward his wife."

"Jo—"

"It's all right, Rose." Joanna glared at the sheriff. "Mr. Barnes was right in demanding he leave. I'm sorry Liam is dead, but you won't find the person responsible here."

With tremendous effort, Joanna maintained her poise while both officers of the law measured her veracity against whatever ruler they used. Finally, the bushy-browed one pushed away from the wall.

Sheriff Myers said, "We have enough information at present."

***

The coroner's inquest on the first of August ruled Liam's death a murder; however, no one was accused, and he was buried the next day.

Joanna shuffled into her kitchen a week later. Having overslept, she hadn't taken the time to dress or fix her hair. She looked around the kitchen. "Where's Jamie?"

"Sleeping. You two have that in common this morning." Darcy darted a glance in Joanna's direction, then bent and shoved a couple pieces of kindling into the stove's firebox, which added more heat to the already warm room. She poured Joanna a cup of coffee and set it on the table before preparing breakfast.

"You haven't eaten?"

"I waited for you. I hope Jamie's crying didn't keep you up last night."

"Don't worry." A baby couldn't be blamed for last night's restlessness or that of the nights before, not when Joanna's problem stemmed from a troubled conscience.

Throughout the ordeal of Liam's death, Kit acted as if his personal mission involved seeing to Rose and Annie's needs while continuing his ministry to Donovan O'Connor. Howard Cox abandoned the House the day of the inquest when he all but accused Kit of murdering Liam.

During the turmoil, Kit courted Joanna with respect and romantic gifts. She leaned toward the Mason jar on the table and sniffed the fragrance of the sweet alyssum and forget-me-nots Kit surprised her with yesterday. What had she done for him? She had kept to herself the one thing that could drive a permanent wedge between them.

"Joanna, I wrote my parents."

Joanna straightened in the chair. "You did?"

Darcy pulled a letter from the pocket of her apron. "This came a few days ago." She handed it to Joanna, who unfolded the sheet of paper.

Whatever Joanna had expected from the Bairds, this ardent plea for their daughter to return home was not it. While careful not to condone Darcy's actions, her mother made clear the parents' forgiveness and preparations to welcome both child and grandchild with open arms.

How would her life have been different had Joanna been raised in such a family? Unlike Darcy, who ran off to find adventure, Joanna believed she would have been content to follow convention . . . if her father had shown more faith in her.

Joanna left her seat and enfolded Darcy in a hug. "This is marvelous news. I'm very happy for you. Have you decided when you will go?"

"I don't know." Darcy clutched the paper until the edge crinkled in her hand. "Do you think I should?"

"Of course, you should."

"But I don't want to cause them trouble. What if—"

Joanna clasped Darcy's shoulders. "You, my prodigal, have been offered a gift of forgiveness and unconditional love. Grab it and don't let go."

The young woman's slow grin brought a beauty to her face not often noticed through the veil of anxiety she wore.

"When Jamie wakes, we'll go to the train station and buy you a ticket."

Darcy's parents had expressed their forgiveness once their daughter revealed her news of an illegitimate child. Would Joanna be as fortunate with Kit?

Chapter Thirty-five

Ten days after Liam's death, Kit received a summons to the Brockhurst home. When he arrived, Mrs. Brockhurst awaited him in the drawing room. A folded sheet of paper rested across her lap.

"Good afternoon, Mr. Barnes." Gone was the friendlier "Christopher."

"Good afternoon."

"Please be seated."

She gestured to the chair he'd occupied on other visits. Kit dubbed it the Inquisition Seat, for each time he sat in it, she cross-examined him with the skill of the two lawmen who visited the house the day Liam's body was found.

News of the statement Howard Cox gave the sheriff had blown through Banesville like a hot, southern wind. Some people were pleased to believe the worst, including a few of Kit's benefactors.

He hadn't touched the hard surface of the chair before his hostess asked, "Are we on schedule for the formal opening?"

"We've been a bit behind since Mr. McCall's death, and not all renovations will be completed, but under Mr. Culbertson's supervision, we'll be ready for the tour on Saturday."

Rather than voice approval or disapproval, she observed him with the intensity of Annie's cat when it prepared to pounce on an unsuspecting field mouse. He shored up his strength to fend off fang and claw. "Is there something wrong?"

Those eyes widened. "Was that supposed to be funny?"

"Mrs. Brockhurst, it's obvious you didn't call me here for a status report." Kit was in no mood to dodge any issues regarding the events of the last week and a half. "I've told you and the other women all I know about the death of Liam McCall, so it's logical there's another matter on your mind."

Mrs. Brockhurst handed him the sheet of paper from her lap. "This was delivered to me yesterday."

Kit unfolded the paper and read the message out loud. "Dear Mrs. Brockhurst. It is with regret that I inform you of the low character of the gentleman"—his voice fell—"of the gentleman in whom you have put both your faith and finances." He read the rest of the malicious message in silence. With each accusation against him, his skin grew colder.

He turned the letter front to back. No signature. Even so, something was familiar, but he couldn't put his finger on what. "Who sent this?"

"Mavis found it tacked to the front door." She snatched the paper from him and refolded it. "I am interested in your response."

His response? What was he to say upon reading that, among other information, the news he'd suspected for two months was true, at least according to the author of the letter?

Mrs. Brockhurst had been his most vocal supporter during his recent meeting with the temperance women. Now, because of everything mentioned in this anonymous communication written to smear his standing in her eyes, Kit sensed he was on the verge of losing her support.

Worse yet, Joanna had lied to him.

"First of all, I don't believe this person regrets any information he provided you." Should he have said "she?" Had it come from one of the temperance women? More likely, Howard Cox sent it. But how would anyone in this town know the information the message revealed? "Second, I've never made secret my trouble with drink."

"I'm well aware of the reason you began your work in Pittsburgh, Christopher. It's one reason I chose to back you in this project over doctors who pushed their ludicrous patent medicines and theories. I believe their philosophy and so-called cures do more harm than good.

"However, in all our conversations, you failed to address the personal indictments against you in this correspondence." She tapped a finger against the paper. "For one thing, you never mentioned your part in a police inquiry conducted last year."

Kit stood and hunched his back. The muscles between his shoulder blades ached, as did his head. Evidently, Ben had been right. He should have revealed the situation in Pittsburgh to the women who supported the ministry.

"It's true that we were questioned, Mrs. Brockhurst, but never under serious suspicion as intimated by that letter. When arrested, the guilty man admitted his sole responsibility. The police were satisfied, and we've had no such trouble since."

"Until ten days ago."

"Yes, we came under suspicion last year after the police found stolen goods in the home. Nothing was found during a search of the residence here."

Liam's alleged thievery cast a shadow over the Banesville ministry. His murder might bury it.

Kit paced in front of the chair. "Obviously, someone wants to poison you against backing our mission. I can assure you we were innocent then, and we're innocent now. There is no connection between Liam's crimes and what happened in Pittsburgh."

"And what of the future?"

"Many of the men we help are destitute, Mrs. Brockhurst. Others are corrupt in their morals. Liam was one of the latter. If you're looking for assurance this won't happen again, I can't make that promise."

The woman studied him with eyes an eagle would envy. "And the other accusation? The one concerning a child."

His face warmed under her keen observation. "No woman's name is mentioned. However, I won't deny its possibility."

Her posture intensified in stiffness until he imagined her backbone would crumble from the stress. "I see."

When she rose from her seat and walked toward the front hall, Kit followed. "I wasn't always a gentleman when under the influence of drink, Mrs. Brockhurst. It's why God has given me a burden to help those going through the same experience. But if you wish, I'll return to Pittsburgh and let Ben handle the operation here."

If the claim in the letter of a child was valid, Kit might prefer to leave Banesville. Distance may be the only thing to rid him of the hostility and bitterness coursing through him.

Mrs. Brockhurst stopped near the door with her hands clasped in front of her until her knuckles turned white. She exhaled a deep-rooted breath. "My son died by the hand of a drunkard, Christopher . . . his own father."

The tension in Kit's muscles melted with his shock. In his previous research, he'd read nothing about her husband's involvement in their son's fall, only that he'd been overcome by grief and abandoned his wife shortly after the funeral. He glanced at the staircase.

"Yes, it happened there." Her voice had softened, and she stared at the second-floor landing as if seeing the tragedy of eleven years ago unfold before her eyes. "My husband and I argued. I should have known better. He'd had too much to drink and was not in his right mind. Walter shook me until I feared I would pass out." She ran her hands up and down her arms, and the normally unyielding body wilted. "When Spencer rushed up the stairs to come to my aid, his father stumbled into him and ..."

And the teen tumbled down the flight of stairs.

For the first time, Mrs. Brockhurst reminded Kit of his mother after her divorce—broken inside, yet glued together by the sheer force of will to save face. "I'm very sorry."

Her body shuddered. "It was an accident. My husband has been confined to a sanitarium since, and our attorney has worked hard to keep everything quiet. So, you see, we all have our burdens, Christopher."

"And our tragedies."

Mrs. Brockhurst held up the paper. "For the time being, I shall forget I received this letter. Though, if the investigation reveals you and Mr. Greer are guilty of any criminal activities in this town, I will not hesitate to recommend our association be

286

terminated."

"As I would expect, ma'am, but you have nothing to worry about."

"Rest assured, should you breathe a word of anything I have told you during this visit, I will deny it and put my efforts into the ruination of your cause, both here and in Pittsburgh."

Kit nodded and stepped onto the front porch. The door clicked shut behind him.

Mrs. Brockhurst might forget the letter, but its contents were impossible for Kit to forget. Blood throbbed inside his skull and beat at the back of his head. His steps pounded harder and faster as he passed through town.

How could any man forget that the woman he loved bore him a child and then denied it?

***

Joanna kneaded the biscuit dough while Rose fried slices of ham. They had passed the last hour in pleasant conversation, pretending a storm cloud didn't hang over their heads.

Mr. O'Connor peered inside the room. "I'm headed to the hardware store. Need anything?" With nothing to add to his list, he tipped his hat and left.

Joanna wiped the dough from her fingers. "That man's come a long way in a short time."

"He has people who care about his progress." Grease popped in the skillet. "Ow!" Rose jumped back and blew on her index finger.

"Are you all right?"

"It's nothing." In a fit of temper, Rose tossed aside the fork she'd been using, wrapped a towel around the cast iron handle, then removed the skillet from the stove and dropped it on the counter.

After a week and a half, they still hadn't heard from the sheriff, and Rose's efforts to attain more information about Liam's death met with resistance. Yesterday, they both snapped at Annie for different and trifling reasons. The longer they remained in ignorance, the more pressure built up around them until it threatened to blow like a steam whistle at one of the mills.

"I don't know how much more of this mystery I can take. What do you think happened to Liam?"

"I'd say his deeds caught up with him." Joanna's answer lacked the proper compassion, but the man had caused them more than enough trouble over the years.

"Believe it or not, I'm sorry for it."

Joanna had finally settled the question of redemption in her own mind. No one was beyond it until their final day in this world. "I'm the last one to throw stones. Now that I'm able to look at life from God's perspective, it saddens me to realize that Liam wasted his years and a chance for a happy family."

Rose swiped her eyes with the back of her hand and began to roll out the biscuit dough. "He was a horrible husband, but I just can't think of anyone who wanted to kill him."

Joanna had kept private the brief fear that Rose had ended her marriage through drastic means. After all, widows received sympathy and divorced women scorn. No sooner than the idea occurred to her, she had rejected it.

She pulled the biscuit cutter from a drawer. "We had no idea he committed the robberies. Sheriff Myers might be right in thinking he had an accomplice. It's possible they had a falling out."

"But wouldn't that person have taken the stolen items Liam

carried with him?"

"Not if he didn't know they were there."

Distracted by the discussion, Rose flattened the dough until it stretched so thin it threatened to tear in spots. "I don't even know where he was staying, and the sheriff won't say whether they've found anything else. He must have kept his ill-gotten gain somewhere."

"Maybe he'd already sold most of what he stole."

"People keep too many secrets in this world." Rose stopped mashing the dough with the rolling pin and stared at Joanna. "It's time to tell Kit."

Joanna didn't even blink at the quick transition in the conversation. The subject had been uppermost in her mind for days. At home, she would work up the courage, only to have it vanish when she saw him.

"I know. Ever since the questioning by the authorities, I've wanted to tell him."

"Then why haven't you?"

Joanna whipped around, and her mouth went dry at the sight of Kit.

He stood in the doorway between the kitchen and the dining room—face flushed and eyes cold as a frozen pond. The cords in his neck rippled. "Why haven't you told me you lied when I asked if you'd ever had a child? That you lied when you said Annie was not my daughter?"

Oh, Lord, I waited too long.

"Let's walk in the garden, Kit, and I'll tell you everything." Her legs wobbling, Joanna departed out the back door, then clasped her clammy hands in front of her and moaned a silent prayer for the words to help him understand . . . and not reject her a second time.

Chapter Thirty-six

Kit followed Joanna to the center of the garden and into the most concealed section. She stopped in front of an iron bench under a maple tree surrounded by shoulder-high evergreen hedges and blue hydrangeas past their bloom.

After a quiet moment, she sat on the far edge of the bench. Her cautious gaze invited him to occupy the other end. Instead, he tramped back and forth in front of her, powerless to constrain his resentment with inactivity.

"I didn't lie to you about Annie, Kit. She is the child of Rose and her first husband. He died five months before the girl was born."

Kit halted his march and glared at her. "She's the proper age, and she has my eyes and hair."

"No, she has her father's eyes and hair. Rose keeps his

photograph if you'd like to see for yourself. Annie is the spitting image of him."

Doubt clouded Kit's mind. The anonymous letter insisted he had a child, but if Annie wasn't his, then why did Joanna look guilty? Why the need to tell him anything?

"When you questioned me, I never actually said I hadn't given birth. You were right, though. I lied by keeping the truth from you."

Now that she stood on the brink of telling Kit everything he wished to know, he almost shouted that he no longer wanted to hear it. Once the words traveled between them, it was probable nothing would be the same. Despite the anguish and disillusionment, he dreaded the change.

The foliage rustled. Jelly broke through into the secluded space and wrapped her body around Kit's legs. The cat had doubled in size since he had given it to Annie.

Annie. The child wasn't his daughter. Was he relieved or disappointed? Right now, too many emotions clawed at him for dominance.

Strange. He'd grown used to the idea that she might be his, yet there was always the prospect of error to fall back on. It was harder to come to terms with the truth.

Joanna closed her eyes, and her mouth stirred in another mute and obvious prayer. She opened her eyes to reveal a calm determination. "After you left Philadelphia, I was devastated and frightened. For weeks, I dreamed you would return and ask to marry me. Then three months passed without a word from you, and it was clear I was expecting a child.

"No matter what you think of me, Kit, I had never before . . ." She choked on a sob that twisted his insides. "I loved you."

Excuses, comfort, resentment, fury, pleading for

forgiveness—it all spun inside Kit's head until he was dizzy, but words failed him at a time when they both needed them most.

She cleared her throat. "As my condition grew more noticeable, Papa found out. He demanded I leave his house and, for several days, I wandered the streets. Then I met Rose and we struck up a friendship." The sobs had evaporated, and Joanna's voice grew stronger. "Since our babies were due around the same time, we helped one another. If it weren't for Rose, I'm not sure what would have happened to me."

Kit sank onto the bench, half turned away, and unable to look at her for fear she'd see his wretchedness. The cat jumped onto the seat between them.

"Why didn't you tell me?"

Dry laughter bounced off his back. "How? You moved away from Philadelphia and told no one where you were going."

And if she had told him, what good would it have done? At that time, he couldn't take care of himself. How would he have managed to care for a wife and infant?

Still . . . He twisted to face her. "I had a right to know."

"You gave up your rights when you discarded me like rotting trash." Joanna stood. "You weren't by my side to suffer the rejection and shame. You weren't cast onto the street by a smug and pious man who proclaimed you condemned to everlasting darkness. You didn't bear the physical pain of childbirth."

Several seconds passed when all Kit heard were noisy gulps as she strained to silence sobs that foretold his greatest crime.

"You didn't crumple in grief by your son's graveside." The last words slipped out in a hoarse whisper.

With the sudden slam of a judge's gavel, the final indictment sank in and the world stopped for Kit. No breeze. No birdsong. No breath. He'd always known he was too like his father. Now he had to wonder if he were worse.

When he finally collected himself, Kit's voice emerged in a murmur as he asked, "What happened?"

"It was a difficult birth. He only lived a matter of hours." Joanna hung her head. "I used to believe it was God's judgment."

Kit tried to rise. Reach out. Console her. Wrap her in an embrace and share the sorrow she endured even now. His arms hung limp. His treatment of her had been no less destructive than Liam's treatment of Rose.

"What was his name?" An absurd time to ask that question, but it was all Kit could work past his lips.

"Aaron Jacob."

He tried to picture the newborn in his mind. For a short time, he'd had a son. Aaron Jacob Barnes. No. Aaron Jacob Cranston. Had the boy lived, his son would never have been known by his rightful surname.

With more bluntness than enthusiasm, Joanna said, "I met Clayton when he visited Philadelphia. We married within six weeks."

"And there were no more children?" Had the grueling birth of their son left her unable to bear more? Was that additional blame to be laid at his feet?

Joanna turned her head to the side, but not so far as to see him. "Once he learned he'd married a woman whose innocence had been lost, Clayton didn't want me either."

Clayton Stewart didn't want her *either.*

Jelly yowled. Rather than being a cry for attention, Kit heard it as a denunciation of his role in Joanna's broken marriage.

"There's more you should know."

What more could there be? She'd wounded him already. Did she now plan to finish him with more reasons to feel disgraced?

"I didn't agree to pay off Liam solely for the sake of Rose. He threatened to tell you what I was too ashamed to confess."

Blackmail? Kit raked a hand through his hair. She agreed to pay for silence rather than tell him of their child? How she must have hated him, and with good reason. Right now, he hated himself.

"We're different people today, Kit. I believe God has forgiven me, and I hope you can do the same."

Joanna scooped up the cat and walked away, leaving Kit alone in the garden with his tormented thoughts and despondency over the loss of a child he'd never known.

If he had stayed in Philadelphia, married Joanna, and seen to her health and well-being, would the baby have lived?

A short time later, Kit gave his legs free rein to transport him down the street while he replayed the events of the afternoon over and over. He should have paid more attention to where he was going because before he knew it, his legs had carried him to the Moondog Saloon.

As he stood outside, his mouth watered for what awaited him through that door. Over the music and laughter from inside the building, he heard Ben's familiar whisper in his ear. "Be strong."

But Ben was back in Pittsburgh. He wasn't here to provide the counsel Kit needed to fight against this all-consuming enticement that seized on his misery.

Kit reached for the door knob and paused only a moment before turning it. Inside, a piano player tapped out a lively tune, which most of the noisy customers ignored. Both businessmen and laborers lounged against the long bar running down one wall or filled chairs at scattered tables before going home at the end of a long day. Smoke drifted through the air from cigars and cigarettes, and the acrid clouds irritated Kit's throat.

He wound through the room to an empty table in the far corner that was, for the most part, clear of the haze. After slumping into a chair, he rubbed a hand over his face in an effort to clear the fog in his mind.

He shouldn't be here. What if he did the unthinkable? What if someone he knew saw him do it? Yet his conscience failed to will his body to rise and walk back out the door.

After a furtive glance around, Kit chuckled. What difference would it make? Once the temperance women found out he'd crossed that threshold, he'd lose his ministry in Banesville.

Who sent the letter to Mrs. Brockhurst? It created a perception of familiarity in his mind, but clarity hid around the corner and out of sight.

Then there was Liam's death. Cox believed Kit was responsible, and if the sheriff gave his theory credence, Kit could lose far more than a ministry to inebriates.

The alcohol called to him. The walls closed in on him.

"Be strong."

Kit's fingers tapped the wood of the table. The rhythm competed with the strident tune coming from the piano. All around him glasses clinked and thumped. He was nothing but a failure who couldn't overcome his weaknesses. New creation? Didn't his being here prove the opposite?

My grace is sufficient for thee: for my strength is made perfect in weakness.

Kit closed his eyes and shut out everything in the room—the smells, the noise, the scratched, sticky surface of the wood under his fingers—everything meant to convince him to give up and become the old creature in need of a drink to empower him.

Just as in the days when he first struggled to overcome his dependence on alcohol, Ben's voice resonated in Kit's head.

"Where does your strength come from, Kit?"

He wasn't sure anymore.

***

Joanna crept closer to the Moondog Saloon. Reluctant to meet any of the drunken inhabitants traipsing in and out, she rounded the corner and tiptoed to a dirty side window.

Peeking through glass spotted and stained with drink and who knew what else, she recognized four of the town's leading citizens. Smoke filled the air. How did the patrons even breathe? The piano player tapped out "Oh, Dem Golden Slippers," a tune suitable to heighten already drink-enlivened moods.

With her cheek pressed against the warmth of the pane, she craned her head left and then right. Areas were cut off from her vision, but . . . There, in a dim corner of the room, Kit sagged in a hard wooden chair. He had no drink in hand or on the table.

The bulk of the breath that stuck fast in Joanna's lungs when Kit walked inside the building whooshed out of her and, despite the warmth of the early evening, fogged the glass. He simply stared into the space in front of him. As he had told her, no decent woman entered a saloon, and she was a decent woman now. She waited to see what he would do next but prepared to intercede if necessary.

Confessing her secret had cleansed her conscience immediately. If Kit rejected her a second time, she'd be heartbroken, yet free of a burden weighing her down for years.

Intent on expressing her release with a cheerful polka or schottische, Joanna had gone straight from the garden to the music room, but rather than sit at the piano, she peered out the window until Kit lumbered through the yard. The hunched posture and plodding movements had shouted his grief and preoccupation with the news she'd revealed.

Whether out of curiosity or compulsion, Joanna followed at a discreet distance. She had expected him to stop along the way, which would allow her to join him as though she, too, had needed to walk off their discussion. He continued into town. At present, she stood outside this abominable place, unable to do more than spy on him and pray.

When she wasn't dodging possible sightings of her from the men inside, Joanna shifted from one foot to the other. How much longer did he plan to sit there?

All of a sudden, a waiter loomed over him with a tray of drinks, and her stomach tightened. She retreated from the window and pressed her back against the outer wall of the building. The old guilt roared back with a vengeance.

She should have found a better way to break the news to him—one that wouldn't have driven him to repeat his destructive past.

Chapter Thirty-seven

In those first trying weeks of seeking sobriety, Kit had memorized numerous verses of scripture that directed God's people to be strong. In this most urgent hour, a number of them rolled through his mind.

Watch ye, stand fast in the faith, quit you like men, be strong. ... Be strong in the grace that is in Christ Jesus. ... Finally, brethren, be strong in the Lord and in the power of his might.

He whispered, "Amen."

"Friend, you musta mistook this building for a church. Order or get your carcass out."

Kit opened his eyes. A barrel-chested man stood before him. He wore a dirty apron around his ample waist. A scowl darkened his features, but the tray in his hand captured Kit's interest. Glasses covered it, both full and empty—beer, whiskey—liquid to tempt him to snatch one and down it.

"You look like you need this more'n that fella yonder." The barman held out a glass half-filled with the golden pull of whiskey.

Kit stared at the drink in the barman's hand. With a will of its own, his arm stretched toward the offering.

God, help me to be strong and courageous.

His head told him to take the drink. His heart pleaded with him to remember the poverty of his past before Christ freed him from drunkenness. He moistened his lips and curled his fingers.

Then a peculiar thing happened. The drink Kit remembered as smooth, warm, and satisfying, turned as sour as vinegar in his imagination. He withdrew his hand and pushed away from the table. Unlike his father, he could own up to his responsibilities like a man. God gave him that power.

He slapped the barman on the back. "I'll happily take my carcass elsewhere, sir."

Though his troubles with Joanna and the sorrow still lingered, he had beaten the craving and self-pity. With God's help, he had come through this experience stronger in confidence and faith. And with God's help, he would remain strong.

Kit left the Moondog Saloon to find that a navy sky had replaced the sinking sun, but he had somewhere to go before turning for home. In the midst of his ordeal, he'd received the clarity he'd sought with regard to the letter sent to Mrs. Brockhurst.

As Kit started down the street, a woman flew around the corner of the building. He stopped before they collided, and then reached out for her. "Joanna? What are you doing here?"

She drew back and studied him with rounded eyes before they filled with her tears. "I saw you take the drink."

His glance slid to the window on the side of the building.

"Why, Kit? You have so many men depending on you. What about Mr. O'Connor? What would he think if he knew what you've done? Mr. Cox is a coarse and shady man, but this won't help him change. And Annie adores everything about you. It's all my fault. I—"

Kit captured Joanna by both arms and backed her around the corner, away from prying eyes along the street. His grip loosened to give her the opportunity to pull away, to rebuff the passion that fueled his purpose, but her gaze locked on his. Gone was the fear he had seen in her eyes before. In its place, her eagerness equaled his own as her arms twined around his neck. She smelled of rosewater and fresh, night air. Her hair, soft and wavy, tangled in his fingers.

Their kiss soared and fell with intensity and gentleness. It unleashed every facet of the emotions Kit buried the night he stole her from his brother. He longed for a lifetime with Joanna, and he wanted her to feel it.

As one, they broke apart to claim a crucial breath. Though he didn't deserve her, God allowed Kit this second chance, and he wasn't about to ruin it.

"Now . . ."—he inhaled a lungful of necessary air—"did I imbibe?"

Joanna tasted her lips and lowered her lashes. She clutched him around the waist. "Don't ever scare me like that again."

"For the first time, I can say with confidence that I won't." He wrapped her in a tight embrace. "How did you find me?"

"I saw you leave the house."

"You followed? I didn't notice."

"You weren't noticing much." Her heart knocked against his ribs. "You don't hate me?"

"Hate you? For being concerned?"

"No. For not telling you sooner about the baby."

He sighed and hugged her closer. "All I care about is keeping my promise, Jo."

"What promise?" The words came out muffled.

"To run to you and not from you." Gently, he separated from her. "I don't care how long it takes, I'll spend the rest of our days atoning for all the hurt I caused you."

"Oh, Kit, please don't even try." He started to reply, but she placed a finger to his lips. "We can't change the past. We can't bring back our son. We've both made mistakes, but not long ago, you told me God forgets our transgressions when we seek His forgiveness. Neither of us will ever forget, and we can't waste our lives focused on the attempt. All we can do is forgive one another and build on what we have now."

She withdrew her finger. "Is that what you want for the two of us?"

"I want even more."

Joanna visibly relaxed. "I'm listening."

"I want a lifetime of happiness and contentment knowing I'm with the woman I love. I want us to reach our nineties and still totter around the house together." Her demure grin encouraged him to add, "I want to marry you and have another child."

"Only one?"

"Let's say one at a time." He laughed and stole another kiss. "Come on. I'll walk you home."

As they strolled down the street, Joanna said, "Helping Darcy has given me a sense of fulfillment. If God decides I should do the same for other women, would you think it foolish?"

Her question deserved a well-thought-out and honest answer. His first inclination, based on self-interest, was to say he'd hoped she'd help him in his ministry. But the more he considered it, the more he saw her in the role of helping unfortunate women and their newborns. "When God leads His children to action, Joanna, it's never foolish."

"But how would that affect our future?"

"I'm proud of what you've done for Darcy, and it's not my place to dissuade you from obeying God's call. I'll stand by your side in whatever you're led to do."

She smiled. "Thank you."

"Let's get you home." Kit's pace picked up.

"You're in a sudden hurry."

"I have an errand after I leave you."

"Oh?"

Perhaps he shouldn't tell her, but if his reasoning were correct, she would hear soon enough. Kit explained about the letter to Mrs. Brockhurst, including the portion about the child.

"That's how you knew I hadn't told you the truth."

"Yes." He paused and then added, "I think I know who sent it."

"Who?"

"Perry."

***

Joanna stumbled to a halt. "You're wrong, Kit. How could Perry provide Mrs. Brockhurst with information about me he doesn't know?" Unless Clayton told him.

"I'm not sure how he found out, but the stationer's mark on the paper was familiar. I think it's the same as on the notes I received from him on two other occasions."

"Surely, he's not the only person to use such paper." Even as she spoke, Joanna doubted her argument. Perry ordered his stationery from a Washington, D. C. bookstore and prided himself on the quality. He said he couldn't buy its equal in Banesville. "What about the handwriting?"

"It was somewhat different. He probably tried to disguise it. I'll find out when I talk to him."

"I'm going with you."

"No, you're going home."

"I'll do no such thing. This involves me, too, Kit." She spun on her heel and headed in the direction of Perry's house.

After knocking on the door of the large two-story Greek Revival structure, they were told by the housekeeper that Perry hadn't arrived home from work, so they walked another quarter mile to the Stewart Broom Factory.

Joanna pointed to a window on the second floor. "There's a light in his office."

"Let's go." Kit followed her into the building at the front of the factory and up the stairs to Perry's office.

Joanna looked around. "He's not here, but he wouldn't leave a lamp burning if he weren't close by." She crossed the room to Perry's desk and began to rifle through the papers on the top.

Kit came alongside. "What are you doing?"

"There must be a sample of his stationery. If we find it, you'll know for sure whether or not the paper came from Perry." She gestured to the door. "Let me know if you see him coming. I'd hate for him to find me going through his things."

Finding nothing on the surface of the desk, Joanna opened the top left drawer, then the middle. After opening the bottom drawer, her heart plunged to her knees. She pulled the top paper out. "Kit."

He glanced at her from near the door. "You found it?"

"No." She held up the paper. "I found this."

Kit stepped closer. "A drawing?"

"Annie's drawing. I haven't seen it since the housebreaking."

Chapter Thirty-eight

To Kit's thinking, there was only one reason Perry Stewart had possession of Annie's drawing. "We were wrong about Liam." Joanna rubbed the area above her right eyebrow. "Perry could have taken this any time."

Kit had his doubts. "He has a habit of barging in without knocking. Do you know if he was ever alone in your house?"

"If he was, I'm not aware of it."

"It doesn't make sense. What would he want with a child's drawing?"

The vertical lines between Joanna's eyes deepened, and she turned the drawing over. Kit saw immediately when an answer struck her. "Unless it was to retrieve this. It's a letter his father wrote. I told him about it a month ago."

Kit read of Clayton Stewart's decision to sell the factory. He didn't like where his thoughts took him. It was a conclusion Joanna would fight with everything in her. "You stay here."

"Kit—"

"Stay, Joanna."

Kit rushed from the office, down the stairs, and out the back door. As he trekked across the yard to the large building where the brooms were made, he went over everything he knew about the housebreaking and the rumors surrounding Joanna. What if there was more truth to the story of her husband's death than spiteful gossip?

A light shone through a window at one end of the broom factory. When Kit entered the building, the main room was dark with the exception of a soft moon glow and the brighter light that spilled across the floor from a doorway to his left. "Perry?"

The sound of Kit walking across the room broke the silence around him. He reached the doorway of a machine shop with its lathes, a band saw, and circular saw. A workbench extended across the opposite wall, interrupted by a door leading outside. Various hand tools hung from the walls.

"Are you in here, Perry?"

He heard the creak of a floorboard behind him a heartbeat before his mind registered a presence. He started to turn. A shove sent him sprawling into the room, and his head smacked the wooden frame of the circular saw. Pain ricocheted throughout his skull.

"Mrs. Brockhurst should have sent you packing. You aren't wanted in Banesville."

The words jumped in Kit's brain and his scalp stung. His arms were jerked behind him and a thin wire bit into his wrists. The room tilted from one side to the other as if he stood on the deck of a storm-tossed boat. His stomach lurched in protest. He focused on the bottom edges of brown-striped trousers and dusty, brown shoes.

"Joanna deserves more than a man who seduces then deserts her."

Perry's kick to Kit's ribs set them afire. His breaths came in quick and shallow gasps.

"Do you think I'll give you the chance to hurt her again?" The leg kicked out. This time the blow caught Kit in the gut and stole the rest of his air. "No one takes what I want. Not you. Not my father."

"Your father want ..." Kit drew in as much air between words as possible. He grimaced with the pain that ran from the back of his head to his waist. "He wanted to sell ... this business. ... D-Did you kill him?"

As an answer, Perry growled and jammed an oily rag in Kit's mouth. Then the light vanished, and the door slammed shut. Kit was left alone in the dark, convinced he'd been attacked by a man who committed patricide.

He prayed Joanna would go undiscovered in Perry's office.

***

Questions whirred in Joanna's brain, always settling on the same answer. She refused to believe Perry entered her house at night, stole the letter, and struck Darcy. He must have taken it another time.

But why? When she mentioned the letter, he dismissed it as inconsequential. If he'd asked for it, she would have given it to him.

Joanna glanced at the clock. Kit must have found Perry by now. She stuffed the letter in the waistband of her skirt and headed for the factory for answers.

As she approached the building, someone doused the light shining from the window of the machine shop, and a door slammed.

Joanna stepped inside the building and allowed her eyes to adjust to the darkness before she crossed the room. With the help of dim moonlight, she avoided the iron vises used to stitch the brooms. "Perry? Kit?"

"What are you doing here, Joanna?"

Her hand flew to her heart. She could make out Perry's shape, but not much more. He stood between her and the door leading outside. "You startled me. Where is Kit?"

"Why would you think I know where he is?"

"Because he came in here looking for you."

"You're mistaken. He hasn't been here."

Joanna's heart thumped a warning. He lied. From Perry's office window, she had watched Kit cross the yard and enter the building. She sidestepped, but Perry did the same and blocked her path to the door.

"Where are you going?" He took a step forward.

Joanna backed a step. Ben told her all men would disappoint her. She'd never included Perry in that caution.

"Why did you steal the letter?"

"Because it was dangerous to me." He answered as though she should have understood. She was far from understanding.

"You don't deny it?"

"Would you like me to lie? I guess that's the type of man who sets your heart aflutter." Perry took another step forward, but Joanna was too shocked to move. "All right. No, I did not steal the letter. No, I did not slap the harlot living in your house—the one who took advantage of your kindness while she ruined your reputation."

Joanna groaned over his admission. She glanced toward the side door, but Perry must have guessed her intention to flee and closed the distance between them. She shuffled backward. Her foot hit the broad stairs leading to the loft, and restraint deserted her. She reeled and pounded up the steps. It was a stupid move. Now he had her trapped.

Where was Kit?

***

The room finally stopped rolling, and Kit inched upright. Pain wracked him with every breath and movement, especially when he struggled to free his hands. Voices stilled his effort. Though indistinct, he was sure one belonged to Joanna. A rush of panic seized him. The wire tore into his skin as he fought even harder to release his wrists.

The door leading into the machine shop from outside opened. Kit ceased his struggle and waited. The new arrival drew closer. Whether friend or foe, Kit tried to stand. His fruitless labor created a scuffle on the floor. The next thing he knew, Donovan bent over him and yanked the rag free. Kit spit out the foul taste that sullied his mouth.

"Looks like you got yourself in a pickle." The whispered words held no humor.

"Can you . . . cut the wire around my hands?"

Donovan walked away and returned a moment later with a pair of wire cutters.

"How did you know I was here?"

"Saw you come out of the saloon. I don't like hypocrites, so I figured I'd see what you were up to."

Sandra Ardoin

In two snips, Kit was free. "Thanks. Help me up." He threw his arm around Donovan's shoulder. His other hand pressed against the tenderness in his chest. "I heard Joanna in the next room with Perry. She's in trouble."

Determined to move under his own power, Kit straightened and scuffled into the main room of the factory. She should have stayed put as he'd told her.

***

Perry followed Joanna up the stairs to the loft. She backed along the edge, past stacked bales of broom corn and wood-slatted crates holding thick dowels destined to become handles.

"Why run from me, Joanna?"

"You're scaring me."

"You've no reason to be afraid. Everything I've done was for your protection and mine. Don't you understand? I wouldn't let anyone hurt you—not my father, not McCall, and not Barnes."

Joanna froze at the mention of the name McCall. "You protected me from Liam?"

He reached toward her. She leaned away, and he dropped his arm to his side. "I paid him well to watch over you, but—"

"You paid him to spy on me?"

"To watch over you." Perry backed her against the right-side wall. "McCall had no scruples. When my father was alive, he was like a fly on the wall—rarely seen, but always watching and listening. The fool took pleasure in tarnishing your reputation and admitted to blackmailing you over an illegitimate child. When you told me of his actions on the Fourth, I decided he must be dealt with before he hurt you."

She'd walked into a nightmare. "You . . . you killed Liam?"

"Your precious Rose should thank me. He deserved his end. After you refused to pay him, he tried to bleed me over my father's death. It's why I needed that letter, Joanna. It would be his word against mine."

"Clayton died from pneumonia."

"He died because he couldn't breathe past ticking and feathers. Somehow, McCall discovered the truth."

"You suffocated my husband?"

"What choice did I have? I did it for you, Joanna . . . for us. That old man made both of us miserable. When he told me he planned to sell the factory, the business I'd worked so hard to build, I saw a solution and took it. I've never regretted my actions."

"Oh, Perry." How could she have known him so well and, yet, never comprehended that he possessed no conscience? She had to get away before his impassive reasoning convinced her that his deeds were justified. "What have you done to Kit?"

Perry swung a fist backward. Joanna jumped as it slammed against the thin slat of a crate holding the broom handles. The punch cracked the top one. Several of the dowels tumbled out and rolled across the floor. "Did you think I wouldn't employ a detective to investigate him? I know the sorrow he caused you."

Her temper awakened to overcome her terror. "Where is Kit?"

"Do not worry about Barnes!"

"He's right. Don't worry about me, Joanna."

Joanna's glance shot to the ground floor where two men stood in the darkness. Her breath stuttered with relief. She tried to push past Perry, but he knocked her against the wall.

Kit held his side as he climbed the stairs. "Donovan, wait here, in case he gets past me."

Once Kit reached the loft, Perry grabbed a dowel from the nearest crate and swung it, hitting him on the side and sending him to the floor. Perry raised the broom handle again, ready to bring it down on Kit's head.

"Stop!" Joanna grabbed Perry's arm, and Kit rolled out of the way.

Perry swiveled and snatched Joanna's right wrist. She squealed with the pressure and pinch of her skin.

"Remember, Mrs. Stewart." Mr. O'Connor's calm voice reached past her distress.

She did a ninety-degree turn and raised her left arm above her head. Before Perry could react, she crooked her left elbow and slammed it down on his forearm. He lost his grip on her wrist. With her fingers bent, she smashed her knuckles into his throat.

Holding his neck, Perry stumbled backward into the crate filled with broom handles. More dowels fell to the floor. Kit grabbed one and swept it out, catching Perry's legs and tripping him. As Perry fought to remain upright, his foot rolled on a loose dowel. His arms flailed and his body tipped sideways.

Joanna lunged, but Kit grabbed her around the waist to keep her from going over the edge of the loft with Perry and several of the dowels. He landed with a heartrending thud on the floor below as the wood pieces thumped around him.

She threw her arms around Kit. He grunted and hunched his back. When she let go, a wet stickiness clung to her fingertips. "Blood."

"It's nothing."

"And the flinch?"

"Just a bruise to the ribs."

A quick, yet tender kiss and then a whispered, "Thank you, God," relayed his relief over their safety. When her gaze drifted to

Perry, Kit said, "Don't blame yourself. You couldn't have prevented any of it."

"I know." If Kit and Mr. O'Connor weren't present, Joanna might convince herself she had imagined Perry's confession to two murders.

With slow and cautious movements, she assisted Kit down the stairs. Donovan stood over Perry, who had landed on his side. "Looks like a break to his shoulder and leg. Guess I'll fetch Sheriff Myers and a doctor."

Joanna knelt beside Perry. His breath hissed with the feeble shift of his body to touch her hand. His face crumpled in pain.

No, his deeds weren't her fault, but the result hurt just as much.

Chapter Thirty-nine

Joanna pulled aside the sheer curtain covering one of the front windows of her house as Kit guided the carriage horse to a stop at the curb. The fit of the well-tailored gray suit and the confident stride of his walk up the front path created a flurry of anticipation in her stomach.

When he spotted her and winked, she turned away from the window, pinched her cheeks, and met him at the door. His wide-eyed inspection was all she needed to be assured the new silk dress, a blue to match his eyes and trimmed with a white lace jabot, secured his approval.

He shut the door on the neighbors' curiosity before taking her in his arms. "You look beautiful. Will you marry me?"

Joanna's low chuckle tickled her throat. "That's the fourth time you've asked in as many days. What answer have I given you each time?"

Despite the persistent discomfort of bruised ribs, he clutched her tighter. "This."

His kiss left her winded. She leaned back in his arms. "My goodness, I'm articulate."

"Why do you think I keep repeating my proposal?" The lightheartedness encircling them ebbed. "You've never given me a firm answer, Joanna."

What stopped her from shouting to the rooftop, "Yes, I'll marry you," as she longed to do? "We have a reception to attend. If we don't leave now, we'll be late."

Kit's parted lips signaled a desire to argue. Instead, he closed his mouth and led her down the path to the carriage. The more distance they covered, the greater was Joanna's impulse to turn and run back to the safety of her home.

Kit drove while she sat with her hands in her lap, her fingers dancing to an imaginative rhythm. "How did this morning's tour go?"

"The mayor, most of the aldermen, the constable, and the justice of the peace still support us. However, I think Sheriff Myers has his doubts. Cox's absence didn't help. He suspects Howard helped Liam commit the burglaries, but he has no evidence."

"At least Mr. O'Connor has stayed."

"He's played an important role in our lives, hasn't he?"

It was a role the fighter admitted to Kit and Joanna after Perry's arrest. Mr. O'Connor knew the depth of Liam's hostility toward Joanna and didn't trust Rose's husband. He sought a job at the House once he learned Liam had done the same. He assumed Liam meant to cause trouble for two people who had shown him a kindness, so he assigned himself the task of watchman. The job gave him reason to stop drinking. Joanna prayed he never returned to it.

"I hesitate to think what could have happened to you, Joanna—to both of us—if he hadn't arrived when he did."

Joanna's mind reeled with each mention of the tragedy. The image of Perry lying broken on the floor still haunted her. What distressed her more was his expected fate once he healed and the trial commenced. "How did I not see what Perry was capable of?"

"He was your friend." Kit guided the horse around a corner. "Myers located the detectives Perry used to gather information about me. Once he had what he sought, he sent that letter hoping to drive me back to Pennsylvania. It might have worked if I didn't love you so much."

She twisted to face Kit and broach the subject she had avoided until now. "Mrs. Brockhurst is satisfied you had nothing to do with Liam's crimes, but we both know Perry's confession won't be adequate in persuading others I'm innocent of Clayton's death. The question will always remain in their minds. I don't want that to affect your work."

Kit covered her hand with his. "I don't care what others think, and if anyone upsets you this afternoon, let me know. We'll leave."

She would never do that. This afternoon meant too much to him.

A maid greeted them at the Brockhurst door. She ushered them into a drawing room filled with plush chairs and tables in rich woods, whatnots with various items of interest, ferns and palms on plant stands. Tassels hung from heavy velvet drapery, and paintings dangled on wires from walls papered in a bold tulip design. Joanna's gaze lingered an extra moment on the upright piano along the far wall.

As they were announced, conversation withered among the eight guests already present in the room. Four men and four women turned to stare at Kit and Joanna. Mrs. Brockhurst crossed the floral carpet to greet them. "Good afternoon, Christopher."

Kit bowed to their hostess. "Good afternoon. I believe you know Mrs. Stewart."

The slender woman neither smiled nor scowled, but reached out with her hand. "Welcome to my home, Mrs. Stewart."

Joanna eyed the gesture a moment before accepting the handshake. "Thank you for the invitation."

Further introductions established the identities of the remaining patrons of the Spencer Brockhurst House. More guests arrived until the room filled with potential supporters. The last to be announced were the Weedons and David Murray and his wife.

A short time later, Kit drifted away in conversation with a number of the men, leaving Joanna on the periphery of a group of women. Determined not to be cowed by a glower from Mr. Murray, she met his gaze until he turned away.

Mrs. Chandler, a boisterous woman in both manner and dress, stepped between them. "What a shocking experience, Mrs. Stewart." The woman's eyes lit with excitement. "I understand one of the men taught you several moves that saved you."

In the twelve days since the incident at the broom factory, Banesville had buzzed with the news of Perry's arrest and the manner in which it happened.

"I'll always be indebted to Mr. O'Connor for his help." It was as far as she'd publicly venture into the private man's role.

"Mercy sakes, after all that's happened it is obvious we are no longer a sleepy town and should prepare ourselves for the unexpected." Mrs. Chandler inched closer. "Do you think Mr.

O'Connor would consent to teach me the same techniques he taught you?"

What had she gotten the poor man into?

At Mrs. Chandler's question, four of the women encircled Joanna, their curiosities raised. Several others stood to the side and glared at her with disdain.

Joanna imagined the battle-scarred fighter's crotchety reaction to Mrs. Chandler's request and smiled. Now that he had no more incentive to watch over her, he needed another purpose. "I think it's a splendid idea."

She followed the ones who had befriended her to the table in the dining room where they helped themselves to dainty sandwiches and desserts. David Murray sidled up to her, and she almost dropped her plate.

He sipped from a glass filled with sweet punch, then whispered, "It looks as if your exploits have won over a number of foolish ladies. What will they think of your association with a young woman who recently gave birth out of wedlock?"

As she stared at him, Joanna's heart tripped at the truth behind his question—the truth about Darcy's baby. Her encounter with this spineless, *married* man strengthened her belief in the call to help other unfortunate women like the one he nearly destroyed. "None of our private deeds escape God's notice, Mr. Murray, and His mercy isn't dependent on your opinion or mine."

Mrs. Brockhurst interrupted the ensuing silence between them with a tap on Joanna's shoulder. "Mrs. Stewart, Christopher raves about your talent on the piano. Perhaps you'll favor us with a song?"

Joanna glanced at Kit, who nodded his encouragement. "I'd be honored."

As she wound through the crowd on her way to the piano, Joanna held her head high and smiled inside. There were those who would never find her worthy, but it was time she stopped letting them run her future.

She placed her fingers on the keys. After a moment's reluctance, the room overflowed with the strains of "Let Me Dream Again."

Kit leaned against the piano, and a deep-seated eagerness inside her burst free. "Yes."

His brow furrowed, and he bent closer. "Yes, what?"

"Yes, I'll marry you."

Kit's burning gaze spoke every word Joanna had ever longed to hear from him.

She need never dream of love again, for it was hers.

Acknowledgments

I wrote this years ago but the thank you still applies.

A Reluctant Melody was born during the writing of my Christmas novella The Yuletide Angel. After the character of Kit Barnes arrived on the scene, it didn't take long for me to realize he must have his own story! The following people provided that possibility.

My gratitude goes to those at Heritage Beacon Fiction and Lighthouse Publishing of the Carolinas for their willingness to publish this book and its predecessor. Their hard work in editing, designing, marketing (and other tasks I'm not even aware of) creates a product a reader wants to add to their to-be-read stacks. I especially thank Ann Tatlock, Susan Craft, Eddie Jones, Paige Boggs, and my fellow LPC authors for their efforts and support.

Critique partners and beta readers refine the manuscript and make it shine. I've had some incredible polishers on this one. Angie Arndt, Marilyn Lentz, Heidi Chiavaroli, Nicole Miller, Phyllis Keels, and my "in-house" reader, Catherine Ardoin—I couldn't do it without you.

And, of course, no book's launch into the world is complete without enthusiastic readers willing to tell their friends. Word-of-mouth recommendations and reviews are the lifelines that keep a book afloat. Thank you so much, readers, for your help.

Hebrews 4:16 is my scripture of choice for A Reluctant Melody, because we all need the grace and mercy only God can bestow. My prayer is that everyone who reads this story will find something in the fictional experiences of Kit and Joanna that blesses their real lives.

Thank you, Lord, for allowing me to do what I truly enjoy.

Thank you for spending your precious time reading *A Reluctant Melody*. I hope you enjoyed it. Your opinion is important to other readers, so if you wouldn't mind taking another moment and leaving a review on your favorite retail book site, I would be grateful.

If you haven't read the story of the first Barnes brother, Hugh, I invite you to check out *The Yuletide Angel*.

As always, happy reading!

As an author of heartwarming historical and contemporary romance, Sandra Ardoin engages readers with page-turning stories of love and faith. Rarely out of reach of a book, she's also an armchair sports enthusiast, country music listener, and seldom says no to eating out. Visit her at www.sandraardoin.com.

Have you Joined the Love and Faith in Fiction community?

Get *Unwrapping Hope*, the historical romance novella that kicked off the **Widow's Might Series** when you sign up to receive updates and special offers at www.sandraardoin.com.

www.ingramcontent.com/pod-product-compliance
Lightning Source LLC
Chambersburg PA
CBHW020405260626
47156CB00007B/2234